MASTERING
the ART *of*
FRENCH
MURDER

Kensington books by
Colleen Cambridge

The Phyllida Bright mystery series

Murder at Mallowan Hall

A Trace of Poison

An American in Paris mystery series

Mastering the Art of French Murder

MASTERING *the* ART *of* FRENCH MURDER

An American in Paris Mystery

Colleen Cambridge

KENSINGTON
PUBLISHING CORP.

www.kensingtonbooks.com

KENSINGTON BOOKS are published by

Kensington Publishing Corp.
119 West 40th Street
New York, NY 10018

All Kensington titles, imprints and distributed lines are available at special quantity discounts for bulk purchases for sales promotion, premiums, fund-raising, educational or institutional use. Special book excerpts or customized printings can also be created to fit specific needs. For details, write or phone the office of the Kensington Special Sales Manager: Kensington Publishing Corp., 119 West 40th Street, New York, NY, 10018. Attn. Special Sales Department. Phone: 1-800-221-2647.

The K with book logo Reg. U.S. Pat. & TM Off.

Library of Congress Card Catalogue Number: 2022950820

ISBN: 978-1-4967-3959-9
First Kensington Hardcover Edition: May 2023

ISBN: 978-1-4967-3961-2 (ebook)

10 9 8 7 6 5 4 3 2 1

Printed in the United States of America

AUTHOR'S NOTE

Although Julia and Paul Child, along with Julia's sister Dort, lived in a two-level apartment at 81 rue de l'Université in Paris in 1949, Tabitha Knight, her "messieurs," and the deadly events depicted herein are complete figments of the author's imagination.

MASTERING
the ART *of*
FRENCH
MURDER

CHAPTER 1

Paris
December 1949

Julia Child had a mayonnaise problem.

I knew all about it—every sordid detail—because, first, I was one of her closest friends in Paris, and second . . . well, I wouldn't be surprised if *everyone* in the seventh arrondissement—from the Place du Palais-Bourbon to the Tour Eiffel—had heard about the mayonnaise problem. Julia was just that kind of person. She was gregarious and ebullient and giddy and enthusiastic.

And I loved her dearly—probably because we were a lot alike in some ways, while in other ways, I *wanted* to be like her. If I could just do half the things in the kitchen that she did—or even a *third* of them!

Julia had been bemoaning her mayonnaise problem for a few weeks now, and I couldn't help but worry about what that meant in the grand scheme of things. After all, if *Julia*, who'd been taking lessons at Le Cordon Bleu, was suddenly having problems making mayonnaise—a sauce she'd been making for months with ease and perfection—what did that mean for *me*, someone who could barely boil eggs?

The implications were ominous.

"I just don't understand it!" she said as we walked down rue de l'Université, the street on which we both lived. Both of us were bundled up against the bitter December cold on our way to the market. I carried a small basket of fresh sage and rosemary bundles from my *grand-père's* greenhouse for some of the vendors, but I would also be buying as well. I was hoping Julia would help me pick out a nice roasting chicken.

"Your mayonnaises have always been so delicious," I said enviously. I had yet to create one single mayonnaise that came together properly. "So beautiful and creamy and stupendous—I can't believe it's still not turning out right."

"It's simply *inexplicable*," Julia replied. "All of a sudden, the sauce is just not doing its thing! The eggs and oil won't emulsify no matter how many times I whisk them up. I wanted to make an herbed mayonnaise last night to toss with spaghetti. But the sauce broke and simply *refused* to come together. I tried three times until I finally ran out of eggs. Paul had to eat spaghetti with black pepper, parmesan, and butter instead—the poor man," she went on with a gusty, affectionate laugh. "He listened to me clang about and whisk and curse, and clang some more, and finally he was so hungry he just wanted to eat."

Paul was Julia's husband, and it was because of his diplomacy job with the United States Information Service that the Childs had moved to Paris a year ago. As Julia told it, the very first meal she'd eaten here in France had been like a switch that flipped inside her, or a light bulb suddenly illuminating. She'd never enjoyed food so much in her entire life. She still spoke about that serving of *sole meunière* in the hushed, reverent tones of someone entering a church.

As she gleefully told it to anyone who would listen, that first dining experience—followed by countless just as delectable ones—was how Julia had found her calling, her muse, her *paradise:* French food and the history, tradition, and preparation of it. *All* of it. Having been raised on flat, stolid American meals prepared by her family's cook, she had experienced what could only be described as a great, even spiritual, awakening upon arriving in France and experiencing the food here.

Since then, Julia had become absorbed first with the taste and pleasure of *eating* French cuisine, then, more recently, the fascination of its history and the joy of preparing it.

Which was why the mayonnaise mystery was so disturbing to her—and to me, for Julia had been coaching me through improving my own cookery techniques over the last few months.

It was either I improve in the kitchen, or I and my grandfather and Oncle Rafe were going to be living on tinned sardines, cheese, baguette, and wine.

At least I knew how to pick out a good bottle of wine.

I had moved to the City of Light from a suburb of Detroit this past spring, right before Easter, but for an entirely different reason than the Childs.

I had recently broken off my four-year engagement to Henry McKinnon and was just about to turn twenty-nine. Since the war was over and all of the troops had come home to take on the jobs we women had been doing while the men were gone, for the last couple of years I'd been restless and at loose ends. And then my French grandmother—who'd helped raise me back in the States—had died in January after a long illness.

The next thing I knew, I was invited to come for an extended visit with my grandfather here in Paris.

My mother, who I love very much and with whom I got along pretty well—considering we were very different sorts of women—encouraged me to go and stay as long as I liked.

Maybe she was getting as tired of my moping and boredom as I was. I know my sisters couldn't wait for me to get out of the house, but I think that was only because they were fighting over my bedroom.

During the war, I'd channeled my energies into working at the Willow Run bomber plant helping to build the B-24 Liberator planes. I'd even learned how to work on their engines. I'd always been a bit of a tomboy, to the dismay of my very ladylike French mother and grandmother. Although I carried lipstick and a comb in my purse, I also always had a Swiss Army knife in my pocket.

I liked to tinker with things like machinery and engines; I was always curious about how machines worked and what made people tick—in fact, that was partly how Julia and I had become such close friends. One day last summer when we ran into each other at the market, she mentioned that their radio wasn't working properly.

I had my handy tool knife with me of course, so I offered to try to fix it. She was so grateful when I did, and when I wouldn't accept any payment for the work, she insisted I stay for dinner. I'd never had such good food outside of a restaurant, and that was when I realized I needed to learn how to cook. If I could fix an airplane engine, I could roast a chicken. It couldn't be that difficult, could it?

Yes. Yes, it could.

The fact that Julia and I lived on the same block and had both recently moved to Paris from the States made it seem like our friendship was meant to be.

Not that it was difficult for Julia Child to make friends—but I was a little less outgoing than my boisterous, enthusiastic friend. And since at that time I didn't know anyone in Paris besides my grandfather and Oncle Rafe, I had truly enjoyed getting to know Julia, her husband, Paul, and Julia's younger sister, Dorothy, who'd come to live with them a few months ago.

"I just worry that this is a harbinger of worse things to come. What's going to be next?" Julia was saying in her dramatic fashion as we walked along the curved path of Place du Palais-Bourbon toward the market. "What if my pie crusts refuse to flake? Or my cake icing starts to run all over? What if my soufflés start to fall as hard as the Roman Empire? What will I *do*? Cooking has become my *life!*"

"Maybe you should just start from the beginning," I suggested, looking up at her. Julia was six feet, two inches tall and sturdily built, and I'm just a hair under five feet, five inches. My slender build and average stature has always caused comment when I mention that I've worked on airplanes, although I'm not exactly sure why. I didn't have to *lift* them or anything. "When I'm trying to figure out why something isn't working, I take the whole mechanism apart, piece by piece, and check every part, one by one. I make sure each piece is working properly and isn't damaged before I move on and put things back together. Maybe you should try that."

"Why, that makes complete sense, Tabitha!" Julia said, stopping abruptly on the sidewalk. She sounded as if I'd just handed her the key to immortal life. "That's how Chef Bugnard has been teaching us at Le Cordon Bleu—to start from the very beginning and master each step before moving on. So that's what I'll do. I'll go back to the very basics of mayonnaise making. I'll make notes. I'll experiment. I'll make vats and vats, and more vats, of mayonnaise until I figure out what's wrong and I fix it!"

"There's just one thing," I said as the market on rue de Bourgogne came into view.

"What's that?" she asked with a frown.

"You're going to need a lot more eggs."

We both roared with laughter so hard we staggered like drunks along the street.

During the war, Parisians had bemoaned first the indignity of the German Occupation, then the untenable, bone-biting cold, and *then* the lack of food as their worst complaints. The fact that the dearth of food was ranked as less a hardship than the chill by a people who lived and breathed cuisine was testament to the cruelty of winter in the City of Light.

I had recently come to concur with the accuracy of that sentiment. Spring, summer, and autumn in Paris had been perfectly gorgeous, and I had fallen in love with the city. I explored the streets either on foot or on my bicycle and literally *inhaled* the city: her smells, her sights, her delicious food, and the lovely, colorful parks that had inspired artists for centuries.

But once winter roared in, my adoration of Paris had cooled— pun very much intended—slightly.

Despite Paris's bitterly cold December, I loved that it was so easy to walk or bike the streets and to *get* places . . . I loved the people, the smells—even the bad ones were charming, simply because they were *Parisian*—and I loved the expansive boulevards and elegant honey or cream bricked buildings that had been part of Baron Haussmann's redesign a century ago.

Parisians complained about the number of cars that thronged their streets now that the American tourists were coming in full force, but I hardly considered myself a tourist. After all, I was half French! I *belonged* here.

There were cats everywhere—so much so that they seemed as integral a part of the city as her famed lights and the Tour Eiffel, which rose in its airy wishbone shape only a few blocks from rue de l'Université.

And of course, there was the food—that someone else prepared—and the wine!

It was simple: Paris was *heaven*.

Rue de Bourgogne was the closest market to the block where Julia and I both lived. I'd found it fascinating and enlightening that when you shop at a market in Paris, you get to know all of the shopkeepers and vendors. There's simply no other option. Everyone is friendly and insists on chatting and gossiping.

It's so much different from the States, where one makes a mad dash into the grocery—a building, rather than a collection of vendors, shops, and carts—snatches up what they need, zips through the checkout line, and then dashes just as quickly home. "Our" market was a little community unto itself, and it was here that I met my neighbors—including Julia—and learned about all sorts of interesting foods and how to buy them.

Preparing my purchases—which I always bought with the greatest optimism—was an entirely different thing, however. I couldn't count how many times I'd ruined a chicken or overcooked a roast.

Despite being French, neither my mother nor grandmother had cooked all that often, and when they did, it was simple American fare because that was what my father liked—and what *his* mother had made. So I had grown up on food much the same way Julia had: basic, boring egg noodles or boxed pasta; beef roasts with thin, tasteless gravies; too-dry roasted chickens, potatoes upon potatoes upon *potatoes*; and lots of corn and green beans. Thin-sliced white bread that came in a plastic bag; bread that was so spongy you could squish a slice, crust and all, into a ball the size of a cherry—and, of course, Spam. Fancy dinner parties in our world often amounted to grilled Spam topped with slices of pineapple. Sauces were cans of condensed Campbell's soup, poured over meat or potatoes.

The coffee I drank had consisted of Folger's mixed with hot water, and I was fond of telling Julia that *my* Parisian moment of sensory enlightenment had occurred when I had my first French *café*.

Unfortunately, coffee was the only consumable still being rationed at the end of 1949, so I couldn't indulge as often as I would have liked at the cafés. Still, my grandfather somehow always seemed to have a more than adequate supply at home. I thought it best not to ask too many questions about that, even though everyone talked openly about the black market.

"Bonjour, Madame Marie!" Julia said gaily as we stopped to look at the shallots and onions offered by the wrinkled, round vegetable woman.

"Bonjour, Madame Child," replied the wizened merchant, who was wrapped up in a warm coat, battered hat, and a wool blanket. Inside a small metal pail burned a tiny fire for her to warm her gnarled hands. "Bonjour, Mademoiselle Knight. And how are you this frigid Thursday morning?"

"Bonjour, madame," I replied. "I am feeling quite pleasant except that my nose is cold and so are my toes!" To make the point, I huddled closer into my heavy woolen scarf, tucking my pointy nose inside its warm folds.

My French was flawless, thanks to my mother and grandmother, but Julia had learned the language only once she moved here. She still struggled when people spoke too fast or talked over one another. I had sat with her many times at the table in her tiny third-floor kitchen, practicing with her while eating whatever delicious food she'd prepared. It was a mutually beneficial relationship.

It was because of those times that I'd begun tutoring some of the children and wives of the American diplomats in French. At Julia's suggestion, Paul Child had enthusiastically offered my name to some of his colleagues at the U.S. Embassy for that service.

I was fortunate enough to now have four American students and a French one—the latter whom I was helping with their English, of course—and that meant I conducted one meeting per day, usually in the morning. It was an easy schedule—if not a little boring—and I certainly would take on more students if the opportunity arose. But for the meantime, it brought me enough money to buy some of the stylish shoes and hats that I simply couldn't deny myself from shops on the Champs-Élysées. I might enjoy climbing trees and taking apart radios, but I'd also inherited my mother's and grandmother's love for pretty clothes and fashionable accessories.

Where Julia spent her money on kitchen equipment—pots, pans, knives, and a variety of items I didn't recognize, I splurged on shoes, hats, pocketbooks, and fabulous dresses, too, of course. I justified the expense because my grandfather wouldn't even consider me paying anything for my room and board at our house on rue de l'Université.

I held my gloved hands out over the warmth of Madame Marie's small bucket-fire as Julia poked through the old woman's basket of shallots. The little dumpling of a grocer was known throughout the neighborhood as Marie des Quatre Saisons because she always had the best produce for every season.

Until I met Marie of the Four Seasons, I had just, well, plucked potatoes from the bin and grabbed the first zucchini I saw, and I even—*quelle horreur!*—had been known to purchase radishes too far past the end of their season . . . withered, dried, tasteless ones. But the very first time I visited the market, Julia and Madame Marie had taken me under their respective wings and set me straight.

Somehow, I'd ended up with them both poking their noses into my bag to see what I'd selected from the *other* produce stand on the rue, which was run by Monsieur Blanche.

"No, no, no, *no!*" cried Madame when she saw the wrinkly radishes and their wilted greens. "But, *no*, mademoiselle, you cannot serve those!" Before I could react, she plucked the offending vegetables and tossed them onto the ground as she cast a ferocious look toward M. Blanche's cart. "To anyone! Not even a street dog!"

"But they're just radishes," I said, trying to contain my giggles at the old woman's outrage. Apparently, this was a very serious situation.

"*I* thought they were just radishes too," Julia had said earnestly. At the time, she was speaking in slow, careful French, but I understood her easily. "Until Madame informed me otherwise!"

"You will never find yourself a man if you serve him wrinkling radishes or wilted greens, mademoiselle!" Madame shoved three of her radishes at me, and I had to admit, they were far superior than the ones she'd dashed to the ground.

"That's very true," Julia said with her infectious laugh. "Men do not like to be reminded of anything that wilts or wrinkles or sags!"

I was so astonished by her comment—especially in front of an older woman—that I burst out laughing in a mix of horror and hilarity.

But Madame Marie was nodding sagely, and she patted my arm. "*Oui, oui,*" she said. "Madame Child"—she pronounced Julia's last name "Scheeld"— "knows what she speaks, *non?* The men, they like the produce that is long and straight and very, very firm because it reminds them of how they are—or wish to be."

Even as I laughed harder, I didn't have the heart to tell either of them that I was perfectly content with the two men currently in my life—both older than me by many decades. Besides, I was already struggling to cook for Grand-père and Oncle Rafe.

Yet, perhaps they would appreciate crisp and firm radishes and not push around on their plates a meal I might prepare with them.

The Incident of the Radishes, as I'd come to think of it, not only introduced me to Julia Child and Madame Marie, but it also launched a market-wide initiative: to find me, Tabitha Knight, a man. Whether I wanted one or not.

I wasn't the least bit brokenhearted about the end of my engagement with Henry. It had been my decision—and one that I'd waited far too long to make. My mother was the one who was devastated. I think she'd been looking forward to getting me out of the house.

The war had changed both Henry and me—as it had done to pretty much everyone I knew. Even though we'd been together since we were twenty-two and everyone assumed we'd marry—and maybe that was why it had taken me so long to break it off—I just didn't feel right about tying the knot and settling down, raising children, and being the teacher I'd gone to school to be. It sounded *boring*, and would be such a letdown—like a deflated soufflé—after my Rosie-the-Riveter job during the war.

I think Henry had been just as relieved as I was to have it over, and we remained good friends. That was how we'd started: by being lab partners in chemistry at the University of Michigan. When I'd decided to booby-trap our teaching assistant's desk with vinegar and baking soda because he gave us a B when we clearly deserved an A, Henry had covered for me.

Two weeks later, he'd enlisted.

And so today when Madame Marie asked how I was doing, she was really asking me whether I'd been on any dates or had met any interesting men. Which was why I'd ducked inside my scarf and pretended not to know what she meant. Nonetheless, the vegetable woman gave me a knowing look.

"And there will be no wrinkled radishes or potatoes for you today, *non*, mademoiselle?" she asked with a twinkle in her eye.

"No, I think I shall have some shallots," I replied.

Julia plucked three shallots from the basket and offered them to me. They bulged fatly inside their papery rust-colored skins, and I could see that the spidery roots on the rounded ends were still supple and had not dried out. "How about these, Tabs? Oh, and Tabitha had a date last night," she said to Madame, and I wanted to kick her.

Julia, not Madame Marie.

"Oh, and so you did, did you?" said the grocer, her eyes fastened on me with interest.

"It wasn't a date," I replied, giving Julia a dark look. She merely laughed and started to root through the basket of red potatoes. "I'm going to murder you," I muttered to her in English.

"It was a *blind* date," Julia said cheerfully, obviously unconcerned by my empty threat. "Dort set her up."

Dort was Julia's sister's nickname. I found it rather amusing that it was the same name as a highway north of Detroit, not far from where I'd lived when working at the bomber plant.

"Oh, she did, did she?" Madame was very interested. "That young woman, that Dorothy, she is very tall—taller than even you, Madame Child, and so she will need a man with good, strong stature, *non?*"

I loved the idea of talking about Dort's husband prospects instead of mine, and so I eagerly followed that train of thought. "Good stature, meaning that he is confident in himself and not afraid to be seen with a statuesque woman. Not necessarily taller." I smiled at Julia, for her husband, Paul, was several inches shorter than she was and they were madly in love. He adored her, and she adored him, and even though I had no interest in "finding a man," I did envy their relationship a little. That was probably part of the reason Julia was so determined to fix me up.

"Don't try and change the subject, Tabs," Julia said, grinning. "You've avoided it during our entire walk here, so now you're required to spill all of the details to Madame Marie *and* me."

I sighed. I supposed it was best to answer the questions now, rather than as we paraded through the market and having Julia lasso everyone else into the subject of my nonexistent love life.

"And so you will tell me about this blind date, then, mademoiselle," said the vegetable woman. It was a statement, not a question.

"Dort had some of her friends over at Julia's house last night, and she invited me so that I could meet one of the men from the theater where she works," I said. "That was all it was."

Dort had a job in the business office for the American Club Theater, which performed at Théâtre Monceau. She'd made many friends, both onstage and offstage at the company, and most of them were American. They often came over to Julia and Paul's apartment after the shows were over, which meant they arrived late and stayed until the very early hours of the morning.

Julia and Paul didn't mind *too* much, Julia told me, except that the young people did drink an awful lot of their booze. And the revelry often kept the older couple up very late. Paul was a little grumpier about it than his wife was, and he'd made Julia promise to talk to Dort about it—especially since last night's gathering had been the third one this week.

"And this man, did you meet him?" Madame was not going to give up the topic. After all, gossip throughout the marketplace was the juice that kept her—and all the other vendors—going.

"Yes, I did. He was very nice," I replied.

That was true. Mark Justiss of Boston had been very nice, fairly handsome, and appropriately attentive once Dort introduced us. We'd talked for a short while between glasses of whisky and wine. But he hadn't really captured my attention in that spark-like way you want to happen when you meet a potential partner. Truthfully, I didn't think I would ever be interested in an American man now that I had moved to Paris. American men were just sort of blah in comparison to their French counterparts.

"Oh, and that reminds me, Julia . . . I might have left my gloves at your place."

"I haven't seen them, but you can certainly stop up on our way back to check."

"Perfect. Now," I said, firmly changing the subject, "I must get some potatoes for Grand-père's and Oncle's dinner. Do you have any suitable ones, Madame Marie?"

The old woman gave a laugh rough from years of cigarette smoke, and her eyes glinted with humor. She knew I was done speaking about men. "As you know, mine are the finest potatoes in Paris. And so what is it you are cooking tonight, mademoiselle?"

"I was thinking of making a roasted chicken," I said. That was one of the few dishes I felt as if I'd begun to master—and one of the few meals I prepared that Grand-père and Oncle Rafe actually ate. If only their housekeeper-cook hadn't left to take care of her mother shortly after I came to Paris!

"Ah, *bien.* And you must have some carrots, then, for the *poulet rôti, non*, mademoiselle?" Marie said with a glint in her eye as she gestured broadly to her basket of carrots.

By now, I'd been fairly well trained by the old woman, so I eyed the long, root-furred carrots closely. "It's near the end of the season, so the insides will be hard and woody," I said slowly, casting a sidelong look at Julia, who nodded encouragingly. "I'll have to remove the cores, won't I?"

"*Oui*, and so you will keep the outsides—the *rouges des carotte*—and they will be sweet and crisp," agreed Marie.

"Yes, of course."

"What have you in the way of turnips?" Julia interjected. "Oh, Tabitha, you'll do a garlic, turnip, and potato mash to go with it all. Ye gods, the chicken gravy will be *spectacular* over it!" Her eyes lit up, and I could tell she was envisioning the beauty of it— imagining the little rich circles of oil glimmering on the top of the herb-speckled gravy . . . at least, that was how it would be if *she* made it.

My mouth watered at the thought. If only I could afford to hire Julia Child to cook for us every night!

"Oh, well, I'm not sure I could manage that," I said, somewhat wistfully.

"Oh, no, no, no, a turnip mash is easy!" Julia said, and then the two other women were off and running with my menu. I didn't have the heart to tell them I knew the meal would turn out to be a disappointment.

"*Oui,* a turnip and potato mash would be *magnifique.* And you'll get rosemary and thyme fresh for that, *non,* from your *grand-père*'s greenhouse?" Marie had already begun to dig in another basket for the turnips of her choice. "And sage too," she added in a tone that brooked no disobedience.

"Yes," I replied, and showed them the herb bundles in my bag. "I've brought some for you, madame, and you too, Julia."

"Oh, *merci!*" Madame Marie was very pleased, and she took the herbs I offered gratefully. I didn't know whether she would use them herself or whether she would sell them, but it didn't matter to me in the least.

Now that the topic of my love life had been retired, the three of us chatted for another few minutes, mostly about the other merchants and members of the neighborhood—all of whom knew one another, for they, or more often their maids, visited the market nearly every day.

"*Pauvre* Mademoiselle Clarice was sobbing so this morning," Marie said as I tucked my purchases into my large cloth market bag.

"Oh no! Do you know why?" asked Julia.

Clarice was the maid, or *femme de ménage,* for a wealthy couple who lived around the corner. The young woman had a sunny personality and was always very polite, if a little reserved, when she spoke to any of us neighbors or vendors. Clarice dressed in somber, dark clothing but always had new, very fashionable shoes—a curious detail that I had noticed early on. And so I'd had to ask about it.

She'd explained that her sister worked for a custom shoe shop and passed on to her any shoes that were imperfect or didn't meet the standards of the customer. I jokingly told her that if any imperfect shoes became available in a size six that I would gratefully take them off her sister's hands—to which Julia interjected that she was certain there weren't many size *twelves* available for women. We had a good laugh at that, the three of us, and one time not long after, Clarice actually *did* bring me a pair of very smart Mary Janes in a dark red tortoiseshell finish from Godot & Block. They'd been rejected due to the smallest of nicks on one side of the shoe. I *loved* them.

"Oh, *oui*," Marie replied, as if it were a given that she should know every detail of the lives of everyone in the neighborhood. "Clarice was sad because the dog of her mistress ran off last night and they can't find her."

"Oh no!" said Julia. "That's awful. I hope they locate her soon! It's so very cold and bitter right now. It would be terrible if something like that happened to our little Minette." She was speaking of the cat that had adopted Paul and her.

I'd seen Clarice walking her mistress's pet many times through the marketplace. I had never seen a dog dressed in a winter coat or sweater before coming to Paris—but then I met Oncle Rafe's pooch Oscar Wilde, who had an entire wardrobe filled with canine fashions.

Thus I wasn't surprised to see that Madame Flouf, Clarice's four-legged charge, seemed to have an endless supply of her very own doggy clothing. Madame Flouf was a medium-size poodle the color of champagne, and she also wore a blue collar with glittering gems on it. I didn't know whether the gems were real or paste, but Clarice's mistress seemed wealthy enough that they might have been genuine jewels.

"*Oui*," replied Marie as she tucked away the coins Julia had placed on the small, rugged table the grocer used as a counter. "Poor Clarice. And did you see that Marcel has made himself a new roof for his stall?"

"No, I did not," Julia replied, smiling as she held her hands out to warm them at the bucket of fire. "We haven't been to that end of the market yet."

"And that is because we came first to you, Madame Marie, since you have all of the gossip and information *and* the best vegetables in rue de Bourgogne! But now we must be off. Julia needs more eggs," I said with a grin. "And my toes are turning into little icicles!"

"So the mayonnaise is still giving you the problems, madame?" said the vegetable woman with a lifted brow. "Tsk, tsk. 'Tis such a shame. Perhaps Mademoiselle Tabitha can help guide you through this problem, eh?"

We all laughed heartily at that purposely ridiculous suggestion and took our leave. By the time we got through the market to Fidelia's egg cart, my bag was heavy with a bottle of Bordeaux-Médoc and also the roasting chicken Julia had helped me select from what she gaily called the lineup of *mesdames gras poulardes*.

"Madame Poulet will be *magnifique!*" Julia assured me as I tucked the chicken into my bag.

I wasn't nearly as confident. The last time I'd attempted to roast a chicken, I'd caught it on fire when I was trying to singe off the bits of hair and feathers still clinging to its pebbly skin. I was holding that particular *madame poulet* over the gas flame and the whole damned thing caught—and so we had a roasted chicken that was black on one side and underdone on the other. I'm still not certain how that happened.

"Ah, madame, how goes the mayonnaise?" Fidelia asked Julia after her initial bonjour to both of us.

It seemed everyone in the seventh arrondissement actually did know about Julia's mayonnaise problem. Perhaps the news had even spread to Montparnasse and the rest of the Left Bank.

"Well, I'm back for more eggs," replied Julia with a pained grin and dramatic shrug, "and so you can guess!"

"Ah, madame, I am so sorry about your problems. But I am not so sorry to sell you more of my eggs!" Fidelia told her with a smile that she included me in as well. She was a tiny, appropriately birdlike woman who fussed over the eggs as if she'd laid them herself. Each was carefully washed and marked with its date using a pencil, then arranged in their baskets in pretty clusters that resembled flowers.

I poked over the eggs, which ranged in color from pale green to tan to brown to cream to lightly speckled rust, and selected a few for my basket. My scrambled eggs were respectably edible, and Oncle Rafe had expressed the desire for a hard-boiled egg in the morning as well. That I was certain to manage.

"Do you think the color of the shell might make a difference?" Julia said suddenly, holding up a pale-green egg.

"In the mayonnaise?" I asked, looking at her with a frown. I didn't see how that would matter, but who was I to say?

"Oh, perhaps, madame," said Fidelia, giving me a wink. "It is possible, and therefore you should buy all of the same color, perhaps? So as not to mix them up when making your sauce?"

An intent expression on her face, Julia began to pick out several more greenish eggs. "I'm going to approach this like a scientist, Tabs. I'm going to be a—a *medieval alchemist* in the kitchen! I'll be the . . . the Sherlock Holmes of food preparation and *observe* the minutiae of *everything!*"

"Did you hear about poor Clarice's mistress's dog?" asked Fidelia as she carefully wrapped our eggs in newspaper and tucked them into their respective cardboard boxes. Her fingers were deft despite the thick mittens she wore.

"Madame Marie told us about it," I replied as I dug out the money for my eggs. "It's so very sad."

"I hope they find her soon," replied Fidelia. "Clarice came to the market twice today, looking for her and asking if anyone had seen Madame Flouf. She said she was out calling for her all night."

"How terribly awful for her and for her mistress," Julia said. "And for poor Madame Flouf to be out in this terrible bitter cold! I do hope it doesn't snow or ice over tonight."

"I made an offering at Ste. Clotilde in her honor," said Fidelia, glancing in the direction of the church, whose twin gothic steeples were just in view over the roof across the street.

"That was very nice of you," I said, and meant it. Until I'd moved in with Grand-père and Oncle Rafe, I'd never understood how much a pet could mean to someone. My mother had refused to have any sort of animal in our house—cat, dog, rabbit, turtle, or even a goldfish, and my father had prudently decided not to argue.

"And did you hear about M. Peroux?" Fidelia said as she tucked the little carton's flaps closed.

"No, what is it?" Julia was all ears, of course. But then, so was I.

"His wife caught him with his mistress and poured all of his wine out into the gutter!" Fidelia told her. Her bright little eyes were wide with shock and mirth.

"Oh no!" I exclaimed, thinking of all of that beautiful wine, just *wasted*, pouring through the frozen gutters. M. Peroux was famous in the neighborhood for his precious wine collection, some of which he'd managed to hide from the Germans during the Occupation. "Could no one have stopped her and saved some of it?"

Fidelia's laugh tinkled merrily. "I am sure M. Peroux tried—as soon as he got his pants on—don't you think?"

Julia and I laughed. "Poor man. I suppose it serves him right," I said.

"Indeed. Most Frenchmen know to keep their mistresses well hidden from their wives," Fidelia said sagely.

"Or not to have one at all—at least if one has an award-winning wine collection," Julia said, winking at Fidelia.

"Ah, men," said the egg merchant, glancing at me. "They are simply not the trouble they are worth sometimes, *non*, Mademoiselle Tabitha?"

I merely shook my head and smiled, unwilling to be drawn into yet another conversation about potential husbands.

"Tabitha happens to already have two of the most *spectacular* gentlemen in her life right now," Julia said with a smile. "I can see why she doesn't seem interested in anyone else—for how *could* anyone compare to Maurice Saint-Léger and that dashing Rafe Fautrier?"

"Indeed," I replied. "And so I'd best get on home and attend to them before they toss me aside for another woman! I would be heartbroken."

We all laughed, and then Julia and I bid au revoir to the egg merchant.

"Didn't you want to come up and check for your gloves?" Julia said as we reached the door to her building at 81 rue de l'Université and I would have gone on.

"Yes, I have time now," I replied, even knowing that it wouldn't be a simple dash into the apartment, a quick look around, and then a leaving. Julia and I would sit and chat, probably have a cup of chocolate or coffee, and if she hadn't left for work, Dort would join us to talk about the party last night.

But Grand-père and Oncle Rafe wouldn't need or expect me for at least another hour, and so I followed Julia into the small lobby of her building.

And that's when I heard someone screaming bloody murder.

CHAPTER 2

"What the—?" Julia said, looking at me as if to see whether I was hearing the same thing.

The screaming was muffled and seemed to be coming from an unobtrusive door at the far left corner of the lobby. I dashed toward the door, market bag bumping heavily against my hip. I thought belatedly about the eggs inside and hoped they'd survive.

Julia had longer legs than me, so she reached the door first. When she flung it open, someone ran smack dab into her.

Being six feet two and quite sturdy in build, Julia hardly staggered from the impact. As she caught the woman who'd run into her, I recognized her as Mathilde, the Childs' day maid.

We both were asking different versions of "What is it? What's wrong?" as the young woman goggled at us with wide eyes and tried to catch her breath and her thoughts.

The poor girl could hardly form any coherent words. At last, Julia set down her bag and took the maid firmly by the arms and looked down at her. "*Mathilde*. Take a deep breath, close your eyes, and then—"

"There's a *body*, madame!" Mathilde burst out and then began to sob and gesticulate.

My French was excellent, but I still wasn't certain I'd heard what I thought I'd heard. "A body? What sort of body?"

I imagined a dead snake, a rat, perhaps even a cat—

"The body of a *woman*! She's *dead*, madame!" Suddenly the words spilled out from Mathilde as if a great dam had burst. "She is just lying there, and all the blood! Someone has surely killed her! Oh, oh, all the *blood*! It's horrible, it's terrible, it's so, so much!"

"Dear heaven," Julia breathed, looking at me.

I felt light-headed. A dead woman, *here*? Murdered? Could it be true? Surely there was some sort of mistake. . . .

"Where is she?" I said. Maybe Mathilde was overreacting—and maybe the woman wasn't dead but just badly injured and needed medical help. "Show us—no, we should call the police first. And a doctor, to be certain."

"*Oui, oui,*" Mathilde said, looking around wildly as if to expect either a telephone or a constable to magically appear.

Just then, the door to one of the first-floor apartments opened.

"What is all of this?" demanded Madame Perier, who was the landlady at 81 rue de l'Université. Eccentric is the kindest word I can think of to describe her. Madame was dressed like a gray scarecrow, in long, flowing, tattered-hemmed clothing that fluttered when she gesticulated. "What is all of this noise? We are a *quiet* building here, Madame Child, mademoiselle—and *Mathilde*! You know better than—"

"Madame Perier, please, we need to call the police," said Julia.

"Why on earth—"

"There is apparently the body of a dead woman in the—where is it, Mathilde?" Julia asked.

Madame Perier's eyes widened as Mathilde began to speak in disjointed phrases.

"If you could call a constable, madame," I said, cutting into the conversation. I don't know why I had a sudden, sinking feeling. I suppose it wasn't that surprising, considering the situation. *A dead body.*

"I'll go with Mathilde to make certain the . . . the woman doesn't need a doctor. It's—she's—downstairs by the trash bins," said Julia, gesturing toward the narrow, shadowy stairwell that apparently led down. Her blue eyes were wide, and her normally boundless energy had been replaced by something more subdued. I'm sure I appeared just as shell-shocked as she did.

Madame Perier fluttered back to her apartment to make the phone call, and Julia and I followed Mathilde down the dim, narrow stairs.

Julia had to duck a little, for the cramped stairwell had a low ceiling, but I was able to slip down the steps quickly and I got to the bottom first.

The entire space was small, dark, and crowded, lit only by a single, stingy bulb that hung above the fifth step leading into the room. At the bottom, I found myself in a small area where it appeared the trash bins were kept, and to where each resident of the building or, more likely, their maid, brought their garbage down as needed. The stairs descended from the first floor, and there was another door that led to the outside for the days the trash bins needed to be collected. We had a similar arrangement at our house, though our garbage door was much smaller as it was only a single, albeit large, residence with the three of us.

The first thing I saw was the row of trash bins. Then I saw a pair of feet, still shod, resting in what would be a supremely uncomfortable position had the poor woman been alive. Then there were legs, bared by a coat and dress that had ridden up nearly to the woman's hips. But my attention was caught and held by the dark stains soaked on the front of her bodice, splatters on her legs and hands, puddles on the floor. Mathilde was right: the blood was everywhere.

The partially subterranean space probably always smelled damp and musty, and like garbage . . . but now, it had the distinct odor of death and blood.

The pools of blood were dark and dull and had clearly been there for some time. The woman had been left behind the trash bins, half propped against the shadowy brick wall, tucked in the corner, where she wouldn't be easily noticed. Her face was partially obstructed by a wing of dark blond hair that had fallen over it, and her hands were flung aside as if she'd simply been tossed there like a sack of flour.

"How awful," Julia murmured, standing behind me. The stingy light bulb behind her created a long, broad shadow, casting what little I could see of the pitiful figure into darkness.

I wanted to do something to make the poor woman more comfortable, or at least to show respect—cover her, perhaps, or move her hands so they didn't seem so strange—but the police would want the scene to remain untouched.

So Julia and I just stood there, our breathing harsh and unsteady. Behind I could hear Mathilde's soft sobs and jerky gasps of air.

"Why would someone do this to someone . . . just *leave* her?" Julia murmured.

"I don't know," I replied inanely. But there were simply no other words. "How could someone do such a thing?"

I read my share of murder mysteries, where dead bodies seemed to drop like flies, and the use of knives, guns, and poison occurred in the characters' everyday life as easily as pencils or cooking pots . . . but to experience such a thing in real life was horrific. I felt the need to pinch myself to see whether I was having a nightmare.

As Julia shifted, her shadow moved and I had a better look at the dead woman. I saw the blue print of her hiked-up dress, discerned the pattern on the shoes covering her pathetically skewed feet, and frowned over the way her mussed blond hair fell over her face.

My breath caught, and I stepped forward involuntarily. I could see her even better now. My stomach dropped, sharp and hard. *Dear heaven.*

I felt ill. Not because I was going to vomit—at least I didn't think I was—but because *I recognized her.*

The sounds of approaching footsteps—fast and multiple pairs of them—drew my attention. Mathilde, who'd stood as far away as she could with her shoulders hunched and her face, but for her wide eyes, buried in her hands, made a little noise of nervousness or surprise and stood up ramrod straight as if at attention.

We turned to see Madame Perier's gray flowing figure emerge from the stairs, followed by two other people I didn't recognize, but who weren't dressed in uniforms or carrying a medical bag.

Apparently, word had spread.

The newcomers were just reaching the bottom of the steps when a whistle shrieked from above, sending sharp, earsplitting echoes reverberating through the brick stairwell.

"Stand back!" A voice shouted as even more footsteps—heavier—made their way down the steps.

The police had obviously arrived.

"Stand away!" shouted the constable, blowing on his whistle again. This time he was at the bottom of the steps, and everyone clapped their hands over their ears to protect them from the high-pitched noise.

"Everyone, *move back*," ordered the constable again, shining his flashlight into their faces so that they would comply. "This is a crime scene, and you must leave."

"I . . . I think I know her," I said. My ears were still ringing from the sharp whistle that had bounced around the small, hard-walled space, but the rest of me felt empty and numb.

"What?" Julia exclaimed, right behind me. "You do?"

"I think I know her," I said again, louder, and this time the second constable looked at me. "Her name is Thérèse."

"All right, then, mademoiselle," said the constable. "You will wait upstairs and we will speak to you then."

Feeling shaky and unsettled, I started up the steps. I'd be glad to get away from the close space, the stench of blood and bodily fluids . . . the sight of violence.

"You know her?" said Julia. Her voice was loud and strident and just above and behind my ear.

"Don't you?" I said over my shoulder.

Before she could reply, we had to step aside for another man bounding down the stairs. He was not dressed in uniform like the constables, but I assumed he was with the *police judiciaire* due to his air of authority and because no one blew a screaming whistle at *him.*

He wore a fedora, and his long, woolen coat flapped at the hem, fluttering against mine as he hurried past without acknowledging either of us. I wasn't French enough to be offended by his lack of even a bonjour or *pardonnez-moi.* Besides, as far as I was concerned, social graces could definitely be suspended during a murder investigation.

People were clustered in the lobby, and I recognized many of them from the neighborhood. There was a sort of dull roar filling the high-ceilinged foyer as everyone was talking and exclaiming all at once. Having been the "discoverer," Mathilde was, understandably, in the center of the conversation, and she was, also understandably, milking the attention for all it was worth.

Julia seemed to know everyone. She went around greeting people as I trailed in her wake, still numb over the fact that I knew the victim.

Well, *knew* wasn't a really accurate description. I'd met her briefly, and our interaction had been limited and superficial. Still . . . it was terrifying to see someone I'd known even slightly lying on the ground, murdered.

"I didn't recognize her. She doesn't—didn't—live here in the neighborhood, does she?" Julia said, picking up the market bag she'd left when she followed Mathilde downstairs. The two bottles of wine inside clinked. "I've never seen her."

"No," I replied. "But she was here last night."

"She *was?* Here?" Julia stared at me. "Do you mean here at Roo de Loo, or here . . . ?" Roo de Loo was Julia's nickname for their apartment here on rue de l'Université.

"I mean here, upstairs, in your flat," I said. "She came last night with some of Dort's friends. How horrible!"

"Dort will be beside herself," Julia said, squeezing my hand. I was *so cold*, and not simply because of the weather. The ugly chill even permeated my heavy coat and scarf. "It's so terrible."

"But who would have done such a thing? What was she doing down there in the trash area, anyway?" I hugged myself, rubbing my arms to warm them against the chill of death. "I didn't even know that place existed here."

"There's *no* reason for anyone to go down there unless they're bringing trash," Julia said. Her voice sounded as unsettled and thin as mine did. "*I* don't even go down there, and I live here! And how did she even know that place existed? Ye gods, I wonder if I should phone Paul and tell him."

"I'm sure it can wait," I replied, still trying to get warm. "What would he do about it, anyway?"

"Not much, but he does work for the USIS. I wonder if they're going to need to know about this—you know they'll want to stick their noses in everything. It's all that diplomacy stuff. The police are obviously going to want to ask you a lot of questions," Julia said, and just then, I caught sight of the official-looking man in the fedora emerge from the stairwell. "And Dort too."

The man scanned the area, and when his attention fell on us, my heart gave a little lurch. "He's coming over here," I said unnecessarily.

There was something about seeing a policeman—in this case, a detective or some sort of investigator—walking purposely toward us that made me nervous. His long, unbuttoned coat still flapped around his legs, and he'd removed his gloves. Now he carried a pad of paper and a pencil, which made him look even more official.

"Bonjour, mesdemoiselles," he said. "I am Inspecteur Merveille, and I must ask you some questions."

Merveille seemed to be in his early thirties, which surprised me a little. Wasn't that young to be a police detective? Either he must be very good at his job, or he looked younger than he actually was. The *inspecteur* was as tall as Julia and his demeanor gave him an air of competent authority. He was clean-shaven and I could see just a bit of dark hair beneath the brim of his hat.

"Yes, of course," I told him just as I noticed one of the constables had extricated Mathilde from her crowd of admirers. They were going to question her as well.

"I understand one of you knew the young woman," he said, after jotting down our names and addresses.

"I don't *know* her. I only met her last night," I replied. "Her name was Thérèse. I don't remember her last name."

Merveille nodded but remained silent. His gray eyes fixed intently on me, but they seemed merely interested instead of accusatory.

Not that he had any reason to be accusatory toward me.

I swallowed hard, suddenly feeling hot instead of chilled. Why was I so nervous? I hadn't done anything wrong.

I started talking again. "Thérèse came with a friend of hers to Julia's apartment last night." I explained about Dort, her job for the American Club Theater, and how some of the actors, crew, and office workers often gathered at her sister's apartment after the shows.

"And so you had not met this Mademoiselle Thérèse before last night," Merveille said.

"No," I replied.

"And you didn't know she was going to be at this little, hmm, soirée you attended?"

I got the distinct impression that Merveille didn't willingly attend soirées. "No—how could I have known that if I had never met her?" I said.

Instead of acknowledging the logic of my question, Merveille merely transferred his attention to Julia. "And you, madame?"

"No," Julia replied.

"But this woman was at your house," the *inspecteur* pressed. "And you did not meet her?"

I could tell Julia was a little flustered as those dark, penetrating eyes settled on her, for she fumbled her French a little. "She was a guest of my sister's. I went to bed at midnight, for I'm used to getting up very early for my classes at Le Cordon Bleu—although the school is on holiday until January. Anyway, I went to bed early and I didn't see much of Dort's—er, my sister's guests."

"And that was of no concern to you? That a woman you didn't know had come to your house?" asked the *inspecteur*.

"Not really," Julia replied with a shrug. "It's my sister's home too."

I noticed that although the detective brandished the notepad and pencil, he had yet to write anything down except our names.

Did his lack of note taking mean I had said nothing important, or that he would remember everything without writing it down—or that he didn't want to divert his attention from us even for a moment by turning to his pad and pencil?

"I see," he replied, then trained those cool eyes back on me. "But you were at the party and you met her."

"Only briefly."

"Did you see what time she left Madame Child's apartment?"

"Yes, it was just after two o'clock."

He nodded. "And did you notice—did anyone leave with her?"

Exactly the question I had been dreading even though I had no reason to do so.

"We left at the same time," I told him.

Merveille's eyebrows jumped a little. "Just the two of you?"

"Yes, we rode down in the lift together."

"And when you got down here to the lobby, then what happened?"

"I left," I replied. "I walked outside and went across the street to my home. And . . . and Thérèse walked outside to wait for a cab. When I left her, she was alive," I felt compelled to add. "Standing just outside the door, waiting for her ride."

"She was standing outside this building, by the street?"

"Yes."

"And no one else was around."

"No, *Inspecteur*. I saw no one else."

"Not even on the street? In an automobile?"

"I didn't notice anyone or any cars around," I said. "It was very late."

"And what about the other partygoers? Were they still upstairs, or were you the last to leave?"

"There were still some people upstairs. No one else was ready to leave."

Merveille seemed as if he was about to speak again, but one of the constables approached and caught his attention. The policeman was holding something wrapped in a plastic bag, and he drew the *inspecteur* aside to speak to him in a low tone.

Julia and I exchanged looks. She seemed properly sober about the terrible situation, but I didn't sense that she felt the same underlying foreboding I hadn't been able to shake.

When Merveille turned back, he was holding the plastic-wrapped item, and I saw what it was: a knife. It was dark with blood and presumably was the murder weapon. I couldn't take my eyes from it.

How horrible. How terribly awful that that very item was used to take someone's life.

As the *inspecteur* turned the package over in his hands to look at it more closely, I heard Julia catch her breath.

Merveille looked up at her sharply. "Yes, madame?"

"Oh, it's nothing," she replied with a weak laugh. "Just . . . there's a lot of blood."

"But surely you are used to the blood, madame, being a student of Le Cordon Bleu," the detective said, watching her very closely. "Or you would not be much of a chef, *non?*"

"Human blood is far different than that from a side of beef," she retorted.

The sense of foreboding that had merely knitted into the back of my mind like a settling kitten suddenly turned into deep, gouging swipes. For I knew what Merveille was about to say just before he spoke.

"Or perhaps it is not the blood that is upsetting you, Madame Child, but the fact that you recognize this very knife?" The *inspecteur* pinned her with cold eyes. "This is *your knife*, is it not, Madame Child? It was your knife, taken from your very own kitchen, that was used to kill this *pauvre* Mademoiselle Thérèse . . . sometime early this morning."

CHAPTER 3

"No one in their right mind would believe that Julia could kill *anyone*," I said wildly, pacing around the salon with rapid, angry footsteps as I gesticulated my outrage. I hadn't even taken off my coat, although I'd removed my scarf and had been using it like a flag for emphasis. "It's simply ridiculous!"

"Now, now, *ma mie*, perhaps we should not rattle the cage so much," said Grand-père, glancing at the credenza situated against the wall. My marching was shaking the floor so violently that the delicate etched glass aperitif and wineglasses were clinking against each other. He was probably concerned about my flailing scarf as well, for there were many delicate objects on the tables in the parlor. "Perhaps you might sit just there, hmm, and have something to calm your nerves?" He gestured to the blue brocade Louis XV sofa. "Armagnac, perhaps?"

"I think such an outrage calls for whisky instead of a mere brandy," said Oncle Rafe, rising to see to it. In doing so, he tucked under his arm the tiny, fluffy brown and white dog that had been sitting on his lap, then moved to the credenza. "And since when do you hesitate to rattle a cage, eh, Maurice?" He gave my grandfather a wry, affectionate look, then smiled at me. "Shall I help you off with your coat, now, *ma chérie?*"

My grandfather gave a short, Gallic wave toward Rafe as if to erase the man's comment, but I saw his lips twitch with humor.

I didn't know his exact age, but I estimated my grandfather

was in his late seventies. Although his body was now far too slender and ridden with tremors, he still had a full head of thick dark hair and perfect teeth that I was fairly certain were dentures. He currently held a cigarette in one veiny, age-spotted hand and a glass of what was probably cognac in the other. A sleek black cat wearing a wide collar of real diamonds sat in his lap.

"Forgive me for not helping you with your coat, Tabitte, but Madame X would be quite disturbed," Grand-père said, gesturing to the cat, who had been named after the famous Sargent painting—hence the jeweled collar.

"No, no, no . . . we do not want to upset the madame or she will claw at the chintz sofa again," said Rafe with great cynicism. He winked at me from the credenza.

I slipped the coat from my shoulders, letting it settle in a heap on the sofa, and leaned over to press a kiss to Grand-père's smooth, damp cheek. "You're right. It's nice and warm in here, and I don't need my coat."

When I'd gotten home and burst into the parlor, filled with righteous fury as well as anxiety, I'd found both of the men in their typical positions: seated next to a very large radiator. Despite the toasty warmth of the salon, they'd had their laps covered in layers of wool blankets along with their respective pets, and Grand-père had a gray shawl draped over his narrow shoulders.

Rafe, who was bald, wore a black knitted cap tugged all the way down to his earlobes and heavy gray brows. Where my grandfather was very tall for a Frenchman, Rafe was of average height. He had olive skin and a neatly trimmed beard and mustache that, he claimed, kept his head warm since he no longer had hair atop. He, too, had been partaking from a cigarette—a different brand from Grand-père's. It was a skinny dark one with a smell that I found particularly pleasant, for there was a hint of exotic spice in it that wasn't in American smokes. Coriander, perhaps. Or anise? I'd learned something about spices from Julia, but I was nowhere near an expert.

The two men had known each other for more than forty years, and when my grandmother moved to America with my mother in 1919, it seemed as if my grandmother's marriage to Maurice Saint-Léger had been, for all intents and purposes, terminated.

I had the impression that had been a mutual and amicable decision, for my grandmother and mother had always spoken fondly of both men. I had the letters that had passed between them over the years—from both sides of the ocean—and was taking my time reading through them all. Despite that, I'd been living here in Paris for nearly a month before I realized that Rafe was not my uncle at all, nor was he any sort of blood relative to me or Grand-père.

Since my arrival, I had also learned that during the German Occupation of Paris, Grand-père and Rafe had been part of the Resistance, helping to route Jedburgh soldiers in and out of the city and doing other tasks to support their countrymen.

Rafe, who was an artist from a family of vintners, had helped publish one of the underground newspapers that contained coded messages for Resistance members, and my wealthy grandfather had used his connections through the bank at which he'd been a partner to support those efforts. I found it fascinating and admirable that they had taken such risks and done so many brave things at their respective ages.

"Now, here you are, *petite*," said Oncle Rafe as he handed me a small glass shaped like a light bulb. A coppery-brown liquid filled just the bottom quarter of it. "Sit and we shall discuss it all."

"*Merci, oncle*," I said, giving him a kiss just above his short gray beard before I sank onto the blue sofa and continued my rantings. "It's simply *wrong* that the *inspecteur* should even consider Julia. Anyone could have taken that knife from her kitchen!"

"Indeed," replied Grand-père. Despite his frail body, his eyes were still sharp and his vision clear. "And you were there last night, *non*? Did you see anyone go into the kitchen?"

"No, but I wasn't paying very close attention," I replied, taking a sip of the whisky. It burned my mouth and throat, but once it settled into my stomach, I felt its warmth seep through me. I was glad Rafe hadn't added soda, as he usually did for me. "And the kitchen is upstairs from the salon, anyway. Anyone could have gone up there and I doubt we would have noticed." I shook my head, frowning. "He was just so blatant about it—the detective—the way he looked at Julia like he was ready to put her in cuffs and drag her off to jail. Oncle Rafe, have you heard of the detective? This Merveille? He seemed awfully young to me. I'm sure he has no idea what he's doing."

Rafe's eyes glinted with humor. "And why would you ask such a question of an old man like me? I know no one. I sit here in this lovely old house and tend to the excellent Monsieur Wilde"—his Papillon dog—"and the persnickety Madame X when Maurice allows me to, and I do my puzzles and eat far too many vegetables for a Frenchman"—he gave me a pointed look, for green salads and steamed vegetables were some of the few dishes I hadn't managed to set on fire—"and that is all my life! See? So very boring and staid."

I patted him on the arm. "Yes, and you've never seen the inside of a prison or sneaked into a German office or invited anyone to this house who carried a hidden knife or a pistol. Of course not. You're as innocent as a virgin on her wedding night." I took another sip of whisky.

"Ah-ha-ha!" cried my grandfather gleefully as he patted Madame X on her elegant head. "And so the woman has seen right through your ploy of innocence! I told you our girl is smart!"

"You did not need to tell me that," Rafe said, giving Grandpère an indulgent look. "She is your granddaughter, after all."

"Damned right," replied my grandfather, and I swore his cheeks were a little pink.

"Ah, well, perhaps I might be able to think of someone I could ask about this Inspecteur Merveille," Rafe said after a moment, giving me a sly grin. "There might be one or two people who still remember me at the 36."

"I'm quite certain that number is far more than one or two," Grand-père said dryly.

"The 36?"

"The headquarters for the *police judiciaire* has been located at 36 quai des Orfèvres for many years, and thus it is often referred to by its address—the 36," replied my grandfather.

"Ah, I see. Like Scotland Yard," I said. Before I had the chance to ask why anyone at the 36 would remember Oncle Rafe, someone knocked at the front door.

Since their housekeeper-cook had left to take care of her ailing mother shortly after I arrived in Paris, Grand-père and Oncle Rafe had hired two day maids—a pair of twin sisters named Bet and Blythe—who came in every morning. Most of the time they prepared a hearty luncheon for us, leaving only the evening meal for me to struggle through. But by now it was well into the afternoon, and they had gone—which meant one of us must answer the door. I was grateful that I was at home to do it, instead of one of the old men.

Oncle Rafe made to rise, but I was quicker. "No, no, I'll get it. I'm too incensed to sit still, anyway."

The salon was up one flight of stairs from the foyer, so of course the front door was on what was called the ground floor. That was one thing I'd had to get used to. Back home, we considered the first floor to be the ground floor of our houses, but Parisians considered the first floor to be the one *above* the ground floor.

The stately three-story house that Grand-père and Oncle Rafe shared would be considered a mansion by any standard. If anyone ever decided to turn it into apartments like the building where Julia lived, the place could easily become three separate and spacious flats. That was one of the reasons we had the maids come in every day, even though Grand-père and Oncle Rafe rarely ventured beyond the first floor, where the salon, a large bathroom, and bedrooms were. The kitchen and another sitting room were on the ground floor, and I had my bedroom and a bathroom on the top floor, where a full staff of servants had once lived.

The house had high ceilings, which meant each flight of stairs was twenty steps, and there were many tall, narrow windows, including a row of dormers that made my third-floor space sunny and airy. I could even see the Tour Eiffel from one of my windows, and loved that it was one of the last things I saw each night before I went to sleep: its elegant, gossamer shape bathed in golden light.

A small balcony on the flat-roofed portico had been glassed in years ago to create a delightful little greenhouse accessed from the room next to the first-floor salon. The greenhouse overlooked the courtyard, and it was where Grand-père kept the plants—his *délicieux bébés*—that I now helped him tend.

Still holding my whisky glass, I hurried down the stairs to the foyer. When I looked through the sidelight of the front door, I nearly dropped my drink.

Inspecteur Merveille stood there in his dark, heavy coat, hat pulled low over his brow. But not too low to fully obstruct the cool gaze that met mine through the window.

What is he doing here?

I considered whether I should even open the door, but the fact that he'd seen me meant I couldn't pretend no one was home.

"Bonjour, *monsieur le inspecteur*," I said as I opened the door.

The gust of swirling wintery air was enough to have me moving back quickly into the relative warmth of the house. Despite my reluctance, I kept the door open in a silent invitation for Merveille to come inside.

"Mademoiselle Knight," he said, removing his hat with a gloved hand. His thick dark hair was perfectly parted and smoothly combed into place. "I find it necessary to speak with you again," he said.

"Necessary?" I muttered, but he heard me.

"Indeed, mademoiselle. There are many unpleasant necessities in a murder investigation."

"Of course," I replied, feeling chastised—and rightly so. After all, it wasn't me, or anyone I cared about, who'd been left to die behind a row of trash bins. "Yes, I'm sorry. Of course. Shall I take your coat and hat?"

Merveille looked around the foyer, and I remembered how awed I'd been the first time I stepped into this grand house with the sweeping stairway, ornate molding, and massive chandelier hanging from the center of a plaster medallion. Beneath the round Persian rug, the floor was polished marble—white veined with cabernet red—with black marble creating a frame that outlined the floor. And that was just the foyer.

"This is your home?" he asked. He handed me his hat and gloves but kept on his coat.

"I live here with my grandfather and my uncle," I replied smoothly. I immediately felt protective of the two elderly men upstairs for several reasons, so I decided that the *inspecteur* and I would conduct our "necessary" conversation down here in the housekeeper's sitting room by the kitchen.

But that was not to be, for before I could speak, I heard a noise from above—the sharp, short bark from Oscar Wilde that indicated he'd spied the newcomer. His petite self, which today was garbed in a smart black jacket complete with waistcoat and tie, had appeared at the top of the steps. He had large ears the shape of butterfly wings—the breed was known as a Papillon, due to those magnificent ears—and they were perked up with great interest. He was mostly white, with some patches of brown and black. Long swaths of black-tipped brown hair, which were combed daily by my uncle, grew from his ears and fell past his little shoulders in silky waterfalls. Oscar barked again, sharper and higher this time as his long, feathery tail waved eagerly.

M. Wilde's bark wasn't any sort of warning or alert. It was more of an expectation—for a newcomer meant that he could anticipate a treat, a session of petting and cooing over his cuteness, or both.

That wasn't to say that Madame X was any less interested when a visitor arrived. She just didn't demonstrate her enthusiasm and anticipation so obviously.

In fact, I saw just the tip of her twitching black tail through the railing at the top of the stairs. She, too, had left the comfort of her master's lap to investigate, but true to form, she'd graciously allowed the excitable M. Wilde to lead the way.

"Who's there, Tabitha?" Oncle Rafe appeared next at the top of the stairs, and I realized my hopes of keeping the *inspecteur*'s visit to myself had been doomed from the start.

"I'm Inspecteur Étienne Merveille from the *police judiciaire*," replied the visitor before I had even the slightest of chances to whisk him away to the sitting room.

"Ah. Investigating the death across the street, are you?" Rafe said in the same blasé tone as if he might have mentioned the icicles hanging from the eaves. "Well, come on up to the salon, then, *inspecteur*, where it's much more comfortable and we have whisky."

Merveille gave me a look as if to gauge my reaction to this invitation, but I responded with a polite smile and led the way up the stairs.

Even so, if I sensed the slightest bit of animosity, condescension, or revulsion from the detective toward my gentlemen housemates, I would show the *inspecteur* the door immediately—murder investigation or not. He could drag me down to the 36 for all I cared.

As one might expect, it took several moments for the "settling in," as I thought of it, during which time I couldn't quite suppress the nervous tickling in my stomach.

"Maurice Saint-Léger?" said Merveille, repeating my grandfather's name as if surprised and perhaps even awed by his identity. "It is a great pleasure to meet you, monsieur." He sounded sincere, but I noticed how frail and vulnerable Grand-père's hand looked in the *inspecteur*'s solid grip as they shook hands. "And monsieur?"

"Rafael Fautrier." I heard an underlying challenge—or perhaps it was pride—when my honorary uncle gave his name.

And then I saw the slightest hesitation, quickly masked, by Merveille before he shook Rafe's hand as well. "A pleasure here as well," murmured the *inspecteur*.

"Whisky? Cognac? Brandy?" asked Rafe as he went to the credenza.

I noticed Madame X had returned to her perch on Grand-père's lap. She eyed Oscar Wilde with disdain as the little dog placed his paws on Merveille's leg, looking up at him hopefully while wagging his feathery tail.

"*Merci*, but no, I must decline," replied the detective. "I have many more hours of work to do before I can indulge."

"Get off the man, Oscar, you little beastie," said Rafe as he turned from the credenza and saw his pet dancing prettily on two hind legs next to the *inspecteur*'s knee. Since the paws-on-the-leg trick hadn't worked, M. Wilde had moved on to adorable cuteness in his efforts.

Madame X sneered.

I fumed.

This was not a social call, and the men were all acting as if it were—at least, the older men were. The *inspecteur* seemed content to examine the room minutely from the seat he'd taken next to my tumbled coat on the sofa. I didn't like it. I just didn't like the way he was looking around and *drinking* in all the details.

"Perhaps a hot coffee, then, *inspecteur*?" Rafe asked.

"That would be very nice, thank you," replied Merveille, taking off his coat. Instead of dropping it in a heap on the sofa as I had done, he hung it on the coat rack by the door.

I rose to see to the hot beverage—it would only take a moment, as we kept hot water in the kettle at all times—wishing the detective would follow me. I didn't trust him alone with my gentlemen.

But, of course, he did not, and when I returned a few moments later with his coffee, I found the three of them conversing easily.

But were they talking about the weather? Or the pitfalls of the Marshall Plan? Or even the persistence of Oscar Wilde—who'd moved on to lying on the floor with his back legs stretched out behind him and his front legs propping him up as he pawed the rug and looked as adorable as possible in his quest for choice tidbits?

No. They were talking about *me*.

". . . came to stay with us after the death of her *grand-mère*," my grandfather was saying. "My wife. In April, wasn't it, Rafe?"

"Yes," I said acerbically. "It was just before Easter that I moved here."

"I wondered at your excellent French," Merveille said, taking the coffee from me.

"My *maman* and *grand-mère* taught me," I replied, still cool.

Could we just get on with whatever he wanted?

"But you were born in America," the detective said, as persistent as Oscar Wilde was.

Now the fluffy little dog was rolling on the floor in front of the *inspecteur*, his four paws batting playfully as he twisted from side to side on his back.

"Put the poor beast out of his misery, will you, Rafe?" said Grand-père with a grating laugh.

"I find him rather entertaining," said Merveille. "I'm wondering what he'll do next."

"*Inspecteur*, what is it you wanted to talk to me about?" I said in an effort to get the show on the road, whatever it was.

Rafe swooped M. Wilde into his arms and fed the little dog two of the fingernail-size cookies he kept in a jar next to his chair. Then, with a sigh, he offered one to Madame X, who sniffed it as if she'd never seen such a thing before—she had— then deigned to take it.

"Ah, yes, Mademoiselle Knight," said the detective. He pulled the notebook and a pencil from his inside pocket. "I just find it necessary to review some of the information you gave me earlier." He flipped through the pages, which had writing on them. He must have made notes after talking with me and Julia.

"Go ahead," I replied. My stomach tightened and I realized I had left my whisky in the kitchen when I made the coffee.

"You and Mademoiselle Thérèse Lognon left the Childs' apartment together at . . . what time did you say?" He glanced at his notepad.

"Two o'clock," I replied, trying to ignore the fact that everyone in the room was watching me carefully.

"And no one else was around when you left her at the front door."

"No, *Inspecteur.* I saw no one else."

"And what about the other partygoers? Were they still upstairs, or were you the last to leave?"

"There were still some people upstairs. No one else seemed to be ready to leave."

Merveille shifted the pencil in his hand. But instead of writing anything on his notepad, he merely tucked the pencil between two pages, leaving his fingers free to pluck a small envelope from his pocket. "And so you have never met this Mademoiselle Thérèse Lognon, and you have never heard of her before last night . . . and you only spoke to her when you rode down in the lift together, is that correct, Mademoiselle Knight?"

"Yes, that's what I said," I replied, watching his deft fingers as he gingerly withdrew the contents of the envelope, holding the small paper by the tip of a corner. "I only met her last night, and we hardly spoke at all."

"Then, perhaps, mademoiselle, you can tell me why Thérèse Lognon had this in her pocket."

I looked at the paper and felt the color drain from my face. It was a piece of stationery embossed with the logo of Grand-père's bank. Someone had printed my name and address on it.

But the most shocking, damning part of it all was that it was written in my own handwriting.

CHAPTER 4

"*I* . . . I don't know," I said, hating that I stammered, but hating even more that Merveille had put me on the spot like that.

I wished desperately for my whisky, which was still sitting innocently down in the kitchen.

The *inspecteur* looked at me. His ocean-gray eyes were cool and emotionless. I felt as if I were pinned to my chair by his gaze. "But you cannot deny that it is quite odd the dead woman had your name and address on a paper in her pocket. On the stationery of Le Banque Maine-Saint-Léger—the bank bearing your *grand-père's* name."

"No, I don't deny that it's strange," I said. My anxiety lessened a little as I realized Merveille wouldn't know that it was my very own handwriting on the note. "But I don't have any idea why Thérèse would have that in her pocket. As I said, I'd never met her nor even heard her name before last night."

"How coincidental that she should leave the gathering with you," said the *inspecteur*, still pinning me to the chair with his stare.

"Unfortunate rather than coincidental," I said. "Since I didn't have anything to do with her murder, *Inspecteur*, even if she did have my name and address in her pocket."

"Do you know who might have written this or given it to Mademoiselle Lognon?" asked Merveille.

Damn. Now I was on the spot. I had no intention of lying to the police, but I certainly didn't want to incriminate myself further.

"May I, *monsieur le inspecteur*?" asked Grand-père, thankfully, before I could respond. His slender, veiny hand was steady as he held it out for the paper.

Merveille gave it to him, but he was still looking at me. "The handwriting is decidedly *not* French," he said.

I swallowed. He was correct. European penmanship—with its neat serifs, ornamental curls, and crossed sevens—was stylistically different from the way we were taught in America. "It isn't, because I was the one who wrote it."

Merveille nodded as if he'd expected that response.

"And you gave it to someone," said Grand-père, just as the *inspecteur* was about to make some, no doubt pithy, comment. Or biting accusation. Yet, Merveille respectfully remained silent as my grandfather spoke. "Tabitte, to whom did you give this paper?"

I shook my head. "I don't know exactly, Grand-père. I'm sorry. You see," I said, turning my attention to Merveille, "I have been doing French tutoring for some American families here in Paris. I wrote down my information for more than one of those prospective clients, and I don't know which one this was for."

Merveille nodded, but I couldn't tell whether he believed me or not. Not that there was any reason he *shouldn't*, but he seemed so . . . implacable. So suspicious.

I clenched my fingers in my lap, hiding them in the folds of my wool skirt and hoped he didn't notice. Being interrogated by a policeman—this, after seeing the bloody body of a murdered woman—was far more upsetting than I could have imagined.

"Perhaps you could provide me with the names of the families you'd given your information to," said Merveille.

"Well, you see, I wrote down my information on six or seven different papers and gave it to Paul Child to take to his office— he works for the USIS at the embassy, as I'm sure you know by now—to give to anyone who might be interested in my services. I don't have any way of knowing where this particular copy came from or how Thérèse might have gotten it."

Merveille did not seem pleased with this information. "I see. Well, at least perhaps you could provide me with the names of anyone you are currently tutoring, or anyone you've spoken to about the job."

"Of course," I replied, but I experienced a dart of terror when I thought about how the families I taught would feel when they were questioned by a police *inspecteur*. Surely they wouldn't want to keep on a young female tutor who was involved in a murder investigation. I heaved a sigh and was only slightly mollified when Oncle Rafe reached over to pat my hand.

"I'm sorry, *ma petite*," he said, giving my fingers a little squeeze. He looked at Merveille. "I don't suppose there is any other way to handle this than to involve Tabitha's clients in the matter, *inspecteur*? Surely you understand how it could cause consternation on their part."

"Not unless Mademoiselle Knight can somehow identify this particular paper," Merveille replied. "Or can at least fathom a reason Mademoiselle Lognon had it in her possession."

I grimaced. "Maybe I should look at it again."

Grand-père handed the paper to me. I'd hardly looked at it when Inspecteur Merveille first gave it to me, for I was so shocked and unsettled.

"What's this?" I said. I'd turned over the paper, blindly searching for something to clue me in to who had given the note to Thérèse: a wine or coffee stain, a scrape of nail polish or lipstick. . . . "There's writing on the back. It says, *Detroit*."

I looked up at Inspecteur Merveille. "You didn't notice the note on the back?" I said, doing little to hide my annoyance.

"But of course I noticed it," he replied in that insouciant French manner that could be either annoying or attractive. In this case, it was annoying. "It's accurate, *non*, mademoiselle? You are from Detroit, are you not?"

He pronounced the city "Deh-twa" as any good Frenchman would, instead of the Anglicized "Dee-troyt" that native Michiganians spoke.

"Yes . . . well, I'm from a small town nearby. Belleville."

"And so Mademoiselle Lognon presumably has made a notation to herself of your background, perhaps," said the *inspecteur*. "Or someone who was considering engaging your services."

"Yes," I replied.

"It would be very helpful to have that list of names of people who were interested in your services, mademoiselle," Merveille said firmly.

"Thérèse might have picked up the paper at the Childs' apartment last night," I said, in a last-ditch effort to dissuade him from getting the names of my clients.

"Are you suggesting this paper you wrote on was still in M. Child's possession last evening? You said he brought them to his office to distribute," said Merveille.

I was becoming irritated by the amount of time and attention being spent on a paper with my name and address on it; it seemed so irrelevant when a woman had been stabbed to death. At least, *I* knew I'd had nothing to do with it, and I knew just as strongly that neither Julia nor Paul nor Dort had, either.

Which, of course, left all of the people who'd been socializing in the Childs' flat last night as prime suspects. My stomach shivered. Had I been hanging out with a killer last night?

Or had some passerby or other resident of the building accosted Thérèse while she was waiting for her taxi, and lured her to the cellar?

"I can't say for certain, Inspecteur. But it *is* possible this paper was still at the Childs' flat because I wrote out some more copies of my information last night so Paul Child would have extras to pass out at the embassy. I suppose I should order some business cards," I said with my own Gallic shrug.

Merveille gave me a grim look but nodded. "I see. But if you could give me the names of anyone who might have had your information before last night, Mademoiselle Knight. In the interest of being thorough, you understand."

Feeling the weight of everyone's attention on me, I rose reluctantly to get a paper and pencil. I scrawled names on the paper and handed Merveille the list. "There. I believe that's everyone I've either spoken to or have been tutoring. I indicated which are clients and which ones are not—at least as of now. Um . . . there was one person who contacted me—a Madame Coleman—that I didn't actually speak to. I returned her call and left a message with the maid, but no one ever called me back. So I didn't put her on the list."

"Perhaps in order to be precise and thorough, you should also put this Madame Coleman on the list," Merveille said in what was obviously not merely a suggestion. With a sigh I took the paper back, dashing the name Coleman at the bottom, then handed it to him. "Thank you, mademoiselle. I shall be as discreet as possible in my interactions with them."

He rose, obviously preparing to take his leave.

"That's it?" I said. "That's all you wanted to ask me?"

"Should I be asking you something more, mademoiselle?"

I felt my cheeks heat. "No, no, of course not."

"But if you think of anything pertinent, you will contact me," he said in a definite command rather than a request. He placed a crisp white business card on the table.

"Yes, of course," I said. I knew it was futile to even suggest that he might do the same.

I escorted Merveille downstairs and to the foyer and retrieved his hat and gloves. When I opened the door to the bitter cold, I had a moment of sympathy for the detective, who was woefully protected from the unrelenting weather only by his fedora, gloves, and wool coat. I imagined he'd spend the rest of the day traipsing around in the biting chill, going in and out of buildings and up and down the streets, trying to retrace the moments of Thérèse Lognon's life.

But he didn't seem to hesitate, or even to brace himself against the unpleasantness as he stepped outside. "*Au revoir, mademoiselle*," he said, and tramped stoically down the walk.

I had just closed the door behind him, wildly grateful for his departure, when the telephone rang. The sound—a shrill, *brilling* noise—was so different from the ring our telephone made back home in Michigan it never failed to startle me, even after eight months of living here. Not that anyone called that often; perhaps that was why the noise still jolted me.

"Saint-Léger residence," I said.

"Oh, thank heaven you're there!" Julia's voice boomed through the receiver.

"Is everything all right?" I asked, suddenly terrified that Merveille had left our house to cross the street and arrest—or simply harass—Julia or Paul or Dort.

"Yes, yes . . . well, as all right as it can be with a dead woman in our cellar and my poor chef's knife having done the deed," Julia replied with a pained chuckle. "Of all things! The poor, poor girl. I still can't believe it!" Her voice became a hush.

"It's horrible," I replied, shivering.

"But, Tabs, I'm calling because you've left Madame Poulet here—along with those beautiful turnips and everything else in your market bag," Julia went on, hardly catching a breath. She had this trilling, warbling sort of voice that always sounded happy, bubbly, and slightly out of breath; especially when she was speaking English, as she was now, and was more comfortable with the words.

"Oh, for Pete's sake. Of course I did! I'll be right over to get it." It was no surprise I'd forgotten my bag with everything going on and me incensed over Merveille's suspicion of Julia.

"I should hope so," Julia replied. "Otherwise, your poor messieurs won't have any dinner, and I will be drinking that splendid Bordeaux-Médoc you selected!"

I was required to dash upstairs, not only to retrieve my coat from the salon but also to tell my "messieurs" where I was off to.

"Roasted chicken?" Grand-père's eyes went wide with delight. "And turnip mash? Is Madame Child cooking it for us, then?"

"Um . . . no, I'm going to muddle through it—but with her guidance," I added quickly when his hopeful expression faltered. "I promise it'll be better than last time."

"Of course it will, *ma petite*," said Oncle Rafe. But he appeared a little wary as well.

"Shall I bring you some coffee before I go? Some bread and cheese? You know how it is with Julia—we'll get to talking, or, rather, she will, and it'll be an hour before I leave."

"Well, if you'll be there that long, perhaps you should just roast the chicken there at Madame Child's," suggested Grand-père brightly. "Er . . . save some time."

"*Maurice*," said Oncle Rafe as a smile twitched his beard and mustache. "Leave the poor girl alone. If the chicken doesn't turn out, we'll have cold ham and boiled eggs crumbled on toast."

"Yes, yes, of course," Grand-père said, duly chastened. My heart gave a sad little pang and I was *determined* to have success with Madame Poulet . . . even if I had to get Julia to roast her for me. "Run along, then, *ma petite* Tabitte, and give our love—and gratitude—to Madame Child. And listen carefully to everything she tells you about the chicken! Take some notes!"

I laughed and bent over to kiss him on the cheek. "I promise Madame Poulet will be magnificent, Grand-père."

I swept up my coat from where I'd left it in a heap on the chair and finished my circuit of the salon by dropping one more kiss on Oncle Rafe's cheek. Oscar Wilde received a little pat between the ears and gave me a quick lick of appreciation with his tiny tongue, but Madame X wasn't the least bit interested in my imminent departure. She was sitting on the windowsill, eyeing me with feline arrogance as the tip of her tail twitched gently.

Even though I was only going across rue de l'Université, I wrapped a thick muffler around my neck and pulled on the warmest hat I could find—one of Oncle Rafe's that was furry and boxy in shape. I'm certain I looked like a little Russian doll, bundled up in my heavy coat with the hat and muffler.

Not for the first time since arriving in Paris did I miss the ease and pleasure of wearing trousers, which would have kept my legs warmer than my knee-length skirt and wool tights.

I'd become used to donning pants when I worked at the bomber plant. We women wore overalls every day as we climbed over planes, onto wings, and into turbines. I'd even begun to wear trousers at home sometimes—and to my mother's and grandmother's mutual horror. But here in Paris, it was techni-cally illegal for a woman to wear trousers without obtaining per-mission—from the police!—to do so. As I understood it, it was acceptable for a female to don pants if she were riding a bicycle or a horse, but not to simply cross the rue, and certainly not to go shopping.

The French were, I decided as I waited for the steady stream of cars to slow so I could step onto the cobblestone street, a strange mixture of formality and bonhomie, restrictiveness and flamboyance, and rudeness and charm. But I adored the French with all of their quirks, and I had come to love their City of Light.

When I walked into the ground floor of Julia's building, my attention went immediately to the door that led to the cellar. The large foyer was empty of people but for the single gen-darme standing guard at the entrance to the crime scene. He appeared bored but resolute, and once he assured himself I didn't mean to approach him, he looked away.

I shivered once more at the memory of what I'd seen down in the cellar by the trash cans, and turned my attention to the cage-like elevator that would take me to Julia's apartment on the sec-ond and third floors. The last time I'd been in the lift, I thought as I stepped inside, was last night when Thérèse Lognon and I rode down together.

Had she had any idea her life was in danger? That it was about to end moments after we stepped out of the elevator?

Surely if she'd been afraid for her safety, she would have given some indication. . . . She would have asked me to wait with her or *something*. Wouldn't she?

I tried to remember if we'd spoken of anything relevant; it had been late, and I was tired and a little drunk—for the wine and whisky flowed easily in the Childs' flat, and a cocktail made me less shy around people I didn't know.

Thérèse and I stood side by side in the roofless cage, both fac-ing the front, nearly parallel to each other. I remembered saying something like, "I'm so glad I've only to cross the street to get home. It's so cold and dark."

She'd replied, "That's lucky for you. So convenient that you live right here. I'll need a taxi."

At least, I thought that was what she said. Something like that. I felt ashamed that I hadn't paid much attention to what might have been the woman's last words.

Not that her means of transportation was important, I was sure. The poor woman had to get home somehow. However, I supposed our brief interaction indicated she'd come to the party on her own—or at least that she hadn't been relying on anyone from Dort's gathering to take her home.

Was that important information? I wondered. As the lift rolled to a halt, I squinted thoughtfully, trying to remember if I'd noticed anything at all about Thérèse Lognon before we'd walked into the elevator together, and then walked out.

When the doors opened, she'd stepped back and I walked out first—for some reason I remembered that. But as I started away from the lift, she hurried to catch up to me. She'd walked right up next to me, and looked over . . .

At the time, I didn't think anything of it, but looking back, I wondered if she had something to say, if she was trying to determine how to approach me . . . or if she was just afraid to be alone after I left.

But I hadn't paused, and she didn't speak or make any sort of gesture as we walked toward the front doors. I gave her a little wave and said, "Good night—I hope your taxi comes soon," as I hurried out into the chilly night.

She replied, "Thank you."

I remembered that, suddenly. The way she said that: *Thank you*. It sounded . . . forlorn.

Or maybe I was just making things up. It had been late, I had had a few drinks, and surely I was coloring my memory with the knowledge that Thérèse was brutally killed only moments after I left her.

The lift door opened at the second floor, pulling me from my morbid thoughts.

I stepped out of the elevator into the salon of Julia and Paul's flat. It was empty of anyone at the moment, but last night, the eight of us had filled every seat available—the chairs, the sofa, even cushions on the floor. The room was much like the chambers in Grand-père's house: airy with a high ceiling and many large windows that allowed in light—as well as the chill.

In the room was a gas radiator that Julia and Paul had purchased out of desperation a month or so ago, remembering how awful their first winter had been in Paris. This appliance was the only reason their flat wasn't unbearably drafty and cold. Julia told me during their first winter they used to sit by a tiny, coal-burning, potbellied stove dressed in layers and layers of clothing. The gas radiator had already made an improvement in their conditions over last winter.

The salon retained some evidence of the previous night's debauchery: an uncapped whisky decanter, sofa pillows tossed askew, a stack of glossy magazines spilled to the side, and two ashtrays that needed to be emptied. A cigarette case, a small handbag, and a pair of gloves—mine!—were on one of the tables near the lift. The scents of stale cigarette smoke, whisky, and perfume permeated the room.

It wasn't a surprise that Mathilde hadn't had the energy or wherewithal to see to the work after what she'd discovered in the cellar.

Minette was curled up in a flowerpot as she often did for some incomprehensible feline reason, and she looked at me with mild interest when I called out for Julia. It was nearly four o'clock and I knew Dort would be at work, so I didn't worry about disturbing her.

Since Julia didn't answer and I could hear movement above my head, I knew she must be upstairs in the kitchen—which was no surprise. Paul joked that if he ever wanted to see his wife, he had to stake himself out in the kitchen.

I climbed the stairs and found my friend moving energetically, gracefully, and loudly through her paces in the crowded kitchen.

"Oh, there you are, Tabs," she said, stirring two pots on the stove—with a third one simply sitting on a burner—a spoon in each hand. Because of her height, she was bent at an uncomfortable angle over the low gas burners, but that didn't seem to slow her down. She wore a denim apron over her skirt and blouse and had a kitchen towel tucked into the waistband. "Did you find your gloves on the table in the salon? And is that your pocketbook on the table there too?"

"Yes, I've got my gloves. No, that wasn't my handbag. Something smells so good," I said, sniffing appreciatively. Even as I spoke, I felt a pang of regret that I couldn't manage to elicit such amazing scents—let alone tastes—in my own kitchen for my own family.

Julia's *cuisine* was a small room boasting an entire wall of windows, which helped to light the drab space but also allowed for drafts. Fortunately, when the oven and stove were going, as now, it was comfortably warm. I immediately took a seat at the table, for there was simply not enough room to stand while my friend was ricocheting from stove to soapstone counter to sink and back again. The stove she had purchased herself, not long after moving in here at Roo de Loo, and I knew that the only reason there was hot water in the kitchen was because early on, Julia had set up her own system: a tub of water over a gas geyser. Whether any water actually ran in the sink was a matter of weather—if it was cold, the pipes, which ran up the building outside, would freeze and she would be out of luck when she opened the spigot.

Numerous pots and pans hung from hooks moored beneath long shelves, and more pots, pans, jars, measuring devices, and canisters lined the tops of the shelves. The two long counters that extended near the stove were also laden with jars, utensils, gadgets—most of which I couldn't identify—contraptions such as a meat grinder, mortars and pestles, and more. So much more. Paul called his wife Jackdaw Julie due to her obsession with cooking tools and her affinity for collecting every shiny new item—just like a crow.

As I watched, one of the spoons stopped stirring, the oven

door opened, Julia stooped, thrust inside her hand and a third spoon she'd somehow acquired for a moment, then rose, thumping the door closed, and was back stirring the duo of pots on the stove. All of this happened in a smooth, balletic flow that was so fast I nearly missed the steps.

That was Julia Child in the kitchen.

"Garlic soup, shrimp and scallops with braised rice—they call it *risotto* in Italy, but it's the same as *pilaf* and just depends whether you add cream or cheese to it—and *jambon braisé Morvandelle*. That's ham roasted in wine in a covered pan with a cream and mushroom sauce. I'm using some of your *grand-père*'s thyme and parsley. It's going to be *divine.*"

"Good grief, are you going to eat all of that tonight?" I exclaimed.

Julia gave her gusty laugh. "No, I'll save the *jambon* for tomorrow—it's even better when reheated. I had to do *something.*" She was pouring some sort of liquid into the pot of rice she was stirring. I hadn't even seen her hand move to the ladle.

"I thought you'd be making mayonnaise," I said with a chuckle. "Vats and vats of it!"

She glanced at me and chortled out a laugh. "Tomorrow! Tomorrow I'll start with the experimentation. Today, I had to do something mindless to distract myself."

Making delectable roasted ham, braised rice with seafood, and soup was *mindless*? Good heavens, I had a lot to learn.

"I just had to take my mind off everything. Can you even believe it, Tabs? Someone murdered a woman in this building— with my knife! That means they had to have been in *my* kitchen! *This* kitchen!"

She turned to look at me, her blue eyes wide with horror and her cheeks carrying two high patches of red as she continued to stir, spice, and sample the rice and soup, both of which were on top of the stove with a third pot containing simmering broth. The ham was in the oven, but every few minutes, she opened the door, took off the top of the roasting pan, and basted the meat.

The incredibly rich scents of garlic, onion, and heaven knew what else had my mouth watering. Earlier, I might have been sure I'd lost my appetite for the time being, but that changed the minute I stepped into Julia's kitchen.

"It's beyond belief," I said. "I don't know what to think about it all other than to be horrified. But I won't keep you," I said, looking about for my market bag. I assumed since Julia knew I'd left it, she'd brought it up here. "I can see you're busy—and I've got to see about getting that chicken in the oven. Grand-père and Oncle Rafe are very excited about the prospect of roasted chicken for dinner."

"And turnip mash. Don't forget the turnip mash, Tabs!" Julia said, spinning, reaching, yanking, while clattering dishes, utensils, and pots. "I singed off the rest of the feathers on Madame Poulet for you," she said, nodding toward a paper-wrapped bundle on the counter.

"Thank you," I said, recognizing that the bundle was my roasting chicken, apparently now plucked free of any latent feathers, wrapped in butcher's paper. "At least I won't get that wrong tonight."

"Oh, don't go yet," Julia said, suddenly whisking a cup of hot chocolate onto the table in front of me—a treat she knew I couldn't decline. If French coffee was amazing, French hot chocolate was out of this world.

"We've simply *got* to talk about this, Tabs! How can there be a murder in my very own building, with my very own knife? We *can't* ignore it!"

"It would be impossible to ignore it," I agreed, dipping the spoon in my hot chocolate to take a small taste. "Especially when the detective *inspecteur* thinks you or I had something to do with it. Mostly me," I added forlornly.

"*You?*" Julia snatched a small frying pan from where it hung from a hook on the wall. It banged metallically when she slammed it onto the stove even as she reached for a whisk that hung on the wall, then for the crock of butter on the counter. "Why would he think you had anything to do with it? It was my knife, after all!" She gave a gusty laugh. "Thank God he didn't go so far as to arrest me!"

"I rode down in the elevator with Thérèse Lognon. *And* she had one of the notes that I wrote out for Paul—with my address and telephone number on it—in her pocket. Apparently, that makes me suspect number one." The hot chocolate was decadent, and I allowed myself to take a healthy sip directly from the cup this time. I nearly moaned with delight. It had been an awful afternoon, and I truly appreciated the simple pleasure.

"That's ridiculous," said Julia, emphasizing her words with the frying pan. "Why, you wouldn't hurt a fly. Not only that, you're just a tiny thing—I don't see how you could go about stabbing a woman to death even if you had a reason to. Which you didn't— have a motive, I mean."

I wasn't exactly tiny—at least in comparison to my grandmother, who'd been barely over five feet tall and just about a hundred pounds—but Julia had a point.

Wouldn't someone have to have had a good amount of strength to do in Thérèse Lognon the way she'd been killed?

"You're right. It had to have been a man." I smelled melting butter and my mouth began to water. Had I eaten anything since my coffee and croissant this morning?

"Or a giantess like me—or Dort," Julia said without a bit of self-deprecation.

"Don't say that," I admonished her. "Inspecteur Merveille doesn't need any more ideas."

"Well, he's not around to hear me, is he? Besides, he's got two eyes—I'm sure he noticed me nearly looming over him."

"Julia, be serious."

"I *am* being serious. I'm being practical and serious about it all—because what else can I do? Someone used my knife and he—I'm firmly in the camp that it was a man, by the way—so he had to take it from here, somehow, last night." Still stirring the rice, she cracked two eggs one-handed into a small bowl. Then, with her fingers, she added a sprinkling of salt, something green she'd chopped without me noticing, then paused her stirring just long enough to put a few grinds of pepper into the eggs.

"Oh, and I talked to Paul on the telephone," she went on, pouring another ladle of broth from the third pot into the rice. "He called from the office and asked if I wanted him to come home. I told him there was nothing he could do, but that he might just as well be prepared to have a conversation with the *inspecteur*—and for a magnificent meal tonight. I do hope the *inspecteur* resists the urge to corner Paul at the embassy."

I winced. That couldn't be good for Paul to be visited at his office about a murder committed by his wife's cooking knife. But Julia didn't seem overly concerned about it.

"All right," I said, looking down into my chocolate as Julia continued her dance and flight around the kitchen. Now she was whisking the eggs—which took two hands—while eyeing the rice carefully.

"Let's figure this out ourselves," I went on. "We're reasonably smart women. It had to be someone who had access to your kitchen to get the weapon. When's the last time you saw that knife?"

"Yesterday after I got home from the market," Julia replied promptly. "It's my favorite chef's knife, and I used it to chop some green onions and chervil for the omelette I made for Paul's lunch—speaking of which, the one I'm making for you will be done in a flash—then I washed it and put it by the sink to dry. I used a different knife when I cooked dinner because that one wasn't in its place on the magnetic strip, and I just grabbed the medium-size knife instead. I told all of this to Merveille, but who knows whether the man believed me. He's got a set of eyes on him, doesn't he?"

"Yes," I replied with great feeling. "They're like daggers. Scary, mean daggers."

Julia laughed heartily. "I meant their color. Didn't you notice? They're a dark gray, but there's a hint of deep blue too."

"Oh, yes. Dark gray—like an angry ocean," I said dryly. "Very fitting. Did you say you're making me an omelette?"

"You look like you could eat something," she said, dumping the whisked eggs into the small frying pan and giving me a bright smile. After no more than a few seconds, she began to jerk the omelette pan sharply over the burner even as she picked up the spoon to stir the rice.

I watched in amazement and anticipation. Julia's omelettes—cooked in less than a minute while moving the pan in a way I hadn't yet mastered—were simple in their deliciousness. I certainly wasn't going to say no to such a treat.

"Anyway, who had the chance to come up here last night and take the knife?" I asked. "It had to be someone who was at Dort's party, don't you think? Who else would have been able to get it?"

"No one. No one at all." Julia watched the egg pan with an eagle eye as she continued to jerk it back and forth over the burner, while giving the rice an occasional stir with her other hand.

"Wait a minute . . . you said you grabbed a different knife to use because that one wasn't in its place. But when was the last time you actually *saw* the knife? You washed it and set it by the sink, and . . . ?"

For the first time since I'd come into the kitchen, Julia stopped moving and turned to stare at me. "Hell . . . I'm not certain. I washed it, put it aside, and I don't actually remember if I ever saw it again—at least, until *monsieur le inspecteur*"—she dropped in the French phrase with exaggerated breathlessness—"showed it to me, drenched in blood." She frowned, then cackled as she went back to stirring and jerking. "Not that that knife hasn't been drenched in blood before—just not human blood."

I held back my own chuckle. Trust Julia to be as subtle as a tank.

"I want to know how Inspecteur Merveille knew it was *your* knife. How did *you* even know, Julia?"

"Mathilde, I would guess. She probably recognized it, or at least thought it would be mine. It's not everyone who has a gorgeous carbon steel chef's knife from Dehillerin." She turned from the stove and poured a fluffy roll of egg from the frying pan onto a small plate and set it in front of me. I rose to grab a fork so she didn't have to, and noticed that the knob on the drawer was loose. I would have taken the moment to tighten it, but I didn't want to get in her way—she was a virtual tornado in the kitchen.

"Right. That makes sense that Mathilde would have recognized your knife. So . . . it could have been taken anytime after lunch," I said thoughtfully as I sat back down.

"I don't see how it could have been. Someone would have had to come in here and steal it—and why would they? Come in off the street and look for a murder weapon? We're on the third floor. No," said Julia, back in full swing now that my omelette had been served: clanging, slamming, stirring, beating, and mortar pestling. "I'm certain it was someone who was here last night. One of Dort's so-called friends. Can you believe it? My *sister* is friends with a *murderer!*"

CHAPTER 5

"*I* agree—it had to be someone who was here last night and had the opportunity to take the knife," I said, forking up my first bite of omelette. Its simple yet satisfying flavor—butter, salt, tangy herbs—almost distracted me from my thoughts, but focus prevailed. "But that fact tells us one important thing about the murder."

"And what is that, Miss Sherlock?"

"The murder wasn't premeditated. The killer didn't come with a weapon."

Julia had been poking inside the oven with a spoon in one hand and a fork in the other. She closed the door with a thud and looked at me, her cheeks flushed from the heat. "That is an excellent point, Tabs. So something must have happened here last night that made someone want to kill Thérèse Lognon."

"Most likely," I replied.

"I didn't really talk to any of Dort's guests," Julia said. "I only caught glimpses of some of them because Paul wanted me to come to bed." She gave me a sly smile. "But you must have interacted with them. Give me the rundown; let's see if we can nail the killer right here in *La Maison Scheeld*," she said gleefully, using the nickname her husband had fancifully given the kitchen, including the French bastardization of their surname. She plopped a wad of dough onto the table near me. "Start with that adorable Mark Justiss that Dort's trying to set you up with."

Fortunately, I had a mouthful of luscious, buttery, herby eggs, so I wasn't required to answer immediately. "You thought he was adorable?" I said as soon as I swallowed.

"Oh yes," she replied. "All that blond hair, and those slender wrists and long fingers? What a combination! Too bad Dort doesn't want to date him herself."

"She seems to really like Ivan," I said, speaking of one of the actors from the American Club Theater. Ivan Cousins was jovial, interesting, and almost a full head shorter than Dort.

"Hmm. Ivan. Well, let's hope he's not the killer or Dort's heart will break. Anyway, more importantly," said Julia, removing the pot of braised rice from the stove at long last, "didn't *you* think Mark was cute? Or at least interesting enough to go out with? Cripes, I hope *he's* not the murderer." She covered the rice, then turned to a small bowl of raw scallops, shrimp, and clam bits. Into a pan with melted butter and a sprinkling of green herbs—chives, parsley, dill—they went.

I took another bite of egg and thought about my interactions with Mark Justiss last night. "He was nice enough," I said. "In a boy-next-door sort of way. And you're right about his hands—they are nice looking, and his fingers are long enough to be a surgeon's, I suppose. But it's not important whether I was attracted to Mark—it's about who might have had the motive and opportunity to kill Thérèse. And to snatch your knife."

"Well, who did?" Julia demanded. "We need to figure that out. I didn't get a chance to interrogate Dort before she left for work; she was in such a tizzy after talking to the *inspecteur*. Not that I blame her! Being interrogated is not fun."

"I don't really know who might have had the chance to sneak in and get your knife. All right, let me think about it," I said when she gave me an exasperated look. "There were eight of us there when I left last night: me, Dort, Ivan, Thérèse, Mark, and three other men. Um . . ." I had to think about their names; I'd only met them last night. "Johnny was one of them . . . He's got a beard and mustache. I think he works backstage doing lots of things like set repairs, that sort of thing. Maybe he's even the stage manager. And there was Neil, one of the lead actors, and . . . hmm . . . oh, yes, Thad. I'm not sure what he does at the theater. Something with the lights?"

"I know Neil Kingsley. He's tall and dark and delicious—and I think he's gay, which is why Dort didn't try to set you two up. He's the lead in *Ten Little Indians*, I think. Or, at least, he's one of the last ones to die, and the most intriguing male character of the bunch. The romantic lead—if you can have one in a murder mystery play.

"Now . . . Thad—he's the kind of wafery and wispy one, right? Kind of reminds me of a good cracker."

I laughed. I knew exactly who she was talking about. Thad Whiting had blond hair that looked dry and brittle, and he was very slender and lanky. He looked like he'd break if he bent over. "A cracker! Great description of Thad. And, yes, Neil's the handsome one."

"I don't know Johnny." Julia was vigorously rolling out the pastry dough as she spoke—I had no idea what it was for—and she paused to give the seafood a quick stir in its pan. It smelled heavenly. "So what happened?"

"All right." I slipped the last bite of egg into my mouth as I took myself back to last night in the salon. "We were all sitting around talking. Everyone was on the sofa or chairs or sitting on pillows on the floor. Mark and I were standing by the window talking for a little while, then someone asked for a light and he offered his, and after that we were interrupted by Dort and Ivan."

"What was Thérèse doing during the evening?" asked Julia. "Did she talk to anyone? She must have! Dort told me she works at the theater, in the box office or something like that."

"She sat in the green brocade chair in the corner most of the time. I couldn't really see her because Johnny and Thad were right there at the bar the whole time, sort of blocking my view."

"That sounds right," said Julia. "Paul is annoyed about the amount of wine and whisky those guys drink when they come over. He wanted to go out there last night and chase them all home at midnight, when they'd only just got here. I wouldn't let him, but I did promise I would talk to Dort about it. Anyway, now I wish to hell he'd done it—then maybe Thérèse Lognon wouldn't be dead."

She flipped over the dough and continued to roll it with angry vigor, then stopped abruptly and looked down at the poor pastry. "I'm doing my own form of murder here," she muttered, then tsked. "Going to need to chill this again, or it'll be like rubber." She gathered the pale dough into a loose bundle and wrapped it in a towel. The whole thing went into the food box that was out the window and suspended over the courtyard below since there wasn't an icebox in the kitchen.

I was quiet for a moment, thinking about what Julia had said—that Paul could possibly have kept the murder from happening by kicking everyone out of the flat. How must he feel, knowing that? I shook my head. No use regretting it; no one could have known.

Even the killer hadn't planned ahead. I spewed out a breath and offered up a little prayer of Godspeed for Thérèse. Then I turned my attention to what I remembered about her.

"She was talking to Neil for a while," I said slowly. "Thérèse, I mean. And I think Thad made her a drink. She flirted with Johnny a little bit, too, and I could tell he had a thing for her. She was pretty vivacious and friendly. You probably couldn't tell from when we . . . uh . . . when we saw her . . . down in the cellar . . . Thérèse was really pretty, and she was very nicely put together—her face made up perfectly: false eyelashes, perfect lipstick, everything. She was very attractive and seemed to enjoy talking to everyone, but English isn't her first language. So she went back and forth between French and English.

"A few of us—Dort, me, Thérèse, Neil, I think Johnny, too—were having a spirited conversation about whether Clark Gable is actually a good actor or just a good-looking man who got lucky to be on screen, and Thérèse made a comment about how it didn't matter—we got to look at him, didn't we? Everyone laughed. She would make those sorts of one-line comments. Another time she said something about how people sometimes weren't who you thought they were. I didn't know what she was referring to; I just thought she was making a joke about Clark Gable. But now . . . maybe she made that comment purposely."

Even as I said this, I realized how different she had been in the elevator with me. Quiet, keeping to herself, even hesitant.

Maybe she *had* known something was wrong. Maybe she'd made that comment and it was the reason someone killed her.

And maybe she had wanted to say something about it to me when we rode down in the elevator, but I was too brusque and self-involved, so she didn't. I grimaced.

"All right, so she was a little bit of the life of the party," said Julia. She had turned off the burner beneath the seafood. Now she brought the dish of rice, along with a ring-shaped pan, to the table where she'd been rolling out the dough. "Was she cozying up to any of the men in particular? Mark, Thad?"

"Not that I noticed. She seemed to be always in a group, not really ever off in a private conversation." I drank the last of my hot chocolate. "I'm trying to remember when anyone left the salon."

"Someone had to, in order to get my knife," Julia said grimly. She'd begun to press the sticky, creamy rice into the ring pan. "Ye *gods*, this is going to be *delectable*," she muttered.

"Well, everyone left at one time or another," I said. "To use the bathroom. Which is right here on the third floor," I pointed out unnecessarily. I sighed, then shrugged. "It's kind of a blur. Honestly, I don't have any serious impressions of anyone. We just sat around and talked about movies and the weather and the season at the theater. I guess I wouldn't be a very good detective."

"Don't be silly," said Julia, looking up at me. Rice clung to her hands and, somehow, there were two grains stuck to her chin and another dangling from one of her brown curls. "First of all, you've got the genes, don't you?"

I looked at her in surprise. "Just because my dad is a cop doesn't mean *I'd* be a good one."

"Why not? You grew up with it—you told me all about how you'd make him tell you about his day. It's probably ingrained in you. Besides, you're one of the smartest people I know—next to Paul—and you always seem to read people really well. Remember that time you spotted the pickpocket in rue Cler? He seemed so nice and polite when we were crossing the street, but you saw right through him.

"And when I was haggling at the shop over the chair I bought for Paul? You could tell the shopkeeper was going to give in, even though I was ready to pay the higher price. I think I still have a bruise from where you elbowed me." She cackled happily.

I shrugged. "That's not really anything—I was watching him, and you were distracted doing all the talking."

"No, no, I'm right, Tabs. You've got a thing about reading people. Just like your dad. You'll start to remember things about last night, and when you do, something will come to you."

I shook my head, unconvinced, but Julia went on. "Someone's got to be in our corner. If that Inspecteur Merveille is sniffing around you as a suspect, he's wasting his time. And who knows—next thing he might be looking at Dort. Or even Paul! That's why I think you ought to actually do a little investigating yourself."

"*Me?*"

"Why not? The sooner you can find a better suspect to point Inspecteur Merveille to—preferably not one of us, of course—the sooner he'll leave you alone."

I was far from convinced. But at the same time, I couldn't deny a little spike of interest in the idea. Not only did I have a father who was a detective himself, I'd been reading detective novels from the age of twelve, when I discovered Nancy Drew. Or maybe it was *because* of my father's occupation that I found mystery novels fascinating.

Starting in my teens, I'd immersed myself in every sort of crime and adventure fiction I could find, from Sherlock Holmes to Tommy and Tuppence and Hercule Poirot to the works of Josephine Tey and Patricia Wentworth. I'd read the Tom Swift stories and even dipped my toe into noir fiction with Dashiell Hammett after my dad suggested *The Maltese Falcon.*

I supposed if one could count having a father for an investigator and reading mystery novels as the groundwork for real-life detection experience, I was as prepared as anyone.

And then, all at once something struck me. "*Blood,*" I said.

"Yes . . . ?" Julia lifted her brows.

"Whoever killed Thérèse must have gotten blood on themselves," I said, frowning. "It's not possible that they didn't get splattered or splashed—there was a lot of blood, and it must have gone everywhere."

"So if someone left here and killed her, if they came back upstairs to the party, they'd be all bloody!" Julia exclaimed. "That's exactly right, Tabs. So . . . whoever did it must not have come back to the gathering, or else someone would have noticed—no matter how sloshed they all were."

"And whoever it was must have left shortly after Thérèse and I did, to catch her before the taxi came and took her," I went on. "In fact, the killer must have gone right on our heels if he was determined to catch up to her before she left. Maybe he even left at the same time and took the stairs down." I frowned even more, feeling my brows and forehead knit together tightly. "We've got to find out who left after we did. Dort will know, won't she?"

"I would think so—if she wasn't too drunk, or making out in the corner with Ivan," Julia said dryly.

Just then, the telephone rang. Julia wiped her hands on the towel tucked into her belt and hurried out of the room to answer it. I'd heard the story of how it took months for the Childs to have a telephone installed once they moved in here to Roo de Loo. Julia claimed her extended conversations with the women at the telephone office, where she'd had to visit regularly, helped her begin to learn French.

While she was gone, I pulled out my tool knife and took the opportunity to tighten the knob on the drawer where I'd taken out my fork.

Julia came back when I was on the third drawer knob. All of them had needed tightening.

She laughed when she saw me. "Oh, Tabs, you and your Swiss Army knife," she said with pleasure. "Thanks for doing that. Half the time when I open the drawer, the damned knob falls off. I could have done it myself, but I never seemed to have the time—or the desire—when I'm in here."

"And Paul can't get to the cabinets because you're always in the way," I teased. "It's the least I can do for the omelette and hot chocolate. I hope that wasn't the *inspecteur* on the phone."

"No," she said, diving back into the task of forming the rice ring. "It was my sister. Would you do me a big favor? Actually, it's for Dort, not me. She forgot her handbag when she went to work, and she needs someone to bring it to her if possible because she has to put gas in her car.

"She says everything is in an uproar at the theater because of Thérèse, and she can't leave—the troupe manager is a real high-strung, mean, and bossy sort of woman and the show must go on and all of that. But I can't leave either—look at me!" She gestured to the kitchen at large. "Could you bring it over to her? And while you're there, you can ask her when everyone left. See if she has any ideas about who could have done it."

"Of course," I replied, quickly calculating the time in my head. It was after four thirty; I should be back by five thirty or six o'clock at the latest, even accounting for the time I'd spend chatting with Dort, who was just as gregarious as her sister. Dinner at Chez Saint-Léger was served much later than it had been back in America—usually eight o'clock, instead of six thirty for the nights my father got home from work on time. Which was not as often as my mother would have liked.

"How long will it take me to roast the chicken?" I asked.

"She's only five pounds, so seventy-five minutes, maybe a little more," said Julia. "But you can roast Madame Poulet tomorrow—God knows it's cold enough that she'll keep—and instead I will send Monsieur Jambon and his *magnifique* Morvandelle sauce home for your messieurs. After all, there is a murder to be investigated," she added with a grin.

"But I'm not investi—"

"You never know what you might find out at the theater," Julia said, easily brushing off my weak protest. "That's where everyone who was here last night works, right? Someone's got to know something."

I shook my head, smiling. "How can I say no to ham *à la Morvandelle?*" Especially since I thought about how Grand-père and Rafe would enjoy a meal cooked by Julia. I'd only known them for eight months, but I had fallen madly in love with both of my messieurs and would walk barefoot over hot coals for either of them. Giving them the pleasure of a well-cooked meal was a simple way to show them my affection.

"That was exactly what I thought," Julia crowed, beaming. "Anyhow, Dort thinks she left her handbag in her bedroom—don't let the mess scare you. I don't think there are any mice or spiders, but you never know. . . ."

I laughed. "Thanks for the warning. The only thing I'm not crazy about is snakes, so I'm sure I'll be fine even if I run into a mouse. I saw a pocketbook on the table in the salon. Is that hers? It's dark blue."

Julia shook her head. "No, Dort has a bright red purse. She says it matches her brilliant and bold personality." She laughed and, having finished the rice ring, wiped her sticky hands on the towel.

The realization struck both of us at the same time and we gaped at each other.

If the handbag in the salon wasn't Dort's . . . maybe it belonged to Thérèse Lognon!

CHAPTER 6

I hurried down to the salon and snatched up the purse, as well as the cigarette case, and brought them back upstairs to the kitchen.

Julia was waiting with unbridled excitement, but she hadn't stopped working. When I came in, she was just placing the ring pan of creamy braised rice, now covered, into a large pot of steaming water.

"There we go," she said. "Now to let that set. The shellfish go into the center of the ring once I turn it out onto a platter. Let me see!" She crowded next to me at the table as I opened the purse.

It was immediately evident that the handbag belonged to Thérèse Lognon. The first clue was the shade of fuchsia lipstick she'd worn—and left on the rim of her glass—last night. The second was an envelope addressed to her.

"Ooh! Now we have her address," Julia said gleefully. "You can go check it out."

I gave her a look.

I still wasn't quite certain how I felt about investigating a murder, but, again, I couldn't deny the spark of interest. There was this little sprite inside me that always thought it would be fun to do surprising and unusual things—sometimes things that maybe I shouldn't. Like booby-trap my teacher's desk. Or climb a tree in my handmade embroidered white First Communion dress.

Or sneak one of my dad's Pabst's at age ten . . . and then another and another and another. The smell of beer still made my stomach heave.

I tried to ignore that little internal sprite, but she was the one who'd insisted I apply for a job at the bomber plant, and that had turned out okay.

And it was because of that saucy little imp that I'd driven Henry's beloved 1946 Thunderbird onto frozen Belleville Lake. I'd measured the ice thickness and done the calculations first, so I knew the ice would bear the weight of *two* T-birds, but he was still pretty mad about it. I kissed and made up with him, but he never quite got over it.

So with Julia and my internal sprite egging me on, it was hard to ignore the idea of doing a little Nancy Drew detecting. I imagined I'd do a little poking around and if I found out anything interesting, I'd turn it all over to Inspecteur Merveille.

If I had known then how things would turn out, I would have simply closed the handbag and delivered it to his office—and kept myself far away from the investigation.

Probably.

"What else is in there?" Julia was practically breathing down my neck, so I turned the bag upside down and dumped everything onto the table.

In mystery novels, the sleuth always finds some important clue in the purse or pockets of a victim. I admit, I was hoping for something like that as I scanned the contents of Thérèse's purse—something that would point to her killer, or at least a *motive* for her murder.

But I was to be sadly disappointed. Aside from the envelope—which turned out to contain a letter from her mother—and the lipstick, there was nothing else of interest: a handful of coins, a coat check ticket from the Théâtre Monceau, a yellow matchbook with a red sun on it, a compact, a ring with two keys, and a small comb.

I even felt around the inside of the purse, with the hope that something was sewn into the lining.

But there was nothing there. The purse was empty.

"Well, that's boring," said Julia. "A woman gets killed and you expect her to have *some* secrets in her bag. Or at least something *interesting*. Hmm. La Sol. Never heard of that place." She was looking at the yellow matchbook, then tossed it back onto the table. "Some café probably."

I was feeling nosy, so I was reading the letter from Thérèse's mother—after all, Thérèse wouldn't care; she was dead. Maybe there was something important hinted at in the note. It was short, but filled with descriptions of what seemed to be a cat named Bruno who had an affinity for unrolling Madame Lognon's balls of yarn and napping among the unraveled skeins.

Disappointed, I folded up the letter and slid it back inside the envelope. The coins were francs and centimes—totalling five francs—the coat check ticket was from the theater where Thérèse, Dort, and the others worked, and the compact was unexceptional other than the mosaic-like designs of mother-of-pearl on the cover. I decided the keys were probably to her flat.

"Well, that's it," I said, stuffing everything back into the purse.

"What's this? Have you taken up smoking, Tabs?" Julia picked up the cigarette case I'd found next to Thérèse's purse in the salon.

"No, but I was wondering if you knew whose it was." I explained where I'd found it. It was silver, intricately engraved with vines, and its weight suggested it wasn't a cheap, dime-store accessory. The cigarettes inside were just ordinary Gitanes.

"Probably one of the men left it last night. A woman would have had hers in her handbag, wouldn't she?" said Julia, closing the case.

"Yes." I frowned. Was it strange that there hadn't been cigarettes, but there had been a matchbook in Thérèse's purse? She had been smoking last night; nearly everyone did, and so nearly everyone carried the supplies. Maybe she was just the kind of person who always bummed cigarettes off men as a way to flirt with them.

I'd had a friend back home who'd used that as a way to meet

guys. "Hey, handsome, gotta smoke?" Sandy would ask, and flutter her eyelashes.

Needless, to say, Sandy was a lot bolder than I was. Plus, I didn't smoke, thanks to my little imp and the three cigarettes I'd had one day when I was twelve.

"Well, I'm certain the owner will identify himself," Julia said, and turned back to her stove. When she opened the oven door, a great rush of delicious smells assaulted me—and reminded me that I still had to take Dort's purse to her so my grandfather and uncle could get their dinner.

"I'll take the cigarette case with me to the theater when I take Dort's handbag," I said, rising. "And then I'll give it to the 36 for Inspecteur Merveille on my way back."

Really, I kept telling myself, it was only reasonable that, since I had to pass through the area . . . well, *near* the area . . . where Thérèse Lognon lived on my way to Théâtre Monceau, it would be okay to make a little detour.

Just to see her building.

It didn't mean I was actually going to investigate the crime; it was just to alleviate a bit of curiosity by stopping by a place that was conveniently almost on the way to where I was actually going.

Except that it really wasn't on the way. It was on the Right Bank, the north side of the river, where the theater was, but they weren't all that close to each other. Thérèse's apartment was in Montmartre, an area where the beautiful white domed basilica Sacré-Coeur sat on a large hill and overlooked the city. The streets were narrow and zigzagging or doglegged and, in some areas, very steep. Not far from the famed church were dance halls and cabarets—including the infamous Le Chat Noir—and the redlight district. It was also home to a cache of artists and musicians who lived a bohemian lifestyle.

I rode my bicycle, which I realized later was a mistake. Dort's and Thérèse's purses were buckled safely in the small basket attached to my handlebars, and the cigarette case I'd shoved in the big pocket of my wool coat. As I pedaled, I felt the weight of the silver case bumping against my right thigh.

I was thankful we hadn't had any new snow or any precipitation for two days to clog the streets. It was cold, but at least I wasn't throwing slush up my back from the tires of my bike. I'd stopped in at home and rushed up the stairs to tell Grand-père and Oncle Rafe about my errand to the theater—and what they were to get out of the deal.

It was almost mortifying how ecstatic they were about their supper coming from Madame Child's kitchen instead of their own, although I could tell they tried to temper their enthusiasm. With that in mind, I was even more determined to glean as much help from Julia with cooking as I could. I knew how much my grandfather and honorary uncle—as well as all Parisians— had suffered when it came to a dearth of food during the Occupation. It was the least I could do to thank them for letting me stay there for free.

The worst part of the bicycle ride was when I crossed the Seine from the Left Bank north to the Right Bank. There were no buildings to help block the frigid wind that rolled off the broad gray river, and I was already regretting my decision to ride. I would have been more comfortable walking, where the rush of air wouldn't be blowing up under my skirt and blasting me in the face, and even more comfortable in a taxi. Of course, it occurred to me only as I was pumping my pedals over the bridge that I could "legally" have been wearing trousers for this little expedition!

I had been thinking about getting my own car here in Paris— Julia and Dort each had one, and they managed to drive relatively safely in the city, although Dort had had a minor bumper-thumper shortly after she arrived. Maybe I should stop buying pretty shoes and blouses and save for a little Renault or something like that. I was certain I could park beneath the portico that led into the rear courtyard at home.

As I navigated my way from boulevard de Clichy to rue Lepic, the streets became steeper and narrower—and followed the path of jagged lightning bolts. They also became darker, for the sun was low and the buildings that lined the way were close and tall. My legs were screaming for a break by the time I turned onto rue de la Mire. I was damp from exertion and silently cursing myself for being a busybody—but mostly for riding a bike instead of hiring a taxi.

But I was here, and therefore I was going to at least find Thérèse's address. I wondered if I'd see Inspecteur Merveille, or whether he'd come and gone already.

I wondered what I'd say if I did run into him . . . and even more, I wondered what he'd say. Would he find my presence some indication of guilt?

I decided if I ran into Merveille here, I could always claim I knew he'd be there so I came to give him Thérèse's purse.

Gritting my teeth at the thought—Paris had been liberated for five years, and therefore I had the freedom to go wherever I liked—I slowed my bicycle to a halt in front of Thérèse's building: number 15.

It was one with a familiar look throughout the city: the distinctive creamy Haussmann brick with ornate trim, four or five stories tall, lined up along the block, nearly right atop its neighbors. I suspected there were two or three teacup-size flats on each floor, and some of them might even have their own bathrooms, though that was certainly not a given. Thérèse's building and those next to and behind it formed a small, shared courtyard in the back. Narrow alleys between the buildings would allow access to the tiny, scraggly patch of yard behind—not for cars to pass through, but for bicycles or those on foot, along with the multitude of cats who populated the city.

Doubtless because of the weather, there were few pedestrians making their way along the sidewalk, and the ones who were were bundled in their mufflers, hats, and coats and moved along quickly with their heads down. There was no sign of any gendarmes or police cars, or even a bicycle parked nearby. The cars parked on the block had been there for at least a few days; all were covered with snow undisturbed, except for an occasional trail of cat prints.

I sighed, straddling my own stationary ride with both feet on the ground, and looked up at the curtained windows of Thérèse's building. Had I come all this way for no reason—just to look at a building from the outside? What was I thinking?

Before I quite knew what I was doing, my internal sprite had me climbing off my bicycle. I wheeled it into one of the narrow passages between buildings and leaned it against a tree that was reasonably out of sight of any passerby who might decide they would rather snatch a two-wheeled ride than walk, then slipped back out to the front entrance of number 15. My knees were a little shaky—from nerves, not from biking for twenty-five minutes—as I walked boldly to the front door of the building.

It would either be unlocked or it wouldn't, and then I'd know whether I'd really wasted my time coming here. Although, I had my Swiss Army knife in my pocket, as always, and one of the tools might come in handy to get the door open—

Then suddenly I stilled, scoffing at myself and rolling my eyes at my stupidity. The keys were in Thérèse's purse! I could actually get into her apartment if I wanted to.

Did I want to?

Had I been reading Nancy Drew for over fifteen years— exploring hidden staircases and reading mysterious letters and examining broken lockets?

Hell yes, I wanted to get in.

Keys in hand, I walked with greater confidence and a thrill of excitement to the front door. It took me only a moment to determine which of the two was for the front door, and I slipped inside, grateful to be out of the cold. The foyer of the building was silent, empty, and cramped. There was no lift; only a flight of stairs trimmed with wrought iron railings.

The tip of my nose was cold and icy, and I wiped it with a handkerchief as I started up the stairs. According to the address on the envelope, Thérèse's flat was number 21, so I guessed it was up three flights due to the way Europeans counted their floors.

Fortunately, no one was around to question me. Probably they were all smarter than I was and were huddled around their coal stoves or gas radiators, drinking *café* or brandy.

But they probably weren't having as much fun as I was having, I thought with a little smile.

Harmless fun, I thought . . . at the time.

The hall was narrow and dark and smelled like overcooked leeks and too many cigarettes. A single bulb grudgingly offered a circle of light that did little to illuminate the corridor, and even less to expose whatever I heard skittering softly away at the end of the hall. Since it had feet and didn't slither, whatever it was didn't alarm me.

There was no carpet underfoot, and the plank floor was scuffed and uneven from wear. It creaked and moaned in places, and I winced every time my step made a noise—even though I doubted anyone could hear me over the radio blaring from flat number 20. The numbers of the apartments were painted on small ceramic plaques hung next to each door on the rough, dun-colored wall. Twenty-one was on the right side, which meant its windows faced the courtyard. That was good; no one from the street would see a light or me poking around.

A little shiver skittered down my spine as I had that thought, then I pushed away the worry. Surely Merveille and his men had come and gone. There would be no reason for anyone to be watching Thérèse's apartment, knowing that the police had already been there.

And why would anyone watch a dead woman's apartment anyway, I told myself firmly. She was already dead.

When I reached the door, I looked up and down the hall. No one was there, none of the other doors had cracked open, and I heard no sounds of life other than the overly dramatic voices from the radio program. I put my ear to the door and listened for a long time. But there were no sounds from inside.

Well, I thought, here goes nothing.

I fitted the key into the lock, twisted it, and carefully turned the knob. Then I stepped into the apartment.

When nothing happened, I let out a long breath and closed the door behind me. My fingers prickled and my knees were shaky. The last time I'd done something this crazy was when I marched myself into the personnel office at the bomber plant on March 1, 1942. Even getting on a ship to come to Paris hadn't been as exciting and frightening as asking to be hired to make war machines.

Was this considered breaking and entering? Since I had a key, it wasn't breaking. I was definitely entering, but Thérèse Lognon wouldn't care.

Belatedly, I wondered if she'd lived here alone and whether I might be disturbing a roommate.

I hesitated, feeling my breath rise and fall in a shallow rhythm. Then, when I heard no sounds from within, I pushed the light switch by the door with my gloved hand. It was after five o'clock, and shadows were growing long—especially here in a north-facing apartment with curtained windows. Another single, stingy bulb came on with the click of the buttonlike switch, but it gave off enough light to see around the small space.

I was surprised to find that the single, rectangular room was barely furnished. There was one ratty, sagging sofa that looked as if it would collapse if someone sat on it. One small woven rug, with a table lamp standing on it, and a travel trunk that might have doubled as a table. All of this was arranged in front of a fireplace that held a small heat stove. A pail of coal sat next to it, along with some kindling and a box of matches.

The kitchen was hardly more than a counter with a stand-alone gas burner, and I knew better than to turn on the tap to see whether water would flow into a small soapstone sink. But it was the only source of water in the place; there wasn't even a toilet. Three short shelves and a single cupboard were stacked next to the sink. They were empty of all but a plate, a cup, and a bowl. There was no trace of food other than a box of crackers. Even the food box outside the window was empty of everything but a tiny rind of cheese.

I saw a mattress on the floor in one corner with another lamp next to it. The bed was poorly made, as if someone had just dragged up the coverlet to get it out of the way in order to have a place to sit and pull on stockings, for an array of clothes was strewn over the top and a pair of smart-looking heels lined up next to it. The clothes looked like they would belong to

Thérèse, and they were by far the nicest things in the entire apartment—fashionable, colorful, seemingly expensive.

There was a mirror propped against the wall, and on the bare wood floor next to it were all of the cosmetics and accoutrements one would normally find at a woman's dressing table: lipstick, nail polish, eye makeup, sparkly combs and hairpins, face powder, hair and makeup brushes, hairspray, perfume, and more in small cardboard boxes.

As I stood there, looking around this dingy, dark, mean room, I could hardly believe it belonged to the bright, vivacious, and attractive Thérèse Lognon I'd met last night. She either hadn't lived here very long, or spent her money only on items to make her look beautiful.

There were curtains on the two tall, narrow windows, and I noticed the drapes looked new—far newer than anything else in the apartment except for a tube of lipstick that still had its sharp, slanted tip. The curtains were dark and heavy, blocking the light and the wintry drafts. Both sets were pulled nearly closed. The room felt stuffy and stale, and beneath the faint scent of face powder and Thérèse's perfume was the smell of mildew and rot.

Drawn to the windows for some reason, I peered through the small opening between the curtains into the postage-size courtyard. The snow glowed in the long shadows, lumpy where it covered benches, straggly bushes, and other natural formations. There was no movement other than a bird darting from a balcony to a tree branch, and although some lights winked in windows across the way, the entire view nonetheless seemed bleak.

Bleak was the best way to describe this entire space. So very different from the impression I'd had of the lively woman who'd lived here.

I pulled back from the window, drawing the curtains together again, and turned to look around the room once more. There was no indication that Merveille and his men had been here; but I wasn't certain what traces they might have left behind—there wasn't much of anything to disrupt.

Maybe they'd come and taken letters, papers, books, files, and photos—for I saw none of that anywhere. Maybe that was why the place seemed so empty and impersonal. The walls were bare, except for a tattered poster of the Le Chat Noir cabaret that had been tacked near the bed. I had the sense that ratty picture had been living here far longer than Thérèse had.

I hesitated, then with a glance to be certain the drapes were closed, I turned on one of the lamps sitting on the floor. This particular one had been positioned to provide illumination for the mirror where Thérèse did her grooming, as well as whatever reading she might choose to do in bed.

I looked more closely at her belongings, not sure what I was searching for. If the police had been through, they had already taken everything of interest. The cosmetics were of good quality, but the jewelry was cheap and some of it was gaudy. There were a few hats, along with a pair of gloves that I noticed were smudged on the side of the left palm. As a left-handed person, I recognized the cause of that. My own hand, and plenty pairs of gloves, had the same marks from ink being smudged when I wrote.

The shrill ringing of a telephone was so startling, so unexpectedly close to me, that I gasped out a little shriek. Clapping a hand over my mouth, my pulse jittery and my knees suddenly weak, I looked toward the sound.

The telephone was on the floor next to the mattress, partially hidden by a tumble of clothing and bedcovers. I hadn't seen it in the shadows, obstructed as it was. I stared at the shiny black device, which continued to *brill* in the silence in a way that jarred my nerves even more.

The fact that there was a telephone in this little hovel when there were no other creature comforts—including a toilet—shocked and confused me. Thérèse had had a telephone installed, but she didn't even own a chair?

And at the same time, my fingers itched to pick up that receiver.

The phone rang for what seemed like an eternity as I stared at it, my heart thudding in my throat. Should I?

At last, the ringing stopped.

Silence reigned but for the sound of my ragged breathing and my pulse in my ears.

I stared at the black monstrosity for several minutes before I noticed the corner of a book tucked behind it, wedged between the edge of the mattress and the wall.

When I picked it up, something clunked quietly to the floor behind it and the mattress.

A gun.

I gaped, my mouth in a wide and silent O as I stared at the dull metal of a pistol barrel.

What was Thérèse Lognon doing with a gun?

I was trying to decide what—if anything—to do about the gun when I heard a rhythmic creak in the hallway. Spinning, I looked toward the door, my heart surging into my throat. The footsteps—for that was what had made the creaking sound— had stopped outside the door.

Quickly, I turned off the lamp as my terrified gaze darted around the room. The only place to hide was behind the long, heavy curtains, and I sprinted toward them on light feet as I heard the door move gently in its frame. With another surge of horror, I realized I hadn't locked the door behind me.

Somehow, I made it to the window farthest from the bed, ducking behind the more shadowy side of the floor-length drapes. I felt sick when I realized the light by the door was still on as well as the door being unlocked, but I hoped that, at least, wouldn't cause suspicion. People often left on a light to welcome them to a dark home.

Of course, they didn't usually leave their door unlocked.

I forced my breath to even out and become quiet—almost an impossibility, considering how my heart was pounding and how quickly I'd moved—and I flattened myself into the nook of the window as much as possible. It was then I realized I was still clutching the book I'd yanked from behind Thérèse's bed.

As the door opened, I felt a renewed rush of terror. Even though I couldn't see who was there, the fact that they were moving stealthily and furtively indicated they had no more right to be there than I did . . . and surely, that didn't bode well.

Whoever was here had waited until dark to arrive. They hadn't knocked or otherwise announced themselves . . . which meant they didn't expect anyone to be here. Maybe he or she had been the one who'd telephoned a few minutes ago to make certain no one answered. There'd been a telephone booth across the street from where I parked my bike.

Whoever the intruder was, he or she was moving as slowly and carefully as I had done when I arrived.

The thought that I was very possibly within a few short feet of a killer was enough to turn me cold and wobbly.

I hadn't prayed in a long time, but I prayed then.

I prayed and I listened.

Whoever was there had a flashlight; From behind the drapes, I could see the light bouncing around.

I couldn't tell anything about the intruder—even whether they were male or female. I could hear only the sounds of care-ful footsteps that became more confident as whoever it was be-came assured they were alone. As much as I wanted to look around the edge of the drapes, I dared not move. But I listened as hard as I could over the roaring in my ears.

The sounds of shuffling, scuffling, rustling told me they were searching for something. Soft clinks and clunks indicated he or she was digging through Thérèse's boxes of cosmetics. I heard the dull clunk as he or she discovered the telephone and moved it—maybe even kicked it—with a huff of frustration. I focused on keeping my own breathing soundless.

If you've ever tried to stifle terrified breathing into silence when your heart is racing and your nerves are stretched tight, you know how impossible it is.

But I must have succeeded, for, after what seemed like a very long time but surely was no more than ten or fifteen minutes, the intruder made another short, sharp noise of fury punctu-ated by the sound of glass shattering . . . and then stalked to-ward the exit.

I closed my eyes, praying once more, holding my breath as I waited for the sound of the doorknob turning, then the finality of the latch to click back into place.

Once it did so, once the footsteps were gone, I felt the tension rush from my body so quickly my knees nearly gave way. I held on to the heavy fabric of the drapes to steady myself, not yet ready to leave the safety of their folds.

I waited for what seemed like another eternity before peering out from behind them. The flat was empty and silent once again. The rhythmic creaking of footsteps had faded.

The only sound was the distant rise and fall of the radio from down the hall.

CHAPTER 7

As I slipped out from behind the curtains, I noticed a new smell lingering in the room. Whoever had been there had left behind a sort of aroma, a faint essence that could be a possible clue to their identity. It was only the faint waft of something sort of sweet and smoky. Not marijuana, but a smell that had a sort of earthy element to it. I sniffed hard, trying to identify it—but by then I was completely spooked. I wanted to get out of that apartment as quickly as possible . . . but something made me go back over to the limp mattress and the telephone.

Somehow I wasn't surprised to see that the gun tucked between the bed and wall was gone.

That frightened me more than anything else.

I glanced at the book I was still holding. It looked like a small hardcover novel, but I couldn't make out the title. A quick flip through the pages in the dim light suggested it was indeed a novel and that she'd marked her page with a folded piece of paper, but it was too dark to tell what language the book was in. I hesitated, but I didn't want to leave it there in case the intruder came back and noticed it had suddenly appeared, so I shoved it into the pocket of my coat next to the cigarette case.

Then I hightailed it out of the apartment, down the stairs, and exited the building.

As before, I didn't see another soul until I was out the front door and saw a car trundling down the block. I found myself looking over my shoulder as I mounted my two-wheeler.

My heart didn't stop pounding until I was three blocks away. At least I was going mostly downhill this time.

The sun had completely disappeared during the half hour I was in the tiny flat. The sky was dark and the buildings on either side of the street cast long, heavy shadows. My breath made regular puffs of white as I hunched over the handlebars.

Under other circumstances, I might have enjoyed the bike ride under a starlit sky along the pretty *rues*, lit by streetlamps that were far more generous with their illumination than the incandescent bulbs in Thérèse's building. Paris had her own elegance all the time, even in the slushiest of winter . . . but at night, she was stunning with her creamy, elegant buildings and their ornate black railings, all lit in golden pools along stately *rues.*

Still, the beauty of my adopted city was wasted on me as I furiously pumped the pedals, determined to put a good distance between me and the apartment. I was long overdue getting to the Théâtre Monceau, but at least I was alive and unharmed.

As I rode, I wracked my brain to remember any details about the unseen intruder, but I couldn't identify anything about him or her, with the exception of the faint scent that hadn't been in the flat before their entrance. It wasn't perfume or tobacco, nor was it unpleasant—but it was distinctive. I was certain I'd remember it if I smelled it again.

The American Club Theater, Dort's employer, performed out of the Théâtre Monceau, which was in the wealthy, elegant eighth arrondissement, several blocks and an entirely different world away from Thérèse Lognon's hovel of a flat on rue de la Mire.

It was more than twenty minutes later when I finally arrived at my original destination and wheeled the front tire of my bicycle into a bike rack out front and used a padlock to secure it. I didn't want to leave Thérèse's pocketbook in my bike basket, but I also didn't want anyone to notice or comment on it. I took off my coat and slung the strap over my shoulder, then put my coat back on over it.

The front doors of the theater probably weren't open yet; it was just after six o'clock and I knew the show didn't start until eight. I wondered whether they'd even have the show, considering what happened to Thérèse. I went around to the back-alley-facing door, per Dort's instructions via Julia, and found that it was wedged open with a doorstop.

Slipping inside, I found myself in the vast backstage area. The ceiling loomed three stories above my head, reminding me of an airplane hangar, and there were set pieces stacked up everywhere. Obviously, these were not to be used during the current production of Agatha Christie's *Ten Little Indians*, for there was a balcony that reminded me of *Romeo & Juliet* and a Japanese garden scene that had to be from *The Mikado*.

A jumble of voices in English—for most of the troupe was American—was accompanied by other activity like hammering and the testing of stage lights. The smells of cigarette smoke and fresh paint lingered.

Before I could even think about how to locate the office where Dort worked, I heard my name.

"Oh, hello—it's, uh, Tabitha, right?"

I turned to see Neil Kingsley, one of Dort's friends from last night, standing there. He was just as dark and good-looking as I remembered, even without the benefit of a couple glasses of wine. I gathered he played Philip Lombard, one of the leads in the current production, and I noticed he was already wearing stage makeup—which answered my question as to whether the show would go on.

The show was, apparently, going on.

Neil wasn't quite six feet tall, but he had a demeanor and look about him that gave him a sort of powerful stature. He was certainly strong enough to have easily overpowered a woman in order to stab her. And attractive enough to have lured her into a dark corner . . .

I tucked away a niggle of nerves as I replied, "Yes, Tabitha. I'm looking for Dort—have you seen her?"

"Not recently, no," he said. "But she can't have gone far—Maribelle is on a rampage, and poor Dort is usually the recipient no matter what the problem is. And there's always a problem. She takes the heat for the rest of us. Especially Thad. Maribelle really gets on his case. He likes to go and hide sometimes, just to get away from her."

He lit a cigarette and drew in sharply as if stressed, and that had me digging into my pocket to pull out the silver cigarette case. "This was left at Dort's last night—is it yours?" I asked.

He shook his head. "No, but it might belong to Justiss."

I nodded. I was about to ask where I should look for Dort when Neil spoke again. "Terrible about Thérèse, isn't it?" His handsome face appeared haggard beneath the pancake of greasepaint. "Just terrible. They said she was stabbed in the cellar of the building—right *there*."

"She might have been killed anywhere," I replied. "But she was found in the cellar. I walked out with her," I went on. "We rode down in the elevator together."

"She left with you?" He frowned, taking another drag of tobacco. "I thought she was getting a ride back with Johnny. Last night's a little fuzzy." He scrubbed his forehead with the hand that held the cigarette. "Did she say anything—you know . . . anything?"

I understood he was asking whether she'd given any indication that her life was in danger. "She told me she was waiting for a taxi. Maybe Johnny wasn't ready to leave when she was, so she called for a ride."

"So you rode down with her." He looked at me closely as he exhaled a stream of smoke. "Did you see anything? Anyone?"

I shook my head. "I live across the street, so I didn't linger. When I left, she had gone back into the lobby to wait for her taxi. There was no one around that I saw."

He shook his head. "Someone must have come in off the street—a tramp or something—and cornered her, and . . . did that."

"I got the impression from the police detective that they think it was someone who knew her," I said. There was no reason to tell him about Julia's knife—either he was the killer and already knew about it, or he would soon find out.

His eyes widened. "Are you saying someone from the party last night killed Thérèse? That's ridiculous."

"I'm not saying anything. I'm just repeating the impression I got from Inspecteur Merveille."

Neil gave me an assessing look. "Wow," was all he said, then dragged again on his cigarette.

I was about to ask whether he'd spoken to the detective when a young woman rushed up. "There you are! Neil, we've got to finish your makeup. Your costume is pressed, and your shoes were spotty so I buffed them up good. It's less than sixty minutes until call." Her eyes were red rimmed and I wondered if she'd been crying. Because of Thérèse, or because of the difficult troupe manager—or for some other reason? Too much dust?

"Sorry," Neil said to me. "Duty calls." He hurried off in a waft of cigarette smoke.

I wanted to say something to the woman, but before I had the chance, she rushed off in his wake.

I stood there for a moment, then started to walk in the direction of the most noises and voices. On the way, I found the props table, the costume room, and the stage manager's desk, but no Dort.

"Tabitha? What are you doing here?"

I turned to see Mark Justiss. He wore a delighted but slightly confused smile. His thick blond hair was mussed, and from the golden glitter of stubble on his jaw, I could tell he'd missed shaving this morning. But he'd paid far more attention to his attire, for he was neatly dressed in coat, vest, shirt, along with gleaming black shoes and a perfectly knotted tie. He carried a battered medicine bag in one hand and his hat in the other.

My understanding was that he was there to provide first aid for the theater troupe and their patrons, while lending a hand backstage as needed. I wasn't certain if he had another job or was just hanging around Paris on his parents' money.

I couldn't fault him if he was—I was doing the same thing. Although in my case it was mostly my grandfather's money.

"Hi, Mark. Nice to see you again. I'm looking for Dort. Have you seen her?" I asked.

"She's on stage left with the gorgon," he replied, still grinning as if he was surprised and happy to see me. He pointed toward what I would have thought was stage right, but apparently I had things backward.

"The gorgon?" I said.

"Maribelle. She started the troupe, you know," he said in a hushed voice as he leaned closer to me. "She's a real you-know-what. Dort wanted her to cancel the show tonight—obviously because of Thérèse, but Maribelle would have none of it. 'The show must go on,' she said. 'Thérèse would have wanted it that way.'" He made a disgusted noise as he moved back. "Like every good American capitalist, Maribelle only cares about making money."

"Oh. Maybe I shouldn't interrupt."

"Yeah, you should probably give them a minute." Mark's expression turned even more sober. "We're all really broken up about what happened to Thérèse. Johnny said he was supposed to give her a ride home, but she left early. Is it true you found her?"

"No, I didn't find her . . . but I saw her," I said. "It was awful. *So awful.*" I couldn't control a shiver, and Mark's arm jerked up, then eased back down as if he'd meant to offer a comforting touch, then decided against it. For some reason, I found that endearing.

"Do they have any idea who could have done it? Some tramp from off the street? That's what everyone's saying."

"I'm not sure," I replied, fully aware that I was speaking to another one of our suspects. "I don't really know very much other than she was stabbed."

"Didn't you leave together last night?" said Mark. "It was around two, wasn't it?"

I looked at him in surprise. "Yes."

He gave me a bashful smile and shrugged. "I was disappointed when you left, so I noticed. And I saw Thérèse go into the elevator with you. Did you know her well?"

"Um, no. I didn't know her at all," I replied, suddenly feeling as if I were being interrogated all over again. My eyes narrowed. Surely he didn't think *I* was a suspect?

He was still smiling, but I thought his gaze had sharpened a little. He had eyes that could have belonged to a tiger. "I didn't really know her, either. She worked front of house—the coat room."

"When did you leave?" I asked. I could interrogate too.

He suppressed a smile. "What's good for the goose, I suppose," he murmured, then replied, "Not long after. The party had suddenly become a lot less interesting to me."

"So you don't know when Neil or Johnny or Thad left," I said, ignoring the heat that rose to my cheeks. He was definitely flirting, and I realized I didn't mind—even though he was American and I was sure I'd never find an American man interesting again.

"The get-together was wrapping up by two thirty anyway," Mark said. "Neil and Thad had finished off the whisky, and Johnny was grumbling about wanting to get something to eat. Ivan and Dort were, uh, doing their own thing." He gave me a wry smile and shrugged.

"So when you left, did you see anything?" I asked. "Anyone?"

He shook his head. "The *inspecteur* asked me the same thing."

Merveille had already been here, questioning everyone from the party. I really wasn't surprised to hear it.

"Did he talk to everyone?" I asked.

"As far as I know, he talked to everyone who was there last night *and* everyone who worked here with Thérèse. I heard him ask Dort for her address, and she had to go look it up in the files," said Mark.

I nodded, but I thought it was interesting that Dort hadn't known where Thérèse lived. I'd gotten the impression that they were all great friends here at the American Club Theater.

"Oh, there you are, Tabs!" Dort and her booming voice broke

into our conversation. "Thank goodness you're here, or I wouldn't have been able to get home tonight. Low on gas—I suppose I should say petrol here, shouldn't I? I can't believe Maribelle is insisting the show go on!" She appeared weary and frustrated.

I handed over her purse, then remembered the cigarette case. As I reached into my pocket, my fingers touched the book I'd taken from Thérèse's apartment. "That reminds me—is this yours, Mark?" I pulled out the cigarette case and handed it to him as I asked Dort, "Will the filling station be open when you leave here tonight? It'll be awfully late."

"Oh, I'm going to dash over there in a few and fill up. I've got time, now that the gorgon is finished with me," she said, rolling her eyes at Mark. "Better hide—she might be coming for you next. She already laid into Thad about some of the lighting filters earlier. I think he's been in hiding ever since."

Mark grimaced at the mention of Maribelle, then looked at me. "Yes, this is mine," he said, gesturing with the cigarette case. "I thought I might have left it there last night; I made the mistake of giving it to Thad for a smoke, and he must have set it down and forgotten about it. I was going to stop by and see if it was there, but, well . . ." His expression said it all.

"Well, I'm glad I saved you the trip," I said. "I had to bring Dort her purse anyway."

He slipped the case into his inside coat pocket. "I wouldn't have minded an excuse to stop by. We hardly had the chance to talk, Tabitha."

Dort gave me a wide-eyed, waggly eyebrowed look, followed by a nudge. Subtlety was not her strong suit.

Fortunately, Mark didn't seem to notice, for he went on. "It was kind of loud and crowded last night."

And someone had been planning a murder.

As if reading my mind, Dort said, "It's just bonkers about Thérèse, isn't it? We're all really torn up about it. Except Maribelle." She bent close and murmured only for my ears. "They're not bothering Julia about it, are they? It was her knife, but . . ." She straightened and shook her head.

I wondered if Dort realized she was probably more of a suspect than her sister was, since she'd at least known the woman. "It's horrible."

"Poor Mathilde," Dort said. "To have come across the scene like that . . ." She shivered and shook her head, and I made a sound of agreement. "She's already a little batty and scattered, so this will probably really mess her up. Poor woman."

I wanted to talk to her more about what Julia and I had discussed, but Mark was still standing there.

Before I could think of a way to extricate us for a quiet moment, Dort suddenly looked at me as if seeing me for the first time. "Oh, Tabs! Do you think you could help us out?"

"What do you mean?" I replied.

"With Thérèse, um, gone, we don't have anyone to run the coat check," said Dort. "Do you think you could stick around and help us out tonight?"

I blinked. "Um . . . sure." All my anticipation of a delectable, delicious dinner by Julia Child evaporated in one great poof.

"Oh, thank you! Um . . . what about tomorrow and Saturday too?" she asked with a bright, hopeful smile.

"Sure," I replied. "It's not like I have anything exciting going on." I realized how that must sound to Mark—either a hint or a complaint; neither of which I had intended—and I felt my cheeks warm again. I didn't look at him.

"Oh, thank you!" Dort swooped me into a big hug, nearly smothering me. She smelled like cigarettes, hairspray, and rose-scented perfume. "It's been the most awful day, and that's one thing off my mind. Let me show you where the coat room and everything is."

"See you later, Tabitha," said Mark as Dort whisked me off through the labyrinth of backstage.

I was happy to go with Dort, because that would give us a few minutes to talk privately. I really wanted to get her impressions of everyone who'd been there last night, and who might have stolen Julia's knife.

Running a coat check was not nearly as difficult as shooting rivets into a metal drum, so it took a total of three minutes for Dort to show me the ropes—and most of that was her trying to find a stack of unused claim checks.

Once she handed them over to me, she plumped down on the chair inside the coat check. "Can you believe this?" she said, resting her head in one hand as she looked up at me miserably. "Poor Thérèse."

"No," I said with great feeling. "I can't believe it." I knew I'd said and thought that countless times today, but that didn't make it any less relevant.

"I think that gumshoe guy thinks I had something to do with it—or Julia," she said. "Just because it's her knife. What a mess."

I knew we probably didn't have much time to talk before Dort had to get back to work or fill up her car, so I didn't beat around the bush. "Whoever did it had to have been at the party last night. They took the knife from the kitchen—it was on the counter by the sink. Did you notice anything?"

"I know," Dort groaned. "And I've been trying to think all day if I saw anything important. Everything from last night is such a blur, and besides, Ivan and I were necking in the corner most of the time. I hardly paid attention to what was going on. I do know that Johnny seemed really surprised—or maybe disappointed—that Thérèse had left."

"Do you have any idea who might have wanted to kill Thérèse? Was she dating anyone? Broken up with anyone? There had to be a reason—and whatever the reason was, it wasn't planned." I explained what Julia and I had concluded about it not being a premeditated murder. "They decided to do it and went looking for a weapon."

Dort frowned. "I just *hate* that thought. That someone just decided to go find a knife and kill her! It's just so awful." She shook her head, her face grave.

"She did have a boyfriend a while back," she went on, her frown growing deeper. "I don't know his name or anything about him, but he never came around here. Wouldn't surprise me if he was married—she stayed pretty mum about him, and that's usually why someone doesn't show off a guy. But they did break things off, maybe a couple weeks ago?"

"Was she upset about the breakup? Do you know who dumped who?" I asked.

"Not sure. She did seem a little . . . I don't know—shaken?—about it. A little nervy, a little tense."

"Maybe she was afraid her ex was going to come after her," I said.

"Maybe. But I know it wasn't anyone who was at my place last night. I would know if she'd been dating any of those guys. She and Neil knew each other before she started working here—he recommended her for the job because she's not bad in English and is fluent in French. But I never got any impression they'd been dating or that there was any friction between them."

"How long did she work here?"

"Oh, she'd been here longer than me. At least six months," Dort said.

I leaned forward and whispered, "I sneaked inside her apartment tonight on my way here."

Her eyes grew wide with admiration and curiosity. "You did?"

I explained how I had the keys, patting the purse still hidden under my coat. "It was very sparse and empty. I thought it was really weird."

"I'm surprised you didn't see Inspecteur Merveille there," Dort said. "I gave him her address and I heard him say he was going right over there when he left. That was only a little while before you got here."

I shrugged. "He wasn't there. But someone else was." I described what happened and watched her eyes go even rounder.

"Holy mackerel, Tabs, what if he'd seen you?"

"He didn't. Or she. I'm not really sure whether it was a man or a woman."

"*And he took the gun?*" Dort said in a stage whisper. "Jeepers."

I nodded, and a sudden thought struck me. "Are Johnny and Thad here?" Besides Ivan—who I couldn't suspect because he'd been making out with Dort the whole time—Johnny and

Thad were the only other people who'd been there last night . . . and who could be considered suspects. Either one of them could have been snooping around Thérèse's apartment while I was there.

"Johnny was here earlier. I haven't seen him for a while, but that's not unusual. He's got a lot to see to before a show, so he's usually running through his list and likes to do it in quiet somewhere. Last time I saw Thad, he was up in the catwalk, fixing one of the light filters and replacing some of the bulbs. One of the lights had a loose wire too. He's been busy," Dort said, as if knowing what I was thinking. "But I don't know about Johnny . . . or anyone else, to be honest. I've been in the office."

"I suppose Johnny might have had time to go over to rue de la Mire," I said, imagining whether the short, muscular Johnny would have made the confident footsteps I'd heard. It was definitely possible. And I remembered Neil saying that Thad liked to hide from Maribelle sometimes. "It wouldn't take more than twenty minutes on foot—but he has a car, doesn't he? He could be there and back in ten minutes."

"Everyone has a car," said Dort. "All of us. What about rue de la Mire? What's over there?"

"That's Thérèse's address," I said. "Number 15 rue de la Mire, room 21."

Dort stared at me. "That's not the address we have in her file."

I blinked. "Well, that's interesting."

"I'll say."

"And that also explains why I didn't see Inspecteur Merveille there. What address did you give him?"

"It's somewhere in Montparnasse, not far from where we live," Dort told me.

I wanted to know why Thérèse had two different addresses. Could she have been afraid of her ex-lover coming after her, so she moved?

Dort sighed, that misery back in her eyes. "I just can't believe one of those guys last night could have killed Thérèse. It's just impossible."

"Whoever did it must have left right after she and I did in order to catch her before the taxi came," I said. "He probably took the stairs down and waited until I left the building so she was alone. But who was it?"

"The rest of the guys stayed until almost three o'clock," Dort said. "I remember because Ivan made a comment about the witching hour and I told him I thought the witching hour was midnight, not three, and we all had a good laugh over that. All of us were still there."

"Even Mark?" I asked. He'd said he'd left shortly after I did. But maybe he'd just been trying to make me feel good.

Not that I cared.

And if he was there later, that meant he wasn't the murderer. So there was that.

"I think so . . . I'm pretty sure. Yes, he was still there." Dort nodded. "All four of them were—Mark, Neil, Thad, and Johnny. And Ivan, too, but he and I were together all night. Trust me." She cracked a smile.

"Well, it probably wouldn't have taken that long for whoever did it to do it. Dash down the stairs—three or four minutes. Talk to Thérèse—he probably had to coax her into a shadowy corner—"

"Then it couldn't have been Neil," said Dort. "We all know he's not the type to tease a girl into a corner, if you know what I mean."

I thought I did. But I still wasn't certain that was a good enough reason to dismiss Neil as a suspect. Or any of them. Even Mark.

"Anyway, whoever it was would have had to have gotten her into a dark area of the lobby, away from the entrance and the elevator or anywhere someone might have come through. And then . . ." I grimaced. I didn't need to finish the thought.

"The killer must have gotten blood on himself," I went on after a moment. I could see the scene unfold in my mind like a movie. "On his clothes and maybe his shoes. Even if he left and went down and attacked Thérèse before her taxi came, and then he came back up to the party, he would have been all bloody."

"What if he wore a coat while he killed her and then took it off when he came back?" said Dort. "Or the other way around— put his coat on after he killed her and came back, to hide the blood?"

I heaved a great sigh. "This is why it's so much harder being a detective for real than in books. That's all true. It could have been *any* of them."

"But," said Dort, "it had to be *one* of them."

I nodded. It had to be one of them.

CHAPTER 8

*T*hat night, I learned that running the coat check meant I was either hopping—super busy—or bored stiff. There was no real in between.

The big rush started at seven thirty and would go until just before eight, when everyone was coming in all at once . . . and then I would be left with almost nothing to do for the next two hours.

The theater's patrons were mostly American; many of them expats. I wondered if I'd see anyone I knew, for the expat community was fairly small. I had my tutoring clients, and I'd met several other American couples connected to the embassy through Julia and Paul as well.

There was also a good number of British people coming to see the show, as well as a smattering of other European nationalities. They were all here, however, to see an American theater troupe performing mostly American plays. Everyone came in from the cold smelling of tobacco, perfume or cologne, and the brisk winter air. They were jovial and very social with one another as they waited in line.

I wondered if part of the reason for the festive air was because they could lapse into the familiarity of their native language.

I quickly got into the swing of things: greet the patron and take their long, heavy coat, hat, and/or scarf carefully through the opening of the half-door that separated me from them.

After one disaster that ended up in a spilled cup of coffee that narrowly missed my skirt, I learned that the key to collecting the coats was to do so without knocking over the coat check attendant's beverage, the tip jar (which was a bonus I hadn't expected but appreciated), the hole punch, or the stack of claim tickets that rested on the narrow ledge that acted as a counter.

Once the outerwear was brought safely over the counter, I was to slip the coat and its accompaniments onto a hanger, punch the claim ticket so there was a way to thread it onto the hanger, and tear off the ticket's bottom for the patron.

I managed this a few times without incident before a gentleman gave me a smile as he handed me his coat and hat. "You're new here, aren't you? Let me give you a hand. The regulars know to punch their own tickets when it's busy." He punched his own claim ticket and tore off the bottom, while I handled the simple task of merely attaching it to the hanger after I'd gathered up and hung his coat.

This technique seemed to catch on with the long line of people waiting, and before I knew it, we'd moved into a more efficient rhythm.

A few of the patrons were in such a hurry they punched their claim ticket twice, but it didn't matter because I could still attach it to the hanger and they were pleased because they got to get to their seats before the show started. Even though they were in line, everyone was in a good mood when the front of house lights blinked, signaling the five-minute warning to be seated.

I was feeling quite satisfied with how efficient I'd become and the rhythm I'd fallen into when I looked up and saw a familiar face.

"Oh, hello, Mr. Hayes," I said with a delighted smile. "How nice that you're able to have a night out."

He was from Baltimore, and his fifteen-year-old daughter Betty was one of the French students I'd gotten through Paul Child's connections. I looked behind Mr. Hayes as I slid his coat onto a hanger.

"Is Mrs. Hayes with you? I wanted to tell her how much improved Betty has gotten in the last week with her verb conjugation."

"Oh, uh, no, Mrs. Hayes couldn't make it tonight," said my student's father. He appeared so startled to see me that he accidentally punched his claim ticket three times.

"Well, I'll see her tomorrow morning anyway for Betty's lesson," I replied. "Enjoy the show!"

"Yes, yes, thank you," said Mr. Hayes as he went off. I noticed that, unlike most everyone else, he hadn't dropped a tip in the jar.

"Where's the other girl?" said the next person in line. "The one who was here before?" He seemed quite put out that Thérèse wasn't the one taking his coat.

"She's not here tonight," I said as I bundled up his heavy coat and pulled it over the counter, uncertain how much information to share.

"Well, where is she? Will she be back? Quite a looker, that one," he added, as if realizing he sounded rude.

Apparently, I wasn't considered a looker myself.

"She's . . . uh . . . she's dead," I said. "So, no . . . she won't be back."

His eyes widened. "She's *dead?*" This information seemed to subdue his demands, but he still mispunched his ticket with an extra hole.

More than a few people had been doing that, and it had begun to sort of offend my sense of organization and neatness.

But the patron tore off his half of the claim ticket and walked off without further ado, and I turned to the next person in line.

Some people were just odd.

Once the rush was over and the play had begun, I could sit on the chair inside the coat check and relax. I'd taken the opportunity to look more closely at Thérèse's book and found that it was an American copy of *And Then There Were None,* the Agatha Christie novel whose adaptation was the current production at Théâtre Monceau. She was only halfway through it, her place marked with the paper. I felt a little pang of sadness that Thérèse would never know how it ended—and that its final solution was diabolically clever and different from the play. I'd read somewhere that Mrs. Christie had heard from a survivor of the Buchenwald concentration camp that a group of the inmates had put on their own version of her play during the war as a way to sustain themselves during that horrific time. That just went to show how important and instrumental mystery fiction could be.

Since I'd already read the book, I tucked it back into my coat pocket. I doubted it was important, but I could give it to Inspecteur Merveille when I turned over Thérèse's handbag—without telling him exactly how I'd obtained it.

Right after the play started, I had called home to let Grand-père and Oncle Rafe know that I was helping out at the theater, and found them in the middle of eating the meal Mathilde, Julia's maid, had brought over for them.

They made all sorts of noises about how nice it was for me to help out and to be careful coming home, but I don't think they missed me at all, to be honest. They couldn't wait to get back to their meal of *jambon braisé Morvandelle.* And I didn't blame them. If I hadn't had that delectable omelette from Julia a few hours ago, I'd have been starving by then.

"Hi," said a voice.

I looked up from the magazine I'd been reading—a French one, and probably left there by Thérèse and not any of the other employees, since they were all American and probably preferred English publications. From our brief interactions last night, I knew Thérèse's French was far better than her English.

Mark was standing there and I smiled at him. "Hi."

"How has your first night been going?" he asked, leaning against the counter.

"Everything went just fine so far." I waved at the tip jar, which had a healthy number of bills and coins in it. "This was an unexpected bonus too."

"I'll say." He straightened. "You might be able to buy a nice bottle of wine with that. Anyway, it's really nice of you to help out."

"Well, someone had to run the coat check in the middle of December," I said with a chuckle. "Or there would have been no room for anyone to sit inside the theater, with all those bulky coats."

"Yeah, I know . . . I was afraid they were going to ask me next," he said with a comical look. "I doubt that would have been as full if the patrons had to look at my ugly mug." He gestured to the tip jar.

"So what exactly do you do around here?" I asked.

He gave me a crooked smile. "Mostly, I'm here as a volunteer doctor for the troupe—and use that as an excuse to inhale as much of theater life as I can. I'm decent onstage, but I can't sing or dance," he went on with a shrug. "Which limits my opportunities. So I try and get my fix by hanging around in the back when I can get away from the practice where I work during the day. I've done everything from sutures—I had to stitch up Gerald Cray last week between scenes—to patching up head contusions to wrapping twisted ankles and doling out aspirin for aches and pains. I just like hanging around with thespians. There's always something going on."

His smile faded as if he remembered that the actual worst had "gone on" last night. "I do think it was terrible of Maribelle not to agree to cancel tonight," he said.

"Well, at least they're going to make an announcement at intermission, dedicating the performance to her," I said. But I agreed with Mark: It was a woefully small gesture.

"I don't know if Dort told you, but if you want to sneak into the back of the theater and watch the play, no one will mind. Just close up the door to the coat room and make sure you're back before intermission. That was part of the reason Thérèse took this job," Mark said. "She said she loved being able to watch the shows for free—and that it helped with her English."

"Oh, thanks," I said. Dort hadn't mentioned it, but I hadn't really minded having a chance to just sit and look at magazines. But being a mystery aficionado, I was definitely curious about the play, for I'd heard the ending had been changed from the book. "It's nice of you to volunteer here. Do you like being a doctor?"

Mark shrugged. "My grandfather was and my father is and, therefore, so am I. I'd prefer to be onstage, but as I said, that isn't likely. I'd be ducking tomatoes and eggplants all night, and the stage would be a mess!"

I laughed with him, but I could see a lack of humor in his expression. I wondered if the self-deprecation was due to his love of theater and corresponding lack of talent, or the fact that he'd followed in his father's footsteps. I was saved from having to come up with a reply when the doors to the theater opened and people began to filter out for intermission.

"I guess I'd better head backstage and see if anyone needs any fixing up," said Mark. "I'll see you later. Oh, uh, Tabitha, would you like me to give you a ride home after the show?" He looked uncomfortable for a moment, then went on. "Given what happened with Thérèse last night, I'd feel better not letting a woman walk or take the Métro home so late."

"I'll be all right—I rode my bicycle," I replied. "Thank you anyway." But I couldn't quite control a little shiver at the thought of making my way home in the night—on wheels or not. It would be a good twenty to thirty minutes on my bike.

"We can toss it in the back of my car," he said, giving me that bashful look again.

"I really appreciate the offer . . . but wouldn't that take you out of your way?" I didn't know where he lived.

"I wouldn't mind even if it did," he said. "And it's not far out of my way. But I understand if you don't want—well, if you'd prefer to get the exercise." His grin was crooked, but I saw the embarrassment behind it. He gave me a little salute and started to turn away.

"Well, when you put it that way," I said quickly. I wasn't at all looking forward to the cold, dark ride back down to rue de l'Université. "I'd love to take you up on a ride home. Thank you, Mark."

"My pleasure. And I really recommend you watch the second act. Neil is brilliant in it. He has such great chemistry with the girl playing Vera." He slipped off into the throngs of people now spilling from the exits in earnest, leaving me to realize I'd just agreed to a ride with a possible murderer.

I saw Mr. Hayes come out of the auditorium, and jolted when I realized the woman he was walking with was *not* Mrs. Hayes. That must have been why he'd seemed so uncomfortable when he saw me at the coat check and I asked about his wife.

Mr. Hayes and his companion turned in the opposite direction from me and made their way down the gallery to one of the two bars set up for refreshment. I sighed, feeling bad for Mrs. Hayes. It wasn't any of my business, but they were my clients and I'd come to know their family, so I couldn't help but feel a twinge of discomfort.

"Oh, hello," said a male voice, drawing my attention from the retreating back of Mr. Hayes and the woman he was escorting.

I turned to find Johnny Cantrell standing there with a bemused smile. I'd confirmed from Dort that he was the set designer and stage manager; one of the few full-time employees at the theater. I sized him up, considering his potential as a killer, and thought that stabbing a woman multiple times would be something he could easily manage. He was maybe two inches under six feet tall, but he was stocky and muscular and about the same age as the other young people who'd been at Dort's party. Johnny had a short, frizzy beard and mustache of the same medium brown as his curly head of hair, and he was dressed in pants and a shirt that was open at the throat to reveal the top of a white undershirt.

"I see Dort conscripted you into helping out tonight," he said. "Thank you so much—um . . . it's Tamara, right?" He gave a little grimace. "No, no . . . Tabitha. Sorry. Last night's a little fuzzy, but I definitely remember *you*."

But not necessarily my name, I thought with a little smile. "Yes, and yes I told Dort I'd help out. It's the least I could do after what happened." I was pleased to have the chance to talk to the third of our four suspects, so I wanted to keep the conversation going.

"I can't believe it. It's just awful," I said as I tried to think of a way to work in some questions without seeming too nosy. Compared to the two other men I'd talked to—Neil and Mark—Johnny seemed more aloof and almost brooding.

"I forgot for a minute that she—Thérèse—was gone," he said, looking beyond me into the coat check room. "And I came over to say hi, like I do every night during intermission . . . and it was you instead." His expression was sober, even sad. "Someone said you found her."

I shook my head. "It was Dort's maid who did, but I saw . . . her. Do you have any idea who could have done something like that?"

"Someone evil," he said flatly. "Someone who—" He bit off whatever he was going to say and shook his head. The venom in his voice made the hairs on the back of my neck prickle.

"I was supposed to give her a ride home last night," Johnny went on in a tight voice. "If I had, none of this would have happened."

"Where did she live?" I asked, trying to sound casual.

He didn't seem to think I was being nosy. "Montparnasse, not all that far from Dort." He rubbed his beard vigorously. "I told her she should move after what happened."

"What happened?"

"A man was killed. They found him in the side stairway of her building. Anyone could have come across him—he was just lying there. Shot. Blood everywhere." He made a sound of disgust. "That's why I wanted to drive her home. I thought I might be able to convince her to . . ." His voice trailed off and he glanced at me, then looked away. "Not go home alone."

I nodded. Dort hadn't noticed any relationship or love issues around Thérèse Lognon with any of the people at the theater, but even from this brief conversation, I knew that Johnny Cantrell definitely had a thing for Thérèse. Whether it was reciprocated was another question.

But since he thought she was living on the Left Bank, and I knew she had been living across the river on rue de la Mire—more than five miles away—that probably gave me the answer: no. Johnny's affection for Thérèse had probably not been returned.

"I think she was scared," he said, more to himself than to me, but I was glad to be the recipient of that musing.

"Scared because a man was killed in her building? Or scared for another reason?" I asked.

"Because a man was killed," Johnny replied a little sharply. "What do you think?" He heaved a sigh. "I don't think what happened last night has anything to do with that man found in her building. How could it? But it's a damned thing."

"Did Thérèse know the man who was killed?" I asked, wondering how much more interrogation I was going to manage before he caught on. Or, maybe he was so caught up in his grief—grief that seemed genuine—that he wouldn't notice.

Sometimes murderers grieved for their victims—especially if they loved them, I reminded myself.

"I don't know. But she was upset about it, I know that." He drew in his breath as if he were about to add something, then let it out sharply. "Last night . . . it had to have been a hobo or someone who just came in from off the street. Cornered her . . ."

"The police don't think so," I said.

"What?" Johnny's attention snapped to me. "What do you mean?"

"The knife was taken from Dort's apartment," I said. "So it wasn't someone from off the street."

The change in his expression came slowly, as if he were carefully assembling the pieces of what I'd just said. "Someone from last night. Someone she *knew*. One of *them*."

I nodded, watching him closely. There was rage there. Rage, horror, and grief shining in his eyes.

I took advantage of his heightened emotions. "Who could have done something like that? You're all friends, aren't you?"

"Any of them. They all wanted her. She probably pushed him away and he got angry and went after her." He raised a shaking hand to his forehead.

"Who?" I asked. "Who did?"

But he just turned away, muttering, "I've got to get back. I've got to go."

As he melted into the intermission crowd, I thought to myself that if Johnny Cantrell had killed Thérèse, he was a far better actor than Clark Gable. And if he had killed her, he was worried about the investigation. Very worried.

I also wondered who was the "he" Johnny had referred to. Had Neil or Thad or Mark been pushing themselves on Thérèse? By all accounts, Neil wasn't known for liking women, but who really knew?

"How are you doing?" Dort wove through the crowd, her head several inches above nearly every person, man or woman. Her voice boomed and somehow made it straight to me above the cacophony.

"I'm doing fine," I replied, still thinking about Johnny.

"All right. You can sit in the theater and take a load off if you want when the show starts up again," said Dort as she reached me and the counter that separated us. "Just be back here about ten fifteen to catch the people who leave before curtain call."

"I think I will. Thanks."

"I'd offer to give you a ride home tonight, but I hear Mark has the honors." Dort leered at me.

"Lucky him," I said. "Hey, listen . . . I was just talking to Johnny and he was going to drive Thérèse home last night—but to the address you have in your files, not the place on rue de la Mire. Do you think she could have been living in two places?"

"I have no clue," said Dort. "How did you find out about that place again?"

"There was a letter in her handbag addressed to her at that location. So her mother knew she was living there, at least." I shook my head as the lights flashed to warn everyone it was time to take their seats. "Thérèse sure had a lot of secrets."

One of them probably had gotten her killed.

CHAPTER 9

*T*he next morning, Friday, I rose and dressed with a mild sense of trepidation. I had my weekly tutoring appointment with Betty Hayes, and for the first time since my initial interview with her parents, I felt nervous and uncertain.

Knowing that her father was, in all likelihood, having an affair, and me having to act as if I didn't know anything—or at least to act normal—was going to be a little bit of a challenge.

Julia was right—I generally could read people quite well. But I was also someone who was able to *be* read. I was thoughtful and far more reserved than my bubbly friend, and couldn't always hide my emotions.

I told myself it would be unlikely I'd even see Mr. Hayes. He'd be at work at the embassy, and that would make things less uncomfortable.

It was just past seven when I came down to the salon and found it empty of people and pets, except for Madame X perched on a windowsill. She gave me an imperious look, then lifted her rear leg and proceeded to clean herself while I tried to determine what obscure feline expectation I'd failed to meet—probably that I hadn't brought her a dish of cream on my first appearance.

The fact that I was coming from upstairs and not the kitchen wouldn't be accepted as an excuse by Madame.

Grand-père and Oncle Rafe hadn't risen yet, and as much as I loved them, I liked having a quiet house to myself in the morning. Since they normally didn't get up until nine o'clock or later, I had gotten into the habit of going down to the kitchen and making a cup of coffee. Then I brought it and a croissant up to the little greenhouse to start my day.

I did exactly that this morning, bringing up my breakfast, such as it was, along with a saucer for the cat.

Grand-père's little dome-roofed greenhouse had been built on the flat roof of the portico attached to the side of the house. It was a miracle it had survived the Occupation, considering its fragility. But, unlike London, there hadn't been any bombings on Paris, which had protected nearly all of the buildings and bridges—other than bullet holes from machine guns and some small Molotov cocktail explosives during the fight for Liberation.

However, the Germans had left their collective mark in other ways. Besides causing great rifts between those Parisians who'd helped or collaborated with the occupiers (sometimes only in an effort to simply remain safe and alive) and those who had resisted against the Germans, other indignities were forced upon the city and the country at large.

Countless pieces of art and jewelry had been stolen, and many were still missing, along with rare, expensive wines and cognacs. Oncle Rafe, whose family was the celebrated Fautrier vintners, had told me about the German *weinführers* who'd commanded the soldiers who broke into private cellars, restaurants, and storerooms to steal some of France's most prized possessions: her wines. The sad part about it all was that Hitler loathed wine and had no use for it. He merely didn't want the French to have it, and so he stocked away what he stole in a hideaway.

With this in mind, my gratitude that Grand-père's greenhouse had been spared during those four terrible years was renewed as I opened the tight-fitting wooden door that led from the salon into the glass-walled room.

Despite the bitter December winter, the greenhouse was filled with sunshine and the walls dripped with condensation. The fireplace and radiator that kept the salon warm shared the same wall as the greenhouse, adding additional warmth to the sun-drenched, enclosed place.

There were rows of planters in the dome-shaped room—long, trenchlike vessels on legs that put them waist-high for easy tending—filled with herbs like tarragon, chervil, rosemary, thyme, basil, and of course, catnip. Grand-père came in every morning after coffee and fussed over his *"délicieux bébés,"* as he called them. He sat on a stool with wheels and rolled from spot to spot along the length of the planters, trimming, watering, and misting the pungent herbs. I had even heard him talking to the plants one day—a scene that had made me smile as he encouraged them to grow even when the winter was "snotty."

Oncle Rafe told me once that it was tending to his plants that had helped Grand-père survive the austerity of the Occupation.

The trenches filled with herbs were joined by a few strawberry plants in tall terracotta pots that had little pocket-like openings on the sides to hold the plants, along with the runners that produced new babies. There was also a pair of large, potted citrus trees—one lemon and one that produced cute, plum-size oranges—which were arranged next to a small wrought iron table with two chairs.

Near the table was a generous tub filled with bubbling water and some large goldfish I learned were called koi. The water helped keep the greenhouse's air humid, and I found the quiet rumbling of the water very soothing.

I noticed Madame X had followed me into the room, so I poured cream into her saucer and set it on the ground. She was allowed into the greenhouse to sunbathe, or to roll and loll among the catnip. It was understood that she would leave the koi undisturbed.

Madame didn't bother to thank me or even acknowledge my effort as she sauntered over with great nonchalance and sniffed at the strawberry plants, her bejeweled collar glinting in the sun. Then she circled her velvety black body around the lemon tree pot, taking her time and pretending disinterest, before at last deigning to approach her treat.

I was enjoying my croissant and *café* when I realized with a grimace that I hadn't taken Thérèse Lognon's handbag to Inspecteur Merveille's office. I had completely forgotten about doing so during my stint in the coat check, and by the time the show was over and Mark and I were ready to leave, it was far too late.

I supposed I could chalk it up to being a little distracted and slightly nervous about the thought of riding home in the car with Mark, but in the end, the journey had been short and uneventful. He'd put my bicycle in the back as promised and navigated to rue de l'Université with no fuss or detour. There was very little traffic—either car or pedestrian—so the ride was brief, and our conversation consisted of a review of how the evening had gone, both onstage and offstage.

"Other than a possible broken toe when Thad ran one of the set pieces over the props man's foot, I have no injuries to report," he said. "Did everyone retrieve their coats and hats?"

"Nearly all of them," I replied. "There are a few in the back that no one picked up." I didn't understand how anyone could forget their coat on a chilly December night, but that was what seemed to have happened. Or maybe they'd been left behind on a different day or belonged to employees at the theater.

Mark asked if I wanted to stop into a café or restaurant to get anything to eat or for a glass of wine, but I declined, and he didn't push the idea. His stubble was a more noticeable golden glint now as it was approaching midnight, and his broad shoulders drooped.

"It's been a very long, horrible day," he said, muffling a yawn with the back of his hand. "I'm not ashamed to say I'm ready to hit the hay."

"It was. And we were both up late last night too," I said.

"I hope you'll let me pick you up for your shift tomorrow night. Dort will already be at the theater." He looked at me as he stopped the car in front of Julia's building. "It's really good of you to help out that way."

"That would be nice. Thank you," I said, then bid him good night before he could try to kiss me—I wasn't yet ready for that—and hurried across the rue to Grand-père's house.

Now, as I sipped my coffee, I smiled a little. Mark was polite and seemed to have a good sense of humor, and maybe I was finding him a little more interesting than I had initially. I probably would kiss him if the opportunity arose again.

I was definitely curious about why he'd become a doctor if he had such an interest in the theater. Spending that much time in school when you wanted to do something else seemed like a big commitment to me. And a waste of time, not to mention money.

The telephone rang, bringing me out of my musings. Fortunately, there was a receiver in the salon as well as on the ground floor, so it was only three rings before I was able to get to it.

"Saint-Léger residence," I said.

"Miss Knight? Is that you?"

"Yes," I replied. The female voice speaking in English was familiar, but I couldn't immediately place it.

"This is Rebecca Hayes. I'm very sorry to call so early, and for this reason, but, unfortunately, we are going to have to cancel Betty's French lesson today."

I felt a funny little sinking in my stomach. "I'm sorry to hear that. I hope everything is all right."

"Oh, well, yes, it is . . . but . . . well, I'm very sorry to tell you this, but Mr. Hayes has decided that Betty doesn't need any more French lessons. So we won't need your services any longer."

I could hear the discomfort and strain in Mrs. Hayes's voice. "All right," I said slowly, trying to hide my shock. "Thank you for calling to let me know."

"Miss Knight," she said quickly, as if to catch me before I hung up, "if you come over this morning, I'll be happy to pay you for today's lesson. Since we are canceling at such short notice, I think it's only fair."

I found myself nodding in assent even though she couldn't see me. I was so stunned about this turn of events, I didn't realize I was doing so until she said my name again. "Oh, yes, thank you, Mrs. Hayes. I'll do that."

"I'm really sorry about this, Miss Knight," she said. "I'll leave an envelope with the maid in case I'm not home. Come over anytime before one o'clock." She said goodbye and disconnected the call.

I let the receiver fall gently into its cradle, staring at it blindly.

It was obvious Mr. Hayes was even more nervous to have me around his family and possibly spill the beans about seeing him last night than I was to try to hide what I knew—and it seemed as if his actions were confirmation of what I'd suspected: He was having an *affaire de coeur*. It was a shame he was taking it out on Betty, for she had really begun to improve in her French. And it was equally clear that Mrs. Hayes didn't want her husband to know I was coming over to pick up my money since she wanted me to come before one o'clock, when he might be at home for lunch.

I was grateful she wanted to pay me—not that I was that desperate for the money—but even more than that, I was angry with Mr. Hayes for being so petty.

I was still annoyed and, I'm ashamed to admit, stewing in my own furious juices, when the door from the salon opened.

"Good morning, *ma chérie*," said Oncle Rafe. He was dressed in a quilted dressing robe of satiny aubergine with wide cuffs over black flannel pajamas and thick-soled slippers. He was not wearing the knit cap, so his bald head shined a little in the warm sunshine. Parts of his beard were curling out of place, indicating he had likely just rolled out of bed and had not combed or waxed it yet. I thought it was adorable.

Oscar Wilde trotted in behind him. Today, the little butterfly-eared dog was wearing only a large red bow tie, but the accessory was decked out in sequins to give him a more dazzling appearance. He immediately went over to sniff at Madame's saucer, but it was empty.

Madame had taken a spot among a cluster of chives and was eyeing her nemesis with cold green orbs.

Once determining that the saucer was empty, Monsieur Wilde hurried over to me. He began to gently bat at my stocking-clad leg with his two front paws while looking up at me with eager brown eyes. He was hoping for a piece of croissant, I knew, and I couldn't resist tearing off a pinkie-nail-size chunk and offering it to him. He took it with tiny, delicate teeth but gulped down the pastry without even chewing it.

"Someone has found an easy mark," said Oncle Rafe with an indulgent smile as he settled at the table with me. He had brought in his own coffee, and I wished I had had the forethought to bring up a pot of it so he hadn't had to go down to the kitchen himself.

He was sturdier and more agile than my grandfather, but I still didn't like the idea of either them using the stairs if they didn't have to. Most of the time, there was no reason for them to leave the first floor: the salon, bedrooms, greenhouse, and bathroom were all on that level. They had their pets and a full bar in the salon, and Bet or Blythe always brought up lunch and an afternoon tea for sustenance.

The large windows could be opened during the nice weather, giving them fresh air, and they always had a pleasant view of our home's private courtyard below, as well as down the rue.

It was a little fall in her bedroom almost two years ago that ultimately brought about my *grand-mère's* death. I had learned firsthand how quickly an older person could deteriorate after such an accident, and I didn't want anything like that to happen to either of my messieurs.

"Now, *chère*, tell me what you have learned about the poor Mademoiselle Thérèse when you were at the theater last night,"

Oncle Rafe said with a gleam in his eyes and a quirk of his neat mustache and beard. "And I will tell you what I have learned as well."

"What do you mean?" I was mostly asking about what he might have learned and how and why, but I was also wondering what made him think I had learned anything about Thérèse Lognon.

Of course I had, but how did *he* know that?

"But you are not the only one who can poke around in a murder investigation," he replied with a wink as he picked up Oscar Wilde and settled him in his lap. The little dog was delighted to be at such close proximity to croissant crumbs. I could see that his beady little eyes were focused intently, trying to work out exactly how he could reach the remains.

"What makes you think I'm poking around in a murder investigation?" I said with great innocence. Rafe wasn't fooled. He merely arched one heavy black brow and took a genteel sip of his coffee.

"Oh, all right," I said, unable to hide a smirk. "I'm not really poking around, but—"

The door to the salon opened and Grand-père stood there. He was dressed similarly to Rafe in a heavy, quilted dressing robe of wine red trimmed with black satin over warm pajamas, socks, and heavy slippers of boiled wool.

"I see you've begun all of the fun without me," he said, giving Rafe a knowing look.

"But you were snoring so pleasantly," my honorary uncle replied with a smile. "Not to mention loudly. I didn't wish to disturb you."

Grand-père shot him a dark glare and muttered something that made Rafe laugh, then started into the room. I rose to give him my chair at the small table, eyeing him closely as he made his way toward us. I was only slightly relieved when I saw that he hardly needed his cane for support, for he was still a little unsteady on his feet.

"Trying to corrupt my granddaughter, are you?" Grand-père said.

"Ah, no, *cher*, I think you will do that all on your own," Rafe replied. I noticed he, too, was watching Grand-père like a hawk.

Apparently, my grandfather noticed as well, for he stopped several paces from the table and gave both of us an irritated look. "I'm not about to spontaneously fall on my arse," he growled. "And I'm not a damned Fabergé egg, even if I did."

I exchanged looks with Rafe but didn't reply. Instead, I wheeled Grand-père's work stool over to the table for me to sit on.

"Now, have I missed anything?" Grand-père said as he began to lower himself into the chair I had vacated. But halfway in the process of sitting, he paused, grumbling under his breath, and dug into the pocket of his robe to remove a coffee cup. He plopped it onto the table.

"Well? Have you finished staring at me now?" He settled a little unsteadily into the chair, hooking his cane on the edge of the table. "Even had to get my own cup."

My heart lurched as I thought about Grand-père making his way down to the kitchen and back up again on all those steps. Why had I not thought to bring up service for all of us?

Well, I hadn't because they were rarely up this early, and by the time they rose, Bet and Blythe were here and would serve breakfast. But, I decided abruptly, that would change starting tomorrow.

"*Merde*, don't look so terrified, Tabitte," he said, digging his cigarettes out of a different pocket. "I got the cup from last night's coffee in the salon, not the kitchen. Now tell me what you know about this Mademoiselle Thérèse and who might have killed her."

"All right," I said, suddenly eager to share what I had found out. I knew I was going to have to turn Thérèse's purse over to Inspecteur Merveille today, and once I did that, all of this would be out of my hands. And rightly so. I was a French tutor, a metal riveter, and a want-to-be-cook . . . not a detective.

"Because Julia's knife was used, there are only four people who would have taken it and used it to kill Thérèse—"

"*Attendez*, one moment, if you please," said Grand-père. "How do you know it was Madame Child's knife and didn't belong to someone else?"

"Because it's a knife of carbon steel, a very fine cooking knife—and because it's missing from her kitchen," I replied. When Grand-père nodded in agreement, I went on. "Four suspects. There is Mark Justiss, who is a physician from Boston, Massachusetts, and has an unrequited passion for the theater. He donates his time to work backstage to help with any medical problems.

"Then there is Neil Kingsley, who is from New York and is the lead in the play at Théâtre Monceau. He's dark, handsome, and well-built—an excellent leading man.

"Next is Thad, and I don't remember his last name. He's actually from Detroit, I understand, but I haven't had the chance to talk to him. He's responsible for the lighting and sound for the play, so he was up in the catwalk fixing the lights yesterday. Thad is the slightest of the bunch of them, but he moves and lifts heavy speakers and lights, so I think he is definitely strong enough to be able to stab someone to death.

"And last is Johnny Cantrell. He seemed the most upset over Thérèse's death—although they all were—and he was particularly broken up over it because he was supposed to give her a ride home last night, but she left before he did. He said something about her being accosted by one of the other men—he didn't say who, he just used the pronoun 'him'—and Johnny seemed to think that whoever killed Thérèse might have been someone whose advances she rejected."

My messieurs watched me with grave attention as I spoke, filling them in on what I found in Thérèse's purse.

I decided I wasn't going to tell them about going to poke around her apartment. Not only was it illegal, but they might worry about my safety.

"The weird thing," I went on, "is that no one at the theater where she worked seemed to know her correct address. Even Johnny, who was supposed to give her a ride home last night, thought she was still living in Montparnasse."

"Very mysterious," said Oncle Rafe, his eyes gleaming with delight. "She was clearly a lady with some secrets—secrets which likely contributed to her brutal death." The light in his eyes faded into sadness.

"And I suppose you can tell us about her apartment, then, hmm, *ma mie?*" Grand-père said. "What did you find there?"

When I goggled at him in surprise, the two of them exchanged indulgent looks.

"But of course you would have done some snooping about," said Rafe. "You are, as I have pointed out, Maurice's granddaughter."

"I trust you were careful about the breaking and entering," said Grandpère, lighting a cigarette. "After all, you *are* my grand-daughter—and your *grand-mère's* as well."

They both laughed at this, and though my grandfather's rumbling chuckle ended in a rusty wheeze, I chuckled too. And then I went on to tell them about my adventure in rue de la Mire.

"And you couldn't tell who came in?" Grand-père leaned across the table as if to encourage me to remember more. "Who was sneaking around?"

"No, although I'm pretty certain it was a man," I said. "Because women's shoes make a different sort of footstep sound."

"*Oui, bien sûr*—because of the heels," said Rafe, nodding. "Excellent point, *ma petite.*"

"And you say this man took the gun with him?" asked Grandpère. "Well, then we know what will happen next, *non?*"

Oncle Rafe made an agreeable tsking sound and nodded.

"No, we don't know what will happen next," I said a little testily. "What?"

"Why, someone is going to wind up with a bullet in their head," said Grand-père, as if it were the most natural thing in the world. To his credit, he wasn't smiling when he said it.

"Or his heart," added Oncle Rafe, just as soberly.

"Why do you think that?" I demanded, my own heart suddenly in my throat as I realized *I* could have been the one who wound up with a bullet in my head had the intruder found me there.

"*C'est logique*," my uncle replied with a shrug. "For why else would one steal a gun but to put it to use—and especially one that can't be traced back to him or her."

"Maybe he wanted it for protection," I said.

"*Peut-être*," he said.

"But what I don't understand is *why* someone killed Thérèse and broke into her apartment and . . . and all of this!" And why Thérèse had had my name and address in her pocket! That was still something that niggled at me, even though I'd mostly dismissed it as a coincidence.

"Yes, *ma chère. Why* is precisely the question." Rafe turned his attention to me. "Why did this happen? There is the question of motive! The good *inspecteur* seems to be rather light on motive, *non*, if he suspects you and Madame Child?" He chuckled.

"It's those damned spies," growled Grand-père. "Mark my words—they're crawling all over the city!"

"Spies?" I scoffed with a grin. "But the war is over. The war is over, the Germans are gone—and who would be spying on who anyway?"

"Not the Germans," said Rafe in a more serious tone. "The Russians. It's the Russians we all must be wary of now."

That shut me up. He was right. I had heard Paul Child mention, if only obliquely, how our government was very concerned about whether the Russians were getting the nuclear bomb. I had heard a politician say in a speech that we were in a "Cold War" with Russia.

Paul must hear a lot of things at the embassy, even though he didn't work in the area of espionage.

At least, as far as I knew.

A little shiver went down my spine. There was no possibility that Paul was a spy, was there? All I knew about his job was that he was here in Paris to help expose the French to American culture as part of the Marshall Plan funding.

With the Marshall Plan, the U.S. government had allocated millions of dollars to help Europe rebuild after the war, and part of the tactic was to bring Western Europeans—in particular the French—closer to their American allies by familiarizing them with our culture. It was an attempt to create better diplomacy between our countries. Paul did pleasant and amusing things like arrange for exhibits of American art, fairs, and concerts with some of our musicians.

Frankly, I thought it was a strange initiative to spend money on, but the U.S. government did a lot of things I didn't comprehend or agree with. I suppose it had to do with helping the European nations—many of which, including France herself, had strong Communist movements—to see that capitalism was a freer, far better option than the Communistic society promoted by Russia.

There were Parisians who loathed the concept and implementation of the Marshall Plan. The Communist Party of France, or PCF, claimed that the integration of American popular culture and food—even mundane items like Coca-Cola— were an indication that the United States was trying to colonize France and the rest of Europe.

There was a strong, vocal movement against Coca-Cola bottling plants being built in the country, and the term "coca-colonization" had been coined to describe this supposed insidiousness of the beverage company and its attempt to overtake French beverages in market share. Even vintners saw the soda pop as a direct competitor to their wines and brandies.

"Russian spies or not," I said, "I can't see how they would be connected to Thérèse's murder. The only people who could have killed her were all Americans. Not a Russki in the bunch."

"As far as you know," said Grand-père. "Those Russians are sly, sly foxes." His eyes burned with intensity and I stifled a giggle at his zealousness.

"Besides," I said, "even if there is espionage going on between America and Russia, that's between those two countries—we're in Paris." I imagined that if there *were* spies, they would be installed in places they could gather information—such as near governmental employees in Washington or Moscow—

Or in embassies throughout Europe.

My thoughts must have shown on my face, for Oncle Rafe and Grand-père nodded at me.

"You see? There are spies everywhere," said Rafe. "Americans spying on Russians, Russians spying on Americans, Americans spying on Americans *for* Russia, Russians spying on Russians for American—"

"Russians spying on Americans who are spying on the French," said my grandfather, "or the French spying on the Russians for the Americans . . . it is a cesspool! Everyone is spying on everyone!"

I was shaking my head, partly amused at their fervor and partly shocked at the thought of all of that espionage happening throughout the world. Who could trust anyone?

"Still, I don't see how that could have anything to do with Thérèse's murder. It's a theater company. The whole thing is probably a love story gone wrong. Johnny certainly seemed as if he was in love with Thérèse—or at least, he cared for her very much."

"That is likely the most logical reason." Rafe nodded sagely. "Love incites one to do so many unexpected things—and sometimes they are very good, very wonderful things, and other times they are horrible, detestable things."

"Indeed," murmured Grand-père.

There was a moment of silence, and I felt as if something was not being said. And then it was over, and my honorary uncle was smiling devilishly.

"And now, *ma chére*, let us tell you what we have learned about this situation," Rafe said.

I narrowed my eyes. "And how did you go about your snooping? You didn't go out last night, did you?"

My messieurs laughed uproariously at this.

"You think that we would have taken the chance of missing Madame Child's dinner for us? When it was delivered, hot and fresh?" Grand-père said, waving a hand through the smoke trailing from his cigarette. "Of course we didn't leave. We opened a very old, very excellent bottle of Bordeaux that we managed to keep from the greedy hands of those German bastards and had a magnificent dinner."

I felt better knowing that, even though the fact that I had missed the delectable roasted ham still stuck in my craw. I'd resorted to eating a hunk of cheese and some cold, leftover sausage from yesterday's lunch when I got home last night.

Even so, I didn't feel even the least bit insulted by their obvious glee over Julia's dinner. Then it struck me that if I was going to be working the coat check at the theater tonight, I wouldn't be home to roast Madame Poulet for them. Damn.

"But of course we missed you at dinner, *ma chère*," said Rafe quickly.

I gave him a withering glance. "I very much doubt that. After all, without me here, there was more *jambon braisé* for you to enjoy."

This caused more laughter—this time, mingled with energetic protestations. They were still laughing, and I had joined them, when I heard the telephone ringing.

Still smiling over my housemates and their antics, I answered the telephone.

"Tabitha!" Julia's energetic voice boomed through the receiver. "Are you up? I have to know everything! Dort came in late last night and said you'd been doing some investigating, but she went right to bed without telling me a *jot*!"

"I have, and apparently Grand-père and Oncle Rafe have some information as well," I told her.

"I'll be right over!"

She hung up the telephone before I could reply.

I poked my head into the salon to tell the gentlemen that Julia was coming over.

"So you can slather all over her about how magnificent your dinner was last night," I said, pretending pique. "I'll go down and make more coffee. And bring up more cups," I said, giving Grand-père a pointed look. In fact, I would tell the maids that they were to leave an extra set of cups and utensils in the salon every day before they left. "Along with some croissants and toast."

"*Bonne fille,*" Grand-père said. "And I will dress, then, so as not to tempt Madame Child from the side of her monsieur." He smiled, looking wickedly handsome and almost youthful as he did so.

Rafe rose but refrained from helping Grand-père to do so, even though I suspected he wanted to. Assured that the two of them would take at least fifteen minutes to dress, I headed down to the ground floor to make coffee.

I was just putting on the kettle when I heard the door knocker announcing Julia's arrival.

I barely got the door open before she swept in, demanding information even as she unraveled herself from her muffler and coat.

"I'm making coffee," I said, gesturing for her to follow me into the kitchen.

"Ye gods, if I had a kitchen this big, what I could do with it!" exclaimed Julia, looking around the space.

It was twice as large as *La Maison Scheeld*, with much higher ceilings, and I knew for a fact that there was running water in the summer as well as in the winter. There was even a spigot for hot water that was actually hot, which I pointed out to her.

"An icebox?" she cried, opening the door of one of Grand-père's recent indulgences and poking around inside.

I was certain my grandfather had made the purchase of the appliance in the hopes of having more storage for leftovers from Julia's kitchen or any other location with good food, since there wasn't enough being made in his own kitchen.

"We'll make omelettes," Julia decided suddenly, having removed a hunk of cheese and the bowl of eggs from inside the icebox. "While you tell me all about Thérèse's apartment. No, actually, *you* will make the omelettes for your messieurs, and I will supervise while you tell me about Thérèse's apartment."

Did I mention that Julia could be a little bossy and impulsive sometimes?

The only reason I didn't argue was because I knew Grand-père and Oncle Rafe would be delighted with toast and a tarragon-scented omelette, and they were still getting dressed so I had the time to cook.

And there might have been a little bit of bruised pride mixed in there as well.

I wanted to be the one to make my messieurs' eyes gleam and their mouths water when I served them a meal.

I wanted them to rave about my cooking, instead of move it around on their plates before not-so-secretly slipping generous morsels to Oscar Wilde or Madame X.

It wasn't that I was jealous of their affection for Julia's cooking; it was that I wanted to contribute to the household where I was living for free, as well as show my love for them. And the austerity of the Occupation, not to mention the strict rationing that was just now coming to an end, was still so recent in everyone's memory I wanted to help abolish it.

And so I set about making omelettes.

"Yes," said Julia, chopping tarragon as I positioned myself at the stove, "you need an entire tablespoon of butter. Right in the pan." I was grateful she didn't try to give me instructions in metric measurements; that would have been just too much complication on top of everything else.

I had a small omelette pan that Julia had tsked over a little—"Copper is really best," she said—but apparently the cast iron one I had would do in a pinch. "Swirl it around so it coats the pan and its sides. That makes the eggs slip and slide like a greased pig!"

I scooped an entire tablespoon of butter into the pan and let it sit on the flame of the gas burner.

"No more than three eggs," she told me. "Now add salt and pepper and this tarragon, and whisk it all just until they're blended—twenty, thirty times. Not too much, now, and you're not trying to *kill* it. I'll grate some cheese for you, but next time, you'll have it ready ahead of time. Once you put the eggs in the pan, you don't have time to do anything else but cook them."

She was right. Once the butter was melted and had just begun to foam—she was watching me with an eagle eye—I poured the herb-speckled, lightly whisked eggs into the pan. The smell of tarragon made me hungry, and I decided I'd be making three omelettes instead of only two.

"That's it, now . . . let them sit for just, oh, to the count of twenty or so. And then you start to move the pan," Julia told me.

Nervously, I watched the bright yellow eggs begin to cook, just starting to get custardy.

"Now!" cried Julia as if my life depended on it. "Move the pan!"

My movements were awkward at first, but after a moment, and with her help, I got the hang of it. The idea, I learned, was to jerk the pan toward you at a slight angle so the eggs kind of slid and rolled around in a bright yellow soupish custard. The constant movement kept the eggs from sticking and overcooking.

"Now the cheese," said Julia, sprinkling a bit of hard white cheese over the eggs, which were still soft and fluffy but getting less soupy. "Keep jerking the pan; see how the eggs flip and curl into themselves? We always overcook eggs in America. The French have it right—they're still soft and creamy, and even a little wet—now, there! It's done! Now give it one last jerk so it all rolls up a little more, then let it spill out onto this plate."

She stuck the plate in front of me, thankfully, for I would have wasted several precious seconds looking for one.

I eyed the omelette as it rolled neatly onto the plate. It looked *magnificent.* And *I had made it all myself!*

"You should be a cooking teacher, Julia," I said, gazing lovingly at my egg progeny.

"I've got to finish at Le Cordon Bleu first," she replied, already chopping more tarragon. "I have so much more to learn. I can't wait for classes to start up again in January. You'll have to come sometime to the afternoon demonstrations. It's like sitting in an operating theater and watching a surgery take place."

I made two more omelettes under her watchful eye, and by the time I was whisking the eggs for the third, I felt confident enough in the process to be able to tell her about what I'd found at Thérèse's apartment, as well as the intruder.

"So whoever sneaked in has the gun? And you didn't see who it was? Nothing about him?" she said as we arranged three plates covered with silver domes, along with toast, preserves, and coffee service on trays to take upstairs.

"Not a whisker," I said, picking up one of the trays. "Except for a lingering smell that I didn't recognize but would if I smelled it again. It wasn't cologne or anything like that, but I just can't place it."

Just as we started out of the kitchen, the back door rattled. It was either Bet or Blythe—I had yet to learn how to tell them apart—letting herself in through the back door. Her sister followed behind. I paused to apologize for the mess in the kitchen, but the maids merely smiled, shook their heads and waved me off.

Maybe they, too, were pleased to see that I'd accomplished something edible in the kitchen.

"*Mon Dieu,*" said Grand-père when Julia and I ceremoniously lifted the lids off two of the plates. "I've never seen a better-looking omelette. *Merci, merci,* Madame Child."

"No, no, no, it was all Tabitha," said Julia in her lilting voice. "And your fresh tarragon, too, Monsieur Saint-Léger."

"You are welcome to partake of any of *mes délicieux bébés* anytime you like, Madame Child," said my grandfather. "Tabitte, this is *magnifique.*"

"*Oui, ma chère,* it tastes delicious," said Oncle Rafe, giving me an affectionate pat on the arm as my grandfather thanked me once again.

I was grateful that neither of the men expressed shock or surprise that I had prepared such a good-looking dish. That was a wonderful indication of their confidence in me, and I appreciated it.

The messieurs attended to their omelettes while I filled Julia in on my conversation with Johnny about Thérèse.

"So no one knew she moved," said Julia. She was sipping coffee while the rest of us mowed through creamy, delicate eggs and toast.

"Unless she was living in two places," I said, a thought having just struck me. "If the dead man showing up in her building spooked her, maybe she kept it to herself so no one knew she'd moved. Maybe she was afraid she'd be next."

No one had to say: *And she was.*

Oncle Rafe delicately wiped his beard and mustache—which had been combed and lightly waxed during my stint in the kitchen—and nodded. "That is quite possible, *chère.* Now . . . shall I at last tell you what I myself have learned?"

"*Yes,*" I said. "Don't you know I bribed you with breakfast so that you would spill all the details?"

He chuckled and hoisted Oscar Wilde onto his lap, settling the dog out of snout distance from the small table around which we'd gathered. "You may bribe me so anytime, Tabitte, and I will spill every detail I know and even some that I've made up."

"I guess you probably called one of your contacts at the 36," I said, laughing. "Since you claim not to have gone anywhere."

"He also claims he doesn't 'know' anyone," said Grand-père with a rusty chuckle as he offered a tiny morsel of egg to Oscar Wilde, "but that is quite a pack of lies."

"Now, now," said Rafe. His dark eyes glinted with humor. "Yes, I did happen to telephone an old friend—"

"You dare not say 'colleague,' *non?*" Grand-père put in with a chuckle.

Rafe slanted a look at him and smiled. "Most definitely not a colleague. But certainly a friend. Former Inspecteur Guillaume Devré from *la Sûreté*—which is the old name for *la police judiciaire*—has a grandnephew who works as a detective at the 36. You might have heard of him, *ma chère*—Étienne Merveille."

CHAPTER 10

My eyes popped wide and Julia squeaked a gasp. "Your old friend, this retired *inspecteur*, is Merveille's uncle?" I said.

Rafe seemed inordinately pleased with himself. "*Oui, bien sûr*," he said, as if the coincidence was hardly worth mentioning. "Merveille is close to his uncle, who was quite a celebrated detective in his time. Now Devré is nearly eighty, and so he spends all of his time trying to stay warm, drinking the best of wines, and attempting to eat every meal as if it were his last—as do we, *non?*" he said, nodding at Grand-père with a rueful smile. "And so it was no great difficulty to find out what your Inspecteur Merveille knows about the case."

"And . . . ?" I said when my uncle paused to light a cigarette—and, surely, to draw out the suspense.

"Here is what I know. Mademoiselle Lognon was stabbed six times and died from those wounds. There was a bit of skin and blood under her fingernails, along with some bruising on her face and arms, which indicates she fought her attacker—possibly as he was forcing her down to the cellar, which is where she was killed. So he will have some marks on him, possibly the arms.

"The killer is right-handed and taller than the mademoiselle, but how much taller, they cannot be certain as there were the cellar stairs involved and one of them might have been on a step during some of the attack, you see?"

I nodded, but remained quiet, hoping for more.

"But it is unlikely either of them were on the stairs during the attack—it would have made it more difficult. So likely he was four or five inches taller, it is believed. So in the neighborhood of six feet. She was wearing her coat but had no handbag . . . which we now know the reason for that," Rafe said, giving me an amused look. "You will have to turn that over to Merveille, *chère.*"

"Yes, I'll do that today after I pick up my last wages from Mrs. Hayes."

When Grand-père and Rafe looked at me curiously, I explained about being fired by the Hayeses. "I'm sure it's no coincidence that I saw Mr. Hayes with a woman who was not his wife at the theater last night," I said ruefully, "and today they are no longer in need of my services."

"Ah," said Grand-père. "That's quite a shame."

"I'm sure I'll find another student to replace Betty," I said.

"Of course you will. Paul told me several people at the embassy wanted your information," said Julia, who'd been uncharacteristically quiet during most of the conversation. Then she looked at Oncle Rafe. "Was there anything else you were able to learn? What about fingerprints?" Julia's eyes gleamed with hopeful enthusiasm.

"Ah, yes. They are looking for fingerprints on the knife, but there weren't any obvious ones. It's winter, of course, so the killer probably wore gloves.

"Mademoiselle Lognon is only half French. Apparently her mother was from Poland or somewhere like that," said Rafe. "According to Devré, his nephew wasn't certain how long the young woman had been living in Paris. There wasn't anything else—at least, so far. But I promised Devré that if he will keep me apprised of any new information, I will in turn invite him to a most magnificent dinner some night very soon." He looked hopefully at Julia, who boomed a laugh and agreed readily.

"I would be honored," she said.

"I'd like to find out about the dead man who was left on the stairs of Thérèse's old apartment building," I said. "To see if there's a connection. Maybe you can ask this former Inspecteur Devré if he can find out anything."

Julia chuckled, looking at my messieurs, and jerked a thumb in my direction. "And she says she's not investigating!"

Everyone had a pleasant laugh over this, then I stood.

"I suppose I'd best be going. I have to take the handbag to Merveille at the 36 and pick up my money from Mrs. Hayes. And I need to stop at the market for more eggs, and some milk too," I said, smiling, as I remembered the success of my omelettes and why we were out of eggs.

It might seem a little thing to anyone else, but for me it was actually quite a big deal.

"Ooh, good! I'll go with you to the market," Julia said.

"And what about the roasted chicken we were promised?" asked Grand-père hopefully. "Will we have this Madame Poulet and her companions for dinner tonight?"

I glanced at Julia, my exuberant mood deflating. "I'm working at the theater," I said uncertainly.

"Oh, that's no problem. We can fix Madame and roast her before you have to leave," she said, and I saw Grand-père and Oncle Rafe *both* slump noticeably in relief.

"We will eat anytime she is ready," said my uncle enthusiastically. "Even if it is at four o'clock in the afternoon for tea!"

I kissed my uncle and then my grandfather on their smooth cheeks, and made my au revoir to Oscar Wilde, who hardly took notice of me as there was a small bit of egg on the table that he'd been straining to reach. I suspected the moment I left the salon, Oncle Rafe would lift the little beastie onto the table so he could slurp it up.

Rafe claimed it was only fair, as Madame X was able to jump up onto any surface she liked for such morsels, while Oscar Wilde had to be lifted to anything above knee height.

"I'll be back as soon as I can," I said. "Stay warm and stay out of trouble."

"But of course. There is no trouble into which we can go,"

replied Grand-père. "We are old and uninteresting and we go nowhere, and, even more sadly, no one visits us."

I'm sure he could hear our hoots of laughter as Julia and I bounded down the stairs and out the door.

"I was thinking about something else," Julia said as we burst out onto rue de l'Université. "Not only would there have been blood on the killer's clothing, but what about his shoes? Splatters everywhere, right? He could take off a coat or put one on to hide the blood, but he couldn't go about in stockinged feet— especially in December!"

"That is an excellent point," I said. "If he went back to your apartment after killing Thérèse, he might even have gotten blood on the floor. Surely he must have stepped in it; there was so much everywhere." I shuddered. Poor Thérèse.

"The police probably already thought of that, but maybe we should go look around the cellar and see if we can find anything," said Julia, who seemed to have forgotten about our trip to the market. "Come on, Nancy Drew!"

Instead of going in through the front entrance to her building, Julia drew me around to the narrow walkway that led between her building and its neighbor. There was a narrow path shoveled through the thin layer of snow, and it took us to a set of steps that led down to a small, subterranean door on the back side of the building.

"This is where the trash bins get collected," Julia said. "Maybe the killer came out this way so he wouldn't be seen with blood all over himself. Oh . . . look at all the footprints." She sounded disappointed.

There hadn't been any snow or precipitation in the last two days, so everything was dry. There was an icy crust on the top of the snow that had collapsed under the weight of many footsteps.

"I don't see anything that looks like blood," I said, examining the array of footprints that probably included ones from the police as well as the killer, and maybe even the trash collectors. There were nonhuman prints as well—dogs or cats that might have tried to scavenge for any garbage that spilled out of the trash cans, or were looking for a place to hide from the weather. But all of the prints lacked details; they were merely misshapen holes in the snow—at least, to my untrained eye.

"What's this?" Julia rose from where she'd stooped to pick up something. "Where have I seen this before?" She was holding a small, triangular piece of vibrant yellow cardstock about an inch long on each side. "Looks like part of a postcard or a package."

She handed it to me and it took only a moment for the memory to click in my head.

"It's part of a matchbook cover," I said. "There was a matchbook in Thérèse's purse—remember? La Sol, I think it said. The Sun. See, there's a little bit of the sun logo."

"So does this mean that Thérèse was out here in the courtyard and had another matchbook from the same place, and she dropped it?"

"Maybe. Or maybe her killer had the same matchbook—"

"Because they both went to La Sol!" exclaimed Julia.

"Maybe," I said again. It seemed like a big leap to make such a connection, but I tucked away the thought. This was real life—not a mystery novel where every little thing turned out to be an important clue.

Julia tried to open the door to the cellar, but it was bolted from the inside. Even my tool knife wasn't going to be any help in opening the door.

"Well, at least we don't have to worry about murderers getting in this way," she said. "I suppose it gets unlocked on the mornings the trash man comes."

Having been stymied at that entrance, we went back around to the front of the building and made our way to the cellar by crossing the lobby and going down the same stairs we had yesterday.

Only yesterday?

It seemed as if it had been years.

Julia forgot to duck and she bumped her forehead on the header beam at the bottom of the stairs. I was right behind and heard her say a very spicy word.

Then we stepped onto the floor. Without speaking, we paused for a moment, looking at the scene.

The space was just as dank, dim, and smelly as it had been yesterday. Thérèse's body had been taken away. There were other signs that the police had been there and had thoroughly investigated the place: the trash bins had been moved, and the floor had been swept of any debris that might have yielded a clue.

But the bloodstains remained, having seeped into the concrete floor.

I wondered how long poor Thérèse had lain there before she became oblivious. I hoped her death had been quick, because it certainly hadn't been painless.

"We need more light," said Julia after a moment. "*Why* didn't we bring flashlights?"

She went over to the exterior door we had just tried to open. As expected, it was bolted from the inside, and once she opened the door, a feeble bit of sunlight spilled into the dark, dank space.

But that was all we needed in order to see a footprint on the uneven concrete near the doorway.

"That's blood," Julia said, looming over me as I crouched next to it. "Isn't it?"

"I'm no expert, but it looks like it." The mark was the same color as the stains from Thérèse's body.

"It has to belong to the killer," Julia said. "Because who else would be walking through fresh blood? And it looks like he must have left through this door."

I rose. "And then what? He came around to the front of the building and returned to the party, covered in blood?" I wasn't convinced of that . . . but how could there be any other explanation? "Why didn't he just come back up the cellar stairs if he was going back to your apartment?"

From Dort's information, we knew that the other guests—Neil, Thad, Johnny, and Mark—had all gone home around three o'clock. That was far too long after Thérèse and I had left for her to still be waiting around for her cab . . . wasn't it?

The thought struck me suddenly. Had she actually *called* for a taxi? Had anyone seen her use the telephone? Did we know for certain she planned to get a ride from someone other than Johnny? Or was that just a story? She *had* mentioned to me that she had to wait for a cab. . . .

These thoughts whirred in my head as I stared at the bloody footprint.

If the men had all left at nearly the same time and she was still there, surely they would have seen Thérèse—and the killer wouldn't have had the secrecy he needed to kill her.

So . . . the only explanation that made sense was whoever killed Thérèse had to have come down to the lobby—probably by the stairs—right after she and I got into the lift. He must have waited until I was safely across the street before accosting her, luring her into the shadows and down into the cellar. Afterward, he returned to the party and left with everyone else.

I calculated the timing in my head. Two or three minutes to jog down two flights of stairs. I hadn't lingered, so Thérèse would have been left alone by the time he got there. Talk her into the shadows, down the stairs, plunge the knife . . .

The whole thing probably hadn't taken more than ten minutes. Maybe fifteen. If anyone noticed he was missing during that time, he could easily explain that he'd gone to the bathroom. Or he could deny it and say, "I was sitting right there."

Whoever had done it must have been a very cool character to calmly return to a party after killing someone. But surely he would have been out of breath, and maybe even filled with adrenaline after such an activity. Maybe one of the other party-goers had noticed that sort of change.

Regardless, the fact remained: Whoever stabbed Thérèse would definitely have been covered in blood. So he went out into the back courtyard and walked around to the front? Why would he do that?

"Maybe he tried to clean himself up out there," I said thoughtfully. "Where he could see better? Under the moon?"

"He could have used some snow to wipe off his hands," said Julia. "Or gloves."

I looked at her. "That makes sense. And then he either took off his bloodied coat or put it on over his bloody clothes to hide them."

"And he walked around to the front and the snow wiped off the blood on the bottoms of his shoes at the same time," Julia said. "But there probably would have been splatters on *top* of his shoes. So we look for dirty shoes on the suspects—or really clean ones!"

We both started for the exterior door at the same time. Maybe there was more to be found in the courtyard. Julia snapped open the bolt and we surged outside.

I was walking along the edge of the building, looking for who knew what, when Julia cried out.

She had gone over to the far corner of the courtyard, searching for clues. Now she was holding what looked like a wad of fabric.

We met in the middle and she thrust the cloth at me. "He stole my apron too!"

Sure enough, it was an apron I'd seen her wear, and there was a lot of blood all over the front of it.

"That explains how he didn't have any blood on his clothing," I said, eyeing the dark brown stains.

"So he stole my knife *and* my apron—"

"With the express purpose of killing Thérèse Lognon," I said, still staring at the apron. I would have to give that to Inspecteur Merveille as well. "I wonder how the police missed this."

"Maybe they didn't look around the whole courtyard," said Julia. "They just followed his footsteps to the front. Besides, it was stuffed under a bush. I guess that explains why he was out here in the courtyard."

"This has certainly been productive," I said, rolling the apron into a small bundle. "I'll take this with me when I take the handbag to the detective." I was looking forward to pointing out that he or his men had somehow missed finding the apron. Subtly, of course.

"Don't forget this piece of the yellow matchbook," Julia said.

"Now that we've found two clues for Inspecteur Merveille, I think it's time to go to the market!"

"And you saw the body?" Marie des Quatre Saisons said. Her dark eyes gleamed with interest as well as sorrow. *"La pauvre mademoiselle."*

Of course the entire market on rue de Bourgogne was filled with gossip about the murder.

"To be so attacked, and in *our* neighborhood too," Madame Marie went on as she used a skinny twig from her small bucket-fire to light a cigarette. "I thought those problems would be over once those bedamned Germans left."

"It was quite awful," Julia said as she poked through a basket of smooth-skinned red potatoes. "The poor thing. But Tabitha here is investigating."

I gasped at my friend's audacity and elbowed her sharply. "I am not investigating," I said to Madame Marie. "I'm leaving that up to the *police judiciaire.*"

Julia made a tsking sound as she opened her purse to pay for the potatoes and the shallots she'd chosen, but to my relief she didn't mention it again.

"But you met the girl, *non?*" said Madame Marie. "Mademoiselle Knight, you met her?"

"Yes, I did. Just briefly," I replied, suddenly wishing I hadn't come to the market after all. "Did Mademoiselle Clarice find Madame Flouf yet?" I said in a desperate bid to change the subject.

"Oh, *oui,*" said Madame Marie. "The poor dog was near frozen, with icicles hanging from all of her curls, but she was found safe and unharmed very late last night."

"At least there is some good news on the rue de Bourgogne," I said. And before Madame Marie could return the subject back to my so-called investigation, I said, "Excuse me, madame—there's Mademoiselle Clarice now. I must speak to her and congratulate her on the safe retrieval of Madame Flouf."

And then it was like a comic strip light bulb coming on over my head, complete with energy lines radiating from it. I should speak to Clarice, not only to express my relief that she'd found her mistress's dog, but also because if she had been looking for her all night for two days, as Madame Marie had told us yesterday, then there was a chance—a slim, very slim one, but a chance nevertheless—that Clarice might have been on rue de l'Université during the time Thérèse was murdered.

It was worth asking, I thought. And it was even more worth getting away from any more questions from Madame Marie regarding my so-called investigation. I supposed I couldn't be that annoyed with Julia for harping on it since I *had* sort of been poking around . . . but the last thing I wanted was for Inspecteur Merveille to hear about it. I could only imagine his reaction.

Gritting my teeth at the thought, imagining those cool, angry-ocean eyes settling on me, I hurried over to Clarice.

"Bonjour, Clarice! I'm so relieved you found Madame Flouf," I said. "Is she doing all right?"

"Yes, and thank you, Mademoiselle Knight. But I have left the very naughty Madame at home today. She is still recovering, I think, from the horrors of being out on the streets for two days and nights—and without her coat!—and the Madame and Monsieur have been fawning over her with treats.

"They've even settled her bed by the radiator, and the poor darling is receiving very much attention," Clarice said with a charming little roll of her eyes beneath the curly brim of her brown hat. "But Madame Flouf was so very naughty to run away when her collar came loose, and I have told her that several times." She sighed. "I am so very relieved that she was found."

Clarice was younger than me, in her early twenties, and because it was cold, she was wearing boots instead of fine shoes from the shop where her sister worked. Her fair, freckled cheeks were pink from the chill, and despite her tart words there was a gleam of humor and affection in her eyes.

"I'm relieved as well," I replied. "Madame Marie said that you were looking for Madame Flouf all night on Wednesday. Were you really out on the streets so late at night?"

"Oh, yes, I was," Clarice replied, nodding vehemently. "I tried to sleep, but I couldn't. I could only imagine poor Madame out here, shivering, lost, and frightened, and so I couldn't stay inside while she was lost. I walked and walked and walked up and down the *rues* and around the circle . . . but I didn't find her. I was sobbing so much . . . and then yesterday, at last, I finally found her. It was the sausage I was carrying that brought her out of the alley, I think." She smiled.

"A sausage would bring most anyone out of the alley," I said with a chuckle. "Were you by chance on rue de l'Université at all on Wednesday night? After midnight? Very early yesterday morning?"

"Yes, I—*oh!*" Clarice's eyes went wide. "Oh, yes, I heard about the terrible thing that happened there in Madame Child's building. The woman who was stabbed to death. To think that someone would do such a thing . . . lurk about in the shadows in waiting, and then drag a person into the dark and *kill* them! Why, it could have been *me* they attacked!" she said. "I heard about it the next morning, and I thought, '*Merde*, that could have been me.'"

"Well, it appears that whoever did it was someone who already knew Thérèse," I said. "It was planned. They weren't looking for a random person walking down the street."

"Oh," breathed Clarice, her eyes still very wide. "Oh, that's maybe even worse."

I nodded. "Yes, I think so." I hesitated, then pressed on. "It seems that whoever did it might have been seen in rue de l'Université a little after two o'clock. Is it possible that you might have been along there around the same time? And perhaps you happened to see anything or anyone . . . ?"

"Oh!" Clarice's cheeks, pink from the cold, suddenly paled. "Why . . . do you mean I might have *seen* the killer?"

"If you were there at that time, and you noticed anyone or anything at all, I'm certain the police would want to know," I said firmly—and doing my best to properly distance myself from the investigation. Really, I had no business being involved. I couldn't wait to give Thérèse's purse to Inspecteur Merveille.

Clarice's eyes had gotten even wider, and now I could see the whites of her eyes all around the brown iris. "But I don't want to talk to the police," she said, backing away a little. "I . . . I don't want to talk to them at all."

"Did you see something?" I asked, not really caring why she was so opposed to talking to the authorities. It wasn't all that surprising, considering the fact that all of Paris had been under an authoritarian control by the Germans for four years, and a good number of the police had been collaborators with them. Parisians had become used to keeping their heads down, so to speak, and not attracting the attention of the authorities.

I also knew there was a strong movement of the Communist Party in Paris, taking advantage of this wariness of government and authority. There were elections coming next year, and I'd heard little worried rumbles about whether the Communists might win—or at least have a good showing.

This thought process made me wonder whether Merveille had been a Collaborator, a Resister, or if he'd been in the FFI with de Gaulle and not here at all during the Occupation. And then I shoved the thought away. Why on earth did I care?

"Did you see anything?" I asked Clarice again.

"I . . . I don't know," she said. "I might have . . . let me think . . . oh, let me think about that."

I tried to guide her through it. "Did you perhaps hear the bells from Ste. Clotilde's tolling while you were out looking for Madame Flouf?"

"Oh. Yes. Yes, I did . . . but what time was it?" Frown lines appeared between her brows and her lips pursed as she thought. And then, suddenly, everything smoothed out. "Yes, I heard the bells ring two as I came by Ste. Clotilde's—it was so loud and deep and sudden that it startled me. I was walking around the Place du Palais Bourbon and then a few minutes later, I turned onto rue de l'Université. So I *was* there a little after two o'clock," she said. Her cheeks were ice white; not from the cold but from the awful realization.

"Did you see anyone?" I asked.

She shook her head. "No, no, I don't—*wait*. Maybe I did. Maybe . . ." The frown lines were back.

"Maybe someone coming from the side of a building?" I prompted. "Or going in the front door of Madame Child's building? It was very late and cold . . . surely there weren't many people out and you would have noticed someone walking by. Or . . . a taxi? Did you see a taxi?" If Thérèse had called for a ride, and the taxi had shown up but she wasn't there, how long would the driver have waited?

"*Yes!* I did . . . I did see someone going into a building . . . I don't know for certain if it was Madame Child's building, but there was a man and he was in a hurry. I do remember that now, yes, I do." Clarice's fingers crept to the front of her coat and gripped it right over her heart as she stared at me. "Was that him? Did I see the killer?" Her voice spiraled up a little, and I saw M. Blanche of the inferior produce looking over from his stall.

I shushed Clarice. Not that I thought Thérèse's murderer was lurking about the rue de Bourgogne market to hear, but it certainly wasn't good practice for a witness to announce to the world that she'd seen a killer. I'd read enough whodunits to know that never ended well.

"It's possible," I said. "Can you tell me anything about what he looked like? What he was doing?"

"Oh, oh . . . let me think." The freckles were standing out like maple syrup splatters on her ice-white face. "He wore a hat and a coat, of course. The coat was long; I noticed because it was flapping around his legs."

"Could you tell anything about him? His height or color of his hair? Was he bearded or clean-shaven?" I knew I was peppering her with questions, but that didn't stop me. If she wouldn't tell Merveille, then I would.

"He . . . his hat covered his hair, so I couldn't see that. His coat was black, or maybe blue—it was dark. I suppose he was about normal height," she said. "I don't think he had a beard. But I did see him coming from the side of a building and then in the front door and I suppose that's why I noticed him. Usually people out that late are walking down the sidewalk and going into their homes."

I nodded. "Was there anything else about him you might have noticed? Anything at all?"

Clarice shook her head. "No, mademoiselle. It was dark and I was cold and I was mostly looking for Madame Flouf."

"You should tell the police about it," I said. "Inspecteur Merveille would want to know." I stopped short of trying to convince her that he would be kind and gentle—the *inspecteur* had not struck me as being soft in any way.

"Oh, *non, non*," she said, shaking her head. "If I get involved with the police and Madame and Monsieur find out, surely they will send me packing. No, no, I cannot do that."

I nodded. At least I had the information—vague as it was—and I could tell Merveille about it. If he chose to follow up with Clarice, then that would be his decision.

CHAPTER 11

I convinced Julia it wasn't necessary for her to drive me to Mrs. Hayes's house to pick up my money. My friend had offered to do so, but I knew how busy she was in the kitchen and, honestly, how much she preferred to be there than anywhere else. And aside from that, much as I loved Julia and her boisterousness, I craved a little bit of quiet to think about what I'd learned.

"You have mayonnaise to perfect, remember?" I told my friend as we separated on rue de l'Université, each with our own market bags. Hers was much heavier than mine.

"Oh, yes. That is very true," she replied with a laugh. "But you'll be back for me to help you with Madame Poulet, right?"

"Yes, of course. Let's say three o'clock?"

Mark was picking me up at six; that should give us plenty of time to roast the madame.

"And we can use your very large kitchen!" Julia was definitely on board with that idea.

I waved her across the street and darted into my house. I'd decided that since I was going to take my bicycle again, I would exercise my right under Parisian law to wear trousers while doing so. It would keep my legs a lot warmer, and it was much easier to pedal without a skirt flaring about my calves. And since I was going to the police station, I could get my so-called permission to wear pants while there.

I rolled my eyes, snickering at the idea as I dropped off my market bag in the kitchen. Bet (or Blythe) was there, making a small luncheon for my messieurs, and she gladly took the eggs, milk, and tiny potatoes to put away.

As I dashed up the stairs to change, I decided not to stop in the salon to speak to Grand-père or Oncle Rafe; I didn't want to be delayed. It was already after eleven o'clock, and I honestly wasn't certain how either of them would react to seeing me in pants.

By the time I got on my bicycle, with Thérèse's handbag, her book, the scrap of matchbook cover, and the bloody apron stowed inside the basket, I realized the sun had come out and that it was a fairly pleasant day.

Except that a murderer walked free.

It was too bad Clarice hadn't noticed anything more about the man she saw coming around into Julia's building. It was obvious to me, at least, that she'd actually seen the killer, but we had absolutely no factors to help identify him.

Then I scoffed at myself. There was no "we" about it, and I was fooling myself thinking there was—or should be. *Leave the detecting to the experts*, I told myself firmly.

The Hayes family lived in a townhouse on the Right Bank, just across the river. It was only a few blocks from the embassy. By the time I arrived, I was pleasantly toasty from my ride, and the sun was bright and warm—definitely a tease toward spring, as it was only mid-December, and we had at least two months or more of cold awaiting us.

I climbed off my bike and leaned it against the side of the steps that led to the front door.

When I rang the bell, it was the maid who answered. I explained who I was and although her eyes widened when she saw my trousered legs, she immediately invited me in.

"I don't believe Madame Hayes is finished with her toilette yet, mademoiselle, but if you would just wait here?" She gestured to the foyer, which was small but nicely furnished.

A half-moon table sat across from the door with a mirror above it, and I could see how windblown I looked. My hair, never sleek or neat thanks to the riot of chestnut curls I inherited from my father, sprang out from beneath my hat. My slender nose was tipped red, and my cheeks were pink with exertion and windburn. The coral-colored lipstick I'd put on was still intact, however, and my mascara hadn't smudged.

I resisted the urge to take off my hat, for it was a losing battle to try to contain the springy coils that made up my hair, but I did straighten the brim and tucked a wayward curl behind an ear. When I finished, I looked down at the table to see a vase filled with very realistic silk sunflowers. Next to it was an empty ashtray and a small decorative plate that held a collection of matchbooks.

I caught my breath when I saw the bright yellow of a matchbook from La Sol sitting in the pile.

I was still staring at the sunny folder, wondering if it meant anything that this was the third time I'd seen one, when I heard the businesslike clip-clop of heels approaching.

"Oh, Miss Knight, thank you for coming by," said Mrs. Hayes as she came into the foyer.

She was a woman in her midforties and dressed neatly in a periwinkle jacket and matching skirt. Her shoes were a shade darker and matched the gloves and pocketbook she carried. Her hair, unlike mine, was a smooth and shiny swath finished with a restrained bit of curl. I had always thought my employer was very attractive and personable, if a little scattered, and I felt a renewed sense of dismay over Mr. Hayes's presumed indiscretions.

She was smiling in a slightly hesitant manner as she handed me an envelope. "I do hope it's all right that this is in dollars instead of francs," she said.

"That's no problem at all," I replied.

"I'm so sorry things didn't work out—I mean, not that you did *anything* to cause the, uh, termination, of course—it had *nothing* to do with you at all. I really want you to know that. And I know Betty will miss you. She was very disappointed this morning when her father told her." Mrs. Hayes sounded disappointed too.

"Thank you," I said. "If anything changes, please feel free to call. I'll always make room for Betty in my schedule."

"I certainly will." Mrs. Hayes seemed about to say something else, but she stopped herself and gave me a polite smile.

If she expected me to offer my au revoirs, she was disappointed. Instead, I took the opportunity to extend the conversation. "Oh! La Sol," I said, casually picking up the matchbook. "I've heard about this place. Is it really nice?"

She frowned, then seemed to realize I was referring to the matchbook. "Oh, heavens, I have no idea. Monsieur—er, I mean *Mr.* Hayes . . ." She laughed and said, "It's so confusing switching between two languages all the time. I don't know how you do it—and so fluently. Doesn't it get confusing?"

I shook my head with a smile. "Not really."

She smiled back, then tsked. "I simply have no skill for languages. I had hoped Betty would do better than I." She gave a self-deprecating laugh. "But I suppose that will have to wait for a while until Mr. Hayes . . . anyway, what I was starting to say is that I've never been to—what's the name of it?"

"La Sol."

"Yes, that. I suppose it's a place Mr. Hayes has gone to with his colleagues. He has late-night meetings sometimes, of course—some entertaining of clients, some meetings that run over. And you know how long and late these French people eat! Why, a three-hour dinner beginning at eight o'clock is really quite extreme, don't you think? Why does it take so very long just to eat a meal?"

"I think the French just love their food and wine," I said with a smile. "I know I do."

"Oh," Mrs. Hayes replied, suddenly looking stricken. "I didn't mean to imply . . . I mean, I know you're half French and I certainly didn't mean to insult you or your family, or—"

"Of course not," I said, flapping an easy hand. "Do you get to the theater very often while you're here, Mrs. Hayes?"

"The theater? Oh no, not really. I wouldn't be able to understand half of what they're saying. Maybe I should be the one taking French lessons."

"There are some productions in English," I said. "The American Club Theater, over on rue Monceau, for one."

Maybe I shouldn't have brought that up. I was practically pointing her in the direction of her husband's infidelity. But my little internal sprite had taken charge, and I couldn't help but feel for Mrs. Hayes, being left alone at home in a foreign city where she clearly wasn't completely comfortable while her husband gallivanted about with another woman.

"I've never heard of it," she said. "Maybe I should ask Rog— er, Mr. Hayes about it. It *would* be nice to have some entertainment that I could understand." She gave a little laugh. "It's hard to even find an English program on the radio. Mostly I just listen to music."

"I wonder when the last time Mr. Hayes was at La Sol," I said. I'm not sure why I decided to press, and to this day, I'm surprised that she didn't balk at my persistent nosiness.

Maybe she just felt so bad about firing me that she didn't want to be seen as rude. Either way, she didn't seem to be bothered by my continued questions.

"Well, I suppose . . . I remember I first noticed the matchbook the other day. Maybe Tuesday, so he probably took it out of his pocket when he got home Monday night. That's what he usually does—empties his pockets right here on the table. All sorts of things he leaves here—coins, scraps of paper, matchbooks. . . .

"I noticed it because it's that bright yellow." She gave a little laugh. "It coordinates so nicely with those silk sunflowers and the green ashtray, and I thought the whole arrangement looked very balanced. I have an eye for things like that," she went on, pride in her voice.

I tended to agree about her visual taste—it was clear in her own presentation as well as what I could see in the house. "That's what caught my eye too," I said.

"Well," she said, making a polite but firm gesture toward the door, "thank you again so very much, Miss Knight. I hope we'll see you again before we leave."

"Me too," I replied. "Please give Betty my best, and tell her to keep practicing. Thank you again."

I had barely stepped over the threshold when the door closed behind me, leaving me to wonder whether I'd planted a clue in Mrs. Hayes's mind about her husband.

To my relief, the basket with Thérèse's things was untouched and I tucked the envelope of money safely into my pocket. I was just mounting the bicycle when someone called out.

"Miss Knight!"

I looked over to see Betty Hayes hurrying around from the back of the house. She must have come out of the servants' door in a rush to catch me without being noticed by her mother, for her coat was unbuttoned and she wasn't wearing a hat or gloves. Her honey-blond hair bounced atop her shoulders.

"Bonjour, Betty." Needless to say, I was feeling a little hesitant about talking to her, but I still spoke in French. I had taken on the calling of teacher, and teacher I would remain. "How are you doing?"

"I can't believe they fired you!" cried the girl in imperfect but still comprehensible French. She was fifteen and, as I had sometimes been at that age, was filled with fiery outrage over actions of her parents that she didn't agree with. "It's just so stupid! You didn't do anything!"

I hesitated, unsure how to respond, and she kept going.

"I want to keep taking lessons, please, Mademoiselle Knight," she said, struggling a little with the language and her emotions. "I'll pay you myself, out of my own allowance. Or I'll get the money from my grandparents. They send me money sometimes." She had reverted to English for the last two sentences.

"Did your father say why he didn't want you to continue your lessons?" I decided to remain in English so that she could more easily express herself. It seemed important to make certain I fully understood the conversation.

"Just that we can't afford it," she said, but there was a stubborn light in her eyes. "That's not the real reason, mademoiselle. It's not. We have plenty of money. I know we do. We just bought a new car, and Mom always buys new clothes. Besides, I really want to learn more."

"Well, I don't think it's a very good idea to go against your father's wishes," I said.

"I don't *care!* I *need* to learn to speak French. I can't talk to *anyone* here—at least, anyone who's not from the U.S. And Americans are *so* boring."

I smothered a smile. I knew exactly what she wasn't saying, for there had been more than one mention of a young Parisian named Jacques during our lessons. I'd gathered that he was the son of a local shopkeeper, which may or may not have been an issue with Betty's parents and part of the reason Mr. Hayes fired me.

"I'm not quite sure how we'd manage to meet for lessons if your father has forbidden it," I said.

"You can meet me at school—I can have a lesson at my lunchtime. Daddy won't ever know. I can pay you. How much is it?"

I waffled internally. I didn't really need the money—although I *was* thinking about buying a car, wasn't I?—and I was certain I could fill her time slot anyway. But at the same time, I hated to be a person standing in the way of education—or young love.

If I agreed, I would be doing it more for her than for me. "How about this. Why don't you talk to your mother about the idea and see what she says? If she agrees that it's all right, I'm sure we can work something out. You already have a free lesson," I added with a smile, patting the pocket where I'd put Mrs. Hayes's envelope.

Betty hesitated, and I prepared myself for more arguments, but to my surprise she nodded. "I think Mom might agree. Especially if I pay for it myself."

I told her how much I charged and she nodded again. I saw no reason to give her a discount; Mrs. Hayes might end up paying for the lessons herself or even convince her husband to do so.

I should have ended the conversation there, but my curiosity egged me on. "Maybe your mother would like to take lessons too," I said. "It sounds like she doesn't get out much, and learning French might help her feel more comfortable."

"What makes you think that, mademoiselle? My mama is very busy," said Betty, back in her slow but correct French. "She is gone all the time at bridge parties and shops and dinners and—and other places." She made a moue of dislike. "And I sit at home with my books and the cat and the maid."

"Oh," I said. "I must have misunderstood."

"Mama's French is very good," said Betty. "Not as good as yours, though." She beamed at me. "I'll ask her about continuing lessons."

"All right," I said. "You can call me or ask your mother to do so." I found one of the bike pedals with my foot, but before I started off, I had one more question. "Have you heard of a place called La Sol? I think it's a club or a restaurant. Do either of your parents go there?"

"No," replied Betty. "I haven't heard of it. But I don't really pay very much attention to what they do."

"All right. I hope to see you again soon." With a wave, I pedaled off.

As I biked, I ruminated over the conversations I'd had with the Hayes women. I had certainly gotten the impression that Mrs. Hayes wasn't comfortable with French—hadn't she said she wasn't good with languages? But according to her daughter, her French was very good—and she was busy all the time; which was a complete contradiction to what Mrs. Hayes had indicated.

Of course, Betty might simply have the impression that her mother spoke very good French—at least, compared to her own capabilities. And Betty had admitted how uninterested she was in her parents' activities . . . so she might not actually *know* what her mother and father did. She didn't seem to care all that much, which wasn't that surprising for a fifteen-year-old who had a crush on a boy.

Still, it did seem odd to receive two very different impressions.

I scoffed and shook my head as I turned onto Quai de la

Mégisserie, which ran along part of the north side of the Seine. It shouldn't really matter to me anyway. Why would it? If Mrs. Hayes was out at the dance clubs every night, that wasn't my concern. And if her husband was going to the theater without her, well, that didn't matter to me, either.

I put it out of my mind as I cruised along, feeling the warmth of the sun on my face.

I smiled, suddenly—despite everything else—filled with the joy of life on this unusually warm day.

I am in Paris.

Every so often it hit me like that: I was living in Paris, the City of Light, the center of food and culture and fashion. One of the most iconic and beautiful cities in the world.

Paris. With her blocks and blocks of the distinctive Haussmann buildings of pale marble façades, wrought iron window grilles and balconies, trims, grates—and corresponding lampposts and signposts. And the mansard-style roofs, which I'd learned were angled at forty-five degrees so as to allow as much sunlight as possible to shine on the streets below. The buildings could appear any color from cream to pale yellow to honey, depending on the time of day and the amount of sunshine.

The buildings had rows and rows of double windows, stacked neatly atop one another in a sort of pleasing grid, including dormers in the attic level—like my own bedroom. Many of them even had their own miniature balconies, rows and more rows of elegant wrought iron accents. Broad, narrow chimneys rose at regular intervals from the curved roofs, and the stone façades had stately but ornate designs in relief above doors and archways.

With grand boulevards wide enough for four cars, and narrow, angular *rues* of cobblestone, the city boasted both an organized center and a labyrinth of alleys and skinny streets beyond. There were multiple cafés on every block, with their tables tucked up against the windows, and larger, fancier restaurants; shops and market stalls. *Boulangeries, pâtisseries, fromageries, brasseries, bistros,* and much more.

The smells of coffee, baked goods, and cigarettes always

seemed to be in the air, combined with that of vehicular exhaust. The streets were filled with cars, and people milled down the sidewalks, crowding shops and stalls along the upper banks of the river. There were others on bicycles, too, but we were in the minority now that the last of the gas rations had been lifted.

And cats. Oh, there were cats! Even in the winter, wherever I looked, I saw a cat: in a window, looking out over its domain; moving sleekly through an alley, clearly on the hunt; perched on one of the wrought iron balconies with an eye on a nearby sparrow; watching slyly at the door of a food shop for anything that might fall its way. Cats seemed to be just as much an integral part of Paris as her food and lights.

I had arrived in my adopted city eight months ago on Good Friday. Two days later, on Easter Sunday of 1949, all of the lights for which Paris had been known were finally turned back on for the first time in nearly ten years—since the austerity and depression of the war.

The Tour Eiffel, Notre-Dame, the Arc de Triomphe, and more were suddenly bathed in the golden glow of light from streetlamps and floodlights. I had seen only the dark, shadowy city for two nights before she was illuminated once again, but the Parisians had lived in the gloomy, wartime dark for a decade. It was no surprise they'd celebrated and partied all night.

Now, as I navigated my bicycle along the *quai haut*—the road running along the higher level of the Seine's riverbank, or quai; I felt a little extra nip of chill from the river. The street was lined on both sides with market stalls, and below, right at the riverside, was the lower-level walkway, the *berge*. That was deserted except for a few straggler pedestrians and a small flock of ducks.

I was approaching the Pont au Change, the bridge that would take me to the Île de la Cité, a canoe-shaped island in the Seine that could be reached by one of eight bridges, four from each of the Left and Right Bank. The *île* hosted not only the Préfecture de Police, or the 36, as Oncle Rafe called it, but also the Palais de Justice—the Justice Department—and one of the city's most beloved landmarks: Cathédrale Notre-Dame de Paris.

Notre-Dame had been one of the first places I visited when I arrived in the City of Light (after the Tour Eiffel, of course). But at the time, I'd given no thought to the fact that the police head-quarters was merely a wide-open city square away from the iconic two-towered, gargoyle-festooned church. I remembered seeing and being charmed by the patrolling gendarmes in their distinctive silo-shaped black képis.

Little did I imagine I would one day again visit the Île de la Cité not to see the grand Notre-Dame, or even Sainte-Chapelle, whose nave has the most breathtaking stained glass windows, but to mount the steps to the much more ordinary and stately police headquarters. I was just about to turn onto Port au Change, grinning to myself with pleasure and joy as I sped along the edge of the road, looking around, taking it all in. Even though I knew it would be strange and awkward speaking to In-specteur Merveille, I was still in a good mood.

Who wouldn't be, on a sunny December day like this, outside, breathing in the fresh river air as I was biking along like a champ.

The cat saved my life.

He was a mangy-looking tiger-like creature, sitting next to one of the trees that lined the street. I saw him a little ahead of me, but when I noticed his poor tail was broken, the top hanging there like a flag at half-mast, I braked suddenly.

At that moment, some great force slammed into me from be-hind.

The next thing I knew, my bike bounced into the deep street gutter and I was flying through the air.

CHAPTER 12

When I hit the ground, my only thought was shock and terror. And pain. Oh, yes . . . lots of pain.

I slammed onto the cobbled sidewalk and tumbled several agonizing inches, landing not far from the tree where my savior cat had been sitting. At the time, I didn't realize the tiger-like cat with the broken tail had saved my life. That understanding was to come later.

My ears were ringing, but there were more sounds filtering through: shocked voices, screams, the roars of engines, the honking of horns, the clattering of metal . . . but it was all an aural blur.

I was vaguely aware of people surrounding me, helping me to sit up while I desperately tried not to vomit. My body ached, my gloved palms and trousered knees radiated with pain. I hadn't hit my head, fortunately, and I hadn't been tangled up in the bicycle when I fell, which could have caused more serious injury.

"*Merci, merci,*" I said over and over to the solicitous bystanders as I tried to catch my breath and push away the pain. "*Oui, je vais bien,*" I told them, even though I wasn't really fine.

Someone had retrieved my bike, while others were picking up all of the things that had been thrown from my person and the cargo basket and piling them at my side.

"That car," said a tall, slender woman in her fifties. She crouched next to me, patting my arm in support. "It ran right up next to you without stopping. If you hadn't stopped, it would have run you over, but when you stopped, he was still going and he didn't hit you as hard as he could have. But I thought you would be dead!"

At the moment, I almost wished I was. I hurt everywhere.

But then her words penetrated the blur of my mind, and I managed to focus on her. "A car?"

She nodded. "When it hit your bicycle, I could hardly believe it! And then he just drove away!"

I was sitting up by now. Someone pressed a handkerchief into my hand, and I used it to wipe my face. When I pulled it away, I saw streaks of blood and dirt.

"A car hit me?" I knew I sounded inane, but I was still pretty muddled and obviously that information was shocking.

"*Oui*," she replied, filled with outrage. "It came right up next to you onto the sidewalk! If you hadn't stopped so suddenly . . ." Her face was grim.

"What . . . what kind of car was it?" Someone pressed some papers into my hand and I stuffed them into my pocket. Another person handed me Thérèse's purse, while another set the bundled-up apron in front of me. Her book had fallen wide open and was muddy, wrinkled, and torn, but still readable. My hat, crushed and dirty, appeared at my side, along with my own handbag and my Swiss Army knife, which had somehow fallen from my pants pocket.

"I don't remember. I didn't see. It was dark, black or blue," she said. Her voice was high-pitched with shock. "Perhaps you should go to the hospital."

"No, no, no," I said, thinking I might attempt to rise. At least I could use my bike for support if I could get upright. "I'm just a little banged up."

I blindly stuffed Thérèse's handbag and the bloody apron into the roomy pockets of my coat, along with everything else that had been collected. The tall woman helped me to stand. I wobbled only a little, and I managed to keep the nausea under control. One of my knees screamed with pain, and I could feel the wetness of blood seeping into my pants.

"Perhaps you ought to take a taxi home," said another woman, who'd been hovering in the background.

"No, no, I'm going to be all right." I was lying through my teeth, but I really just wanted everyone to go away and leave me alone so I could gather my wits and strength.

When the crowd suddenly melted away, I thought my wish was about to be granted . . . until I looked up into the last face I expected to see.

Cool, ocean-gray eyes looked at me from under the brim of a low-riding fedora.

"Mademoiselle Knight?" Inspecteur Merveille sounded both surprised and concerned. "It seems you've been in quite an accident."

Hovering behind the *inspecteur* were two constables—which was likely the reason the crowd had begun to disperse, now that the police had arrived. It was another example of the subtle, inherent mistrust of authority lingering from the Occupation.

"I fell," I said in a steady voice. The few syllables were about as much as I could trust myself with, for my head had started to spin a little. But I was damned if I was going to sit back down, especially in front of the *inspecteur*. And I certainly wasn't going to allow myself to throw up, even though my innards were churning greasily.

"She didn't *fall*," said the woman who'd been helping me. "A car *hit* her and then drove off without even stopping! You should go and catch him, that driver!" She was speaking to the constables, who looked from her to the *inspecteur* to me and back again.

"Mademoiselle Knight, perhaps you'd allow me to help you to somewhere you can sit down and tell us what has happened," said Merveille. "I understand you were on your way to see me anyway, *non?*"

I could only imagine how he knew that. "Yes," I replied grimly.

The next thing I knew, I was being ushered toward an official-looking car. It was parked right at the edge of the *quai*.

"My bike," I said, halting suddenly just before I had to maneuver myself into the vehicle.

Inspecteur Merveille tsked and looked over. I followed his gaze. My bicycle was there, but it wasn't going to be very useful for a while, if ever again. Its rear tire was a mangled mess, and the frame had been bent.

"You're very lucky, Mademoiselle Knight," said Merveille. He gestured for me to climb into the car, offering me a hand for stability.

I released his fingers as soon as I was settled in the passenger seat, supremely grateful that we'd both been wearing gloves. Merveille spoke to the constables, then walked around and climbed into the driver's side.

"There is a place you can . . . er . . . clean up," he said.

"I have some things to give you," I told him. "That belonged to Thérèse Lognon."

"So I understand. It can wait until you've . . . er . . . set yourself to rights," he said. "Are you certain you don't want to go to the hospital, mademoiselle?"

"No," I replied firmly. I didn't know why it was so important to me not to be fussed over or to seem weak. I also had the impression the *inspecteur* didn't give much credibility to my sex.

Or maybe it was because I knew I had been snooping about in areas that weren't really my concern. I was already at a disadvantage; I didn't need to be undermined even more.

We arrived at the 36 without having spoken any further. I spent the short drive trying not to feel strange being alone in the car with a man as austere and forbidding as the *inspecteur*, while at the same time trying to ignore how crummy I felt, with sore knees and palms, an achy body—and the expectation that said forbidding *inspecteur* was probably not going to be pleased with me.

Maybe I *should* pretend to be a little weak.

But that was not an option. I hadn't taken on the job as a Rosie the Riveter because I was one to bow to pressure or stay in my place.

If only I knew what my place *was*, now that the war was over and things had gone back to normal.

I winced when I climbed out of the car. My knee was already swollen so much I could hardly move it.

"This way, mademoiselle," said Merveille. "If you permit, we can speak in my office. But first, you might wish to . . . er . . . visit the ladies' lounge to wash up your . . . er . . . scrapes." He even offered me his arm as we approached the steps to the Préfecture de Police, and I had no option but to make use of his assistance. It was either that or take the chance of my knee completely giving out and dumping me on the ground.

The place Merveille euphemistically called the ladies' lounge was nothing more than a small gray brick room with an arrow-slit of a window and two stalls. But I forgot all about that when I got a look at myself in the mirror.

I was an absolute disaster. My face was grimy with blood and dirt. I had a good scrape along my jaw and another mark on my cheek. My mascara had been completely transferred to the skin beneath my eyes. And my hair looked as if I hadn't combed it for weeks. The simple barrette I'd used to hold the curls out of my face was now irretrievably tangled in the mess, and the rest of my unruly hair straggled into my eyes and was plastered to my neck and temples.

It was no wonder Inspecteur Merveille had insisted I clean myself up. I wouldn't want to look at me, either. I washed the scrapes on my forearm and cheek with the soap—which stung. My pants and gloves had protected me from the worst of cuts, though one of my knees throbbed painfully.

I was afraid to even look at my aching right knee; there was a quarter-size bloodstain on the front of my pants. But I bravely pulled up my pant leg and dabbed at the blood. It was better to do that than to have my wool slacks stick to the wound as the blood dried.

I folded up a wad of paper napkins and made a temporary bandage held in place with a silk scarf I'd tucked into my purse.

My body ached, and my knee didn't want to hold my weight, but when I was finished with my repairs, I didn't look nearly as scary as I had. Fortunately, I had my purse and its contents. It seemed not to have opened during my fall, so I was able to retrieve and use my lipstick and brush—not that a brush did much of anything to tame my hair, but at least I could get the barrette free and make a neat side part. I used a little water from the sink to calm my curls, and dampened paper napkins to clean the bits of blood and dirt from my scrapes.

A swipe of rose-pink lipstick helped boost my confidence a little. I resisted the urge to spritz a little of the perfume I kept in my purse. The last thing I needed was for the *inspecteur* to think I'd primped for him.

At last, I could delay no longer.

I opened the door to the so-called lounge and was startled to discover that Merveille had been waiting the whole time.

I managed to hide my surprise as his attention swept over me as if to determine whether I'd "cleaned myself up" enough. I'd expected him to have left some lower-level associate to take me to some cold and spare interrogation room. Instead, he'd stood outside the ladies' lounge for fifteen minutes, waiting for me.

"This way, mademoiselle, if you permit," he said, and gestured to the corridor that extended before us.

He actually did lead me to his office, which was surprisingly roomy. The space was filled with heavy wood furniture: a desk, two chairs, a small bookshelf crammed with tomes, and a low credenza along one wall. There were two high transept windows on an exterior wall that allowed in light without taking up much space on the wood-paneled walls.

Merveille obviously shared the room with another detective, for a second desk and another pair of chairs butted up against the opposite wall. The desk's surface was strewn with papers, coffee mugs (and corresponding stains), pencils, and a variety of other items, including half of a croissant. It appeared that whoever sat there wasn't familiar with the purpose—or location—of the trash can beneath the desk, for it was surrounded by crumpled papers and food wrappers.

I knew immediately that the desk with the single framed photograph, the neat stacks of paper and folders, a packet of Clove chewing gum, the clean and empty coffee cup, and the paper blotter aligned precisely in the center belonged to Merveille. Even if I hadn't made that logical deduction, the wall adjacent to the desk would have clued me in, for it was covered with an organized collage of photographs tacked to the paneling.

Several of them were pictures of Thérèse Lognon, both alive and dead. There was a map with some pins stuck in it to mark locations related to the crime, along with images of the murder weapon, footprints, the exterior of Roo de Loo, the Théâtre Monceau, and a building I didn't recognize.

But it was the photographs of myself, Julia, Paul, and Dort that had me whirling toward the *inspecteur*. Not an intelligent move, as it sent a screaming pain shooting up from my knee. I managed to stifle a gasp and channeled the agony into indignation.

"You don't actually think Julia and Dort are suspects!" I exclaimed. "And definitely not Paul Child!"

I didn't even pause to wonder how Merveille had obtained our photos. Mine looked like the one on my passport and, as usual, my hair was a Medusa of curls. But, to be fair, there were also photographs of my suspects as well: Johnny, Mark, Thad, and Neil.

Merveille gestured for me to take a seat in the chair next to his desk. "Please sit, mademoiselle."

I did, gratefully, but I didn't let him see my relief. That sudden, spinning move had really cost me, and I had to grit my teeth against the pain. I needed some ice for my knee, but I was damned if I was going to ask *him* for it.

"How did you even know I was coming here?" I asked, shrugging out of my coat. I was hot with fury and discomfort.

"When I spoke to Madame Child, she indicated that you had

a handbag belonging to Mademoiselle Lognon," replied the *inspecteur*. He gave me the forbidding look I'd anticipated as he removed his overcoat. He took off his fedora, revealing a head of neatly parted and smooth dark hair. I wondered how that was possible beneath a hat, then decided Merveille was the sort of man who didn't allow any sort of disarray in his life.

No soirées, no disarray, no sense of humor.

He hung his outerwear on a coat rack near the door. I left my own coat crumpled in the chair behind and beneath me. My hat was unwearable, and I had not put my gloves back on after washing up. I couldn't help but feel a little flicker of defiance in the face of his unyielding perfection.

"You can't really believe Julia or Dort murdered Thérèse," I said, still indignant. "That's preposterous!"

"What did you bring for me, mademoiselle?" he asked, sitting in the chair at the desk across from me. The framed photograph faced him and was at an angle where it couldn't be viewed by anyone unless they were sitting in his chair. I had a sudden torrid curiosity about who or what was in the picture—it being the single personal item in his work area. "And why do you have it in your possession in any case?"

"At least you know Paul Child couldn't have done it," I went on, ignoring his question. "He's not tall enough."

Merveille gave me a piercing look. "And what makes you think that, Mademoiselle Knight?"

I gulped. I couldn't reveal how I knew that the murderer was four to five inches taller than Thérèse, who was slightly taller than me, without divulging Oncle Rafe's connection to Merveille's great-uncle.

Suddenly, I remembered my saving grace.

"Because someone saw the killer." I probably could be excused for the flair of the dramatic in my announcement.

I was rewarded by a widening of surprise in his eyes, followed by the narrowing of suspicion. "And how do you know this, mademoiselle?"

"A young woman in my neighborhood was searching for her

mistress's dog at the time, and she saw a man come around from the back of the building and then go into the front," I said with slightly less flourish. "It was shortly after two o'clock in the morning. Unfortunately, she didn't notice any details about him— only that it was a man wearing a hat and in a long coat. It wasn't Paul Child—he's not tall enough. And if it was a man, it wasn't Julia or Dort—or *me*." I gave Merveille a pointed look.

The *inspecteur* made a quiet sound that could have been either derision or disbelief. Or perhaps, if one was feeling charitable, thoughtful interest.

Then, with his own pointed look directed to my lower half— and something that could possibly be the beginning of a smirk— he said, "Unless, mademoiselle, you were wearing a hat . . . and trousers."

I was saved from replying—and thankfully so, for I had no idea how to respond—when a young man dressed in a constable's uniform knocked on the frame of the open door. "Inspecteur, as you requested." He was holding a small bundle of cloth.

Merveille rose and took the bundle, giving the young man— who looked as if he were barely out of high school—a murmur of thanks. To my mystification, he handed the bundle to me and I realized with surprise and pleasure that it was a bag of ice.

"*Merci*," I said, and my indignation softened—but only a bit. I was still flabbergasted that anyone would truly consider the Childs or me as possible killers. "But we don't have a motive," I said. "Yes, one of us—Julia or Paul or Dort or I—could possibly have done it, but why?"

Merveille gave me a measured look. "That is precisely what I intend to find out. Why someone wanted to kill Thérèse Lognon—why that someone decided in an instant to do so, and obtained a knife and brutally stabbed her. And so, mademoiselle, if you could give to me the items that belonged to Thérèse Lognon, perhaps I could make that determination?" Although his words formed a request, his tone indicated command. And more than a trace of impatience.

"Yes, of course," I replied. The chill from the ice was already easing the pain in my knee. I fumbled through my coat pockets to retrieve Thérèse's purse and the bloody apron I'd squashed in there. I knew that no matter how hard he looked, he wouldn't be able to find a motive for one of us to kill Thérèse.

Merveille made that same ambiguous sound of surprise or interest when he saw the bloody apron, but gave no other reaction as he looked through the handbag. Sadly, I was feeling too out of sorts to make any snide comments about the efficiency of his men in their search of the murder scene.

If Merveille noticed that Thérèse's book wouldn't have fit in her purse, he didn't comment or ask how I'd come to have it. He pulled out the letter from her mother, the matchbook, the keys—though with them, he gave me a swift look of suspicion— the lipstick, and her compact. I looked at the items. It felt like something was missing, but I couldn't put my finger on what. Definitely the keys and letter were the most important things, and they were there.

"That's not the address Dort gave you yesterday," I said helpfully, gesturing to the letter. "It looks like Thérèse moved after the man was shot in her building, and didn't bother to tell anyone at the theater."

He ignored me. By that point, I half expected him to order me to leave so he could get on with his investigation.

After a short while reviewing the items from the purse, he looked up at me. "And this young woman you know who believes she saw the killer . . . will you tell me her name?"

I hesitated, then decided to be frank. "When I talked to her, she was very concerned that if she got involved with the police, she would lose her position. I truly don't want to be responsible for that."

"Mademoiselle, a woman is *dead*." His steely eyes settled on me. "Another one could be next."

"If I believed she had any helpful information, I would tell you, Inspecteur, I swear it. But even though I questioned her closely, I'm confident she really didn't see anything."

"You *questioned* her." Merveille leaned forward and I caught a whiff of damp wool and clove. "What do you think you're playing at, Mademoiselle Knight? This is not your concern—"

"But it is my concern!" I burst out. "If you suspect me or my friends for a crime none of us have committed, then it *is* my concern!"

"But you have just explained to me why it *couldn't* be you or any of your friends who stabbed Thérèse Lognon," he replied in a reasonable tone.

"That's right—because none of us have any motive." I knew I should keep my voice calm and even, but I couldn't quite pull it off. He was so infuriating.

Merveille settled back in his chair. "No motives, you say? I can think of several, mademoiselle. Monsieur Child, he might wish to have rid himself of a discarded and angry lover, *non*? Mademoiselle Lognon was very attractive and vivacious—the type of woman to easily attract the attention of men. Or Madame Child herself might have wished to remove the other woman—or the temptation of one—from her husband's affections and interest—"

I burst out laughing. I couldn't help it. "You are barking up the wrong tree, Inspecteur. Paul and Julia are absolutely crazy for each other. There is no possibility that Paul Child is having an affair—or that Julia suspects he is. Do you know," I said, leaning forward and dropping my voice slightly, "that when he comes home for lunch every day from the embassy, they always take a nap together afterward?" I lifted one of my eyebrows so he would get the idea.

If I had hoped to chastise or embarrass him, I didn't succeed. His expression didn't give even a flicker of emotion. I supposed it could have been because he was French and his countrymen in general were not the least bit prudish or reticent when it came to the topic of sex.

"And what about you, mademoiselle? Perhaps you were the jealous one—Mademoiselle Lognon had, conceivably, put designs upon the man in whom you were interested? This Monsieur Justiss?"

I blinked. "I only met Mark Justiss that night," I said, more startled than I cared to admit that he'd homed in on the possibility of Mark and me being involved—as premature as it was. "And it's *docteur*, not monsieur. So me being jealous enough to kill a woman over a man I'd only just met is ludicrous. And before you suggest it, no, Dort wouldn't do that, either."

He looked at me closely for a moment, those steely eyes cool and expressionless, and then he gave the most subtle of nods. I wasn't certain whether it was an affirmation of what I'd said, or whether it was an affirmation of his own internal thoughts.

Just then, a thought struck me. "I'd like you to know that this morning I was fired from my tutoring job by one of the families on that list I gave you." I fixed him with what I hoped was a slightly accusing, but very annoyed look. "It's as I expected—the minute the police start coming around asking questions, people get suspicious. And they don't want you teaching their kids. I can sympathize with my friend who saw the killer—talking to the police would probably get her fired from her job too."

Merveille shook his head and made a mild tsking sound. "*Non*, mademoiselle, I have yet to speak to any of the people on your list. So you cannot lay that at the feet of the *police judiciaire*." He lifted one dark brow and settled back into his chair. "But now I am curious—which family is this, and what reason did they give for terminating your employment?"

Feeling only slightly mollified—after all, I was still fired by the Hayeses—I explained, then added with a sigh, "I expect Mr. Hayes wanted to let me go because I saw him last night with a woman who wasn't Mrs. Hayes."

"Ah, that is possible." Merveille nodded.

I decided it was time to change the subject. I didn't want him to circle back and press me about Clarice. "Inspecteur, there was something else you might find interesting. That matchbook for La Sol—I found another piece from the same type of matchbook outside, in the courtyard behind the house where Thérèse was killed. Maybe the killer dropped it. Maybe there's a connection." I saw no reason to mention that I'd seen the same matchbook at the Hayeses' house. Surely that was just a coincidence.

Although, if this was a Nancy Drew story or a Miss Marple tale, it certainly wouldn't be.

He nodded, but before he could speak, there was another knock on the doorframe. This time, instead of beckoning the constable—not the same very young one—to come into the office, Merveille said, "If you will excuse me for a moment, mademoiselle."

He strode from the room, leaving me alone with my curiosity about a picture frame facing the wrong direction.

Merveille was barely out of the room when I sprang to my feet and edged toward the desk while still keeping an eye on the door.

The photograph was, as I'd half suspected, that of a young woman. She appeared younger than me—her early twenties, maybe even younger, and her clothing and hairstyle were at least five years out of date. So the picture had been taken either before or during the war.

She was fair of hair and light of skin, suggesting that she wasn't a sister, mother, or aunt of the dark-haired, olive-skinned Merveille. The only conclusion I could draw from the single personal item on his desk was that she had to be his wife. Or maybe a fiancée, since Merveille didn't wear a wedding ring. Either way, I found it very intriguing to wonder what sort of woman would want to be with such a stiff, austere, unsmiling man.

She wasn't beautiful, or even all that pretty. Just an average-looking girl. But there was a light of humor in her eyes, and the faintest, sauciest smile quirking her lips—and I simply couldn't imagine someone who looked like her, who seemed to have her own lively sprite living inside her head, falling in love with Étienne Merveille.

I was listening carefully, so I heard the quiet scuff of a footstep the fraction of a second before Merveille came back into the office.

But, despite my knee—which was feeling much better thanks to the ice—I was quick. When he came in, I wasn't seated, but I was standing at the wall with all of the crime scene photographs, gaping at them openly.

I hadn't initially noticed the photograph of a second dead body. But now that I was standing there and had dragged my indignant attention from the pictures of Merveille's suspects (at least four of them being wrong), my attention was focused on the image of a man sprawled on an internal staircase. There was a pool of blood next to him and a big splotch on his shirt.

It was no great leap for me to realize that this was a photo of the man who'd been killed at Thérèse's old apartment. And maybe the building I didn't recognize in the photo was the place where he'd been killed—where Thérèse used to live.

"Who's that?" I asked, pointing to the picture of the dead man.

It seemed that Merveille was connecting the murder at Thérèse's place to her own death, just as I had instinctively wanted to do.

"Is there any other information you wish to give me?" he asked. "Anything else you have kept to yourself other than this matchbook?"

"No," I replied. I hadn't actually expected him to answer my question, but I had hoped.

"Very well then, mademoiselle. I thank you for remanding the personal items of Mademoiselle Lognon to me, despite the delay in doing so." He picked up my crumpled coat to help me into it, clearly indicating that my time in his office was at an end.

"What was his name?" I asked, still looking at the picture of the dead man as I slid my arms into the waiting coat.

Merveille simply shook his head in negation.

"Do you think his death has anything to do with Thérèse's murder?" I asked, picking up my crushed hat.

I heard the faintest sound of a pained sigh—the first real sign of humanity from the man. "Mademoiselle Knight," he replied, "I will say this only once: Leave the investigating to the proper authorities. No more questioning of people. No more poking about in handbags, apartments, and courtyards. I implore you, do not involve yourself with things that do not concern you.

"Or the next time you might suffer from something far worse than a scraped face and swollen knee."

CHAPTER 13

*T*o my surprise, Inspecteur Merveille had arranged for one of the constables to drive me back to rue de l'Université. Maybe he was being nice, but more likely, he wanted to make sure I went home instead of "involving myself with things that didn't concern me."

I hesitated to abandon my ruined bicycle, but the constable— a friendly man with a red nose, round cheeks, tiny beard, and a smelly, dark cigarette—convinced me that it wasn't fixable. She would go to the bicycle graveyard, he told me soberly.

I climbed into the waiting car and pulled the gloves from the pocket I'd stuck them in. As I did so, something fluttered to the floor. I bent to pick it up and discovered it was a coat check ticket. For a moment I was mystified—I hadn't used a ticket for my own coat last night, of course. Then I realized that it had probably spilled from Thérèse's purse when I had my accident. Everyone around had been thrusting fallen items at me, and I had probably stuck it in my pocket.

For a moment I wondered if I should give it to Inspecteur Merveille. Then I dismissed the thought; I wasn't in the mood to be scolded again. I put it back in my pocket and thought that if I *happened* to see the *inspecteur* again—which I highly doubted I would, and sincerely *hoped* I would have no need to—I could give it to him then.

Of course, he would probably give me that cold, suspicious look, thinking I'd once again held something back from him.

By the time I got back home, it was nearly two o'clock. I was expecting Julia at three to guide me through the Great Roasting of Madame Poulet.

Since I kept the ice on my knee for the drive from Île de la Cité, I was able to climb the stairs to the salon with hardly a limp.

Even so, the moment Grand-père saw my scraped face, he lunged from his chair so quickly Madame X was forced to save herself from tumbling ignominiously to the floor. She, of course, landed neatly on all four paws, shooting me a furious look.

"Tabitte! *Ma chère*, what on earth has happened to you?"

"And what is it that you are *wearing*?" said Rafe, goggling at my trousers.

"Ah," I stammered over the cacophony of Oscar Wilde's excited barking and jumping. He didn't care about my limp or my scrapes; he simply wanted a biscuit, and I was a fresh mark. "I was riding my bicycle, and I fear it is no more. There was a little bit of an accident."

"But you are limping! And your beautiful face!" Grand-père was stabbing the button on the wall next to his chair to call for one of the maids.

"I'm just fine," I said, patting the silky dog in an effort to squelch his yapping. M. Wilde bumped my knee during a particularly high-springing jump, but he was so tiny that it didn't even hurt. "I've been putting ice on my knee and I just need a little makeup to cover my scrapes."

"Sit, sit, *chérie*," said Oncle Rafe, looking at me with suspicious dark eyes. "You'll have a bit of brandy and tell us all about it."

I had no choice in the matter; had I argued, they would have been even more suspicious, and I didn't want them to worry. *I* wasn't worried myself, despite Inspecteur Merveille's dark pronouncement.

He didn't really think someone had tried to run me over because I had found Thérèse Lognon's purse, did he? Absolutely ridiculous.

Bet (or Blythe) arrived in the salon, slightly out of breath from dashing up the stairs. She had on her coat and hat, indicating that she and her sister had been about to leave for the day. I felt badly about the delay, but Grand-père would have none of it and sent the maid back down for some ice and a bit of aspirin.

Madame X had taken a seat on the ottoman in front of me and she was *not* pleased. Her glowing green eyes were still shooting furious sparks in my direction.

On the other hand, Oscar Wilde was delighted with my presence and I scooped him up onto my lap, barely resisting the desire to stick my tongue out at the arrogant Madame X. I should have brought home the stray cat with the broken tail that had saved my life—*then* she would have had something to hiss about.

Oscar Wilde had a biscuit; I had my ice, two aspirins, and a small brandy; and Madame X continued to sneer at me. By now she'd settled herself back on Grand-père's lap, where he'd mollified her with a tiny morsel of cheese.

I gave a brief explanation of my accident, then purposely spent more time and detail describing my conversation with Merveille.

"Well, at least he didn't have *our* photographs on the wall," said Oncle Rafe when I finished. His eyes gleamed with delight.

Grand-père gave a gravelly chuckle. "Devré would have set him straight on that, now, wouldn't he?"

Rafe scoffed. "I'm not at all certain Devré would be so convinced of our innocence in anything. He knows us all too well."

"Ah, he knows *you* too well, *cher*," said Grand-père. "Do not drag me into your sordid past."

I chuckled. I definitely wanted to hear about Rafe's sordid past. But before I could beg my grandfather to elaborate, someone rang at the door.

"That'll be Julia," I said, rising reluctantly as Oscar Wilde bounded toward the stairs, yip-yapping wildly.

Grand-père and Oncle Rafe brightened visibly, and they sent me off with great enthusiasm—somehow no longer distressed about my bumps, bruises, and scrapes, and certainly not troubled about spies and espionage.

True Frenchmen they were: only worried about their next glorious meal.

"First you dry her to death. She's got to be *bone dry*. Then you have to *massage* her to *bits* with the butter," Julia sang in delight. "This is not the time to be stingy or squeamish about it, Tabs. Get it all over her—into every nook and cranny, and then some."

I looked balefully at Madame Poulet, who, true to Julia's word yesterday, had been completely defeathered. Madame sat there in her toweled-dry, hairless splendor: pale pink with wrinkled, pebbled skin.

"Make certain she is perfectly dry," she said, and I dutifully picked up the towel to once more rub the skin. "Then salt the inside. We won't be stuffing her; she's too small."

"How much butter?" I asked after I'd sprinkled salt inside the bird.

"Lots, of course! Be *generous!*"

Before I could argue or even negotiate, Julia took my hand and plopped a big spoonful of butter in the center of my palm. "Now massage!" she ordered. "Do the inside first, of course—stick your fingers right inside madame. And make sure you get up into her armpits, now. Don't be shy!"

So I did. I rubbed butter all inside that chicken, then all around the outside—even into her armpits and up her butt. And when I thought I was done and eagerly reached for a towel to wipe off my hands, Julia tsked and plopped another spoonful of butter in my hand and made me do it all again.

During the process, I explained about my bike accident—about which Julia had demanded information immediately upon seeing me—and recapped my conversation with Merveille . . . all the while, I massaged, massaged, and massaged. I swear, we used a half cup of butter on that one little bird. It was a good thing the food rationing was over! That would have been the household's butter allotment for the entire month.

By the time I was done, Madame Poulet was slick and greasy. I was glad Julia was there, because I was afraid if I tried to lift the chicken into her roasting pan, she'd slip out of my hands and tumble to the floor. While I was doing the buttery massage, Julia had tucked the potatoes and turnips into the oven for their own roasting.

"Now to tie her up neatly," she said, offering me a large needle threaded with a long white string.

"Oh, no, you'd better do that—"

"Nonsense! You can do it, Tabs. It's easy. And it's not only to make certain she looks beautiful when she comes out—instead of flopping her legs and wings open like an eager bride—but it makes her cook more evenly. Now, proceed."

She showed me where to poke the needle beneath Madame's knee near the tail end of the bird, and then to bring it all the way through and around the drumsticks to hold them in place against the body. At first I felt a little queasy sticking the needle into the soft, fleshy skin, but reminded myself that Mark Justiss sewed up skin on a regular basis.

"Now the top end," Julia instructed, and showed me how to tuck the wings so their tips were flush against the body, and then I sewed them flat, spearing the flap of neck skin on the way to keep everything closed and in place.

"Perfect! She's trussed up tighter than Pauline and her perils on the railroad tracks," she said with great satisfaction. "Now into the hot oven." She checked to make certain it was heated to two-twenty (which I knew was four hundred twenty-five degrees Fahrenheit; the metric conversions made it even more difficult for me to try to learn to cook over here), then watched as I carefully slid Madame onto the roasting pan rack, breast side up.

"Now . . . ten minutes and then we turn her on the rack."

"*Turn* her? On the rack? Do you mean in the oven?" Good heavens . . . that was going to be a disaster in the making. If I didn't burn myself, I'd probably drop the poor chicken on the floor.

"Yes, yes, you have to put her on her side at the tenth minute, and then onto her other side at the next tenth minute. And *then* we turn the temperature down to one seventy-five—that's about three fifty Fahrenheit—and then we *baste*! Every ten minutes after that," she said with great satisfaction. "We have to turn her halfway through the roasting time. And then again . . ." She went on and on.

Jeepers. "I had no idea it was this difficult to roast a chicken," I said weakly.

"Ah, but a perfectly golden Madame with lightly browned and crispy skin is nothing short of simple perfection! It's not so difficult, is it?" she asked, looking at me worriedly.

"Not really . . . it's just I'm sure I'll probably knock her over into the bowels of the oven and she'll catch on fire and it'll be a *disaster.*"

She put her hands on her aproned hips. "Don't be silly, Tabitha. Any woman who can manage a rivet gun can turn a bloody hen in her roasting rack."

I laughed weakly. Maybe she was right. "So, Julia," I said, trying to sound casual. I'd been trying to figure out a way to bring up the topic that had been niggling at me all morning. "Does Paul ever talk about . . . um . . . you know . . . spies?" I couldn't help it; my voice dropped to a whisper even though no one was around.

"What do you mean?"

I shrugged. "I don't know. My *grand-père* says there are spies crawling all over the city. I guess I thought if anyone knew anything about it, Paul might. Working at the embassy."

Julia put her hands on her hips, a little smile twitching her mouth. "You know Paul and I met working for the OSS in Ceylon."

I had indeed known that both of them had worked for the Office of Strategic Services, the U.S.'s intelligence agency during the war. Which was why I had broached the subject.

If anyone had any idea about how spies worked, Julia would. She'd once told me she'd known all the data on every American spy in Japan and India because she'd been the one managing and organizing the personnel database. But I was also just as certain she couldn't—or wouldn't—tell me very much. It was all classified.

Still, I had to at least ask.

"Right. I just wondered whether . . ." I stopped, because I wasn't even certain I wanted to know whether Paul Child—and maybe even Julia herself—was a spy here in Paris. I really didn't think they were, but who knew?

"Well, we left those days in the OSS far, far behind us when we moved here," said Julia. Which was literally true—Paris was a long way from Indochina.

"I know," I said, sensing that she wasn't going to give up much of any information. "I'm just asking in *theory*—do you think there really are spies all over the city?"

"Definitely not," she replied, but there was a gleam in her eyes that belied the words. "But if there were spies, they'd definitely be Russians and Americans—spying on each other." Then, with a start, she cried, "Time to flip that hen!"

And the next thing I knew, I was maneuvering Madame Poulet onto her side on the rack inside the hot oven.

"Oh, Tabs, you'll never guess what!" Julia said as I closed the door, perspiring from the heat, as well as nerves from the process of The Turning.

"What?"

"My mayonnaise turned out today!" In her excitement, she sounded even more like a trilling, operatic bird than usual. "I girded my loins and went into the kitchen. I grabbed the bowl from next to the stove—I was making stock from the ham bone and the metal bowl was just sitting there, and I thought, *What the hell, let's give it another shot!* I broke those damned eggs into the bowl, and I told them I expected them to behave . . . then I whisked them with the oil and *et voilà*! The mayonnaise, as Chef Bugnard would say, she was born! And she was stupendous!"

"Congratulations," I said, acknowledging and accepting that the topic of espionage was closed. "Was it the firm talking-to, do you think, that made it all work?"

"I don't have any idea," replied Julia with a braying laugh. "But here's hoping that the Curse of the Disagreeable Mayonnaise has been put to rest!"

As promised, Mark picked me up just before six o'clock. I was waiting for him downstairs and slipped out before he could ring the bell and alert Oscar Wilde.

A meeting between Mark and my messieurs would have opened an entire Pandora's box, regardless of the fact that Grand-père and Oncle Rafe were as happy as two fat cats with the moist, perfectly golden-skinned *poulet rôti* on their plates. I expected their own not-so-fat cat and the boisterous M. Wilde would soon be just as happy with their own pieces of crispy skin.

"Wow!" Mark said when he saw me. "What happened to you?"

I thought I had done a good job of hiding my injuries with makeup—including a fire engine red lipstick to distract the eye—but apparently my skills had fallen short. Either that, or Mark was particularly observant when it came to my appearance.

I brushed off his concern as we climbed into his car. My limp was hardly noticeable, thanks to more ice and another dose of aspirin, and I knew I would be taking advantage of the fact that the coat check girl was allowed to sit when she wasn't busy.

When we arrived at the Théâtre Monceau, Mark parked in the alley next to the building. I saw Neil Kingsley almost right away, for he was standing out in the back by the stage door, finishing up a cigarette in the chilly air. The sun had set and the only illumination was a sconce affixed to the wall next to the door.

"Hi," I said as Mark and I approached. "What are you doing out here?"

"Needed some fresh air," replied Neil. He wasn't yet made up for the show, and his handsome face appeared drawn and a little pale. When he lit a second cigarette, I noticed the bright yellow cover of the matchbook he used.

Curious.

"That's from La Sol," I said, acting as if I knew all about the place—whatever it was.

"Yeah," said Neil, tucking the matchbook back into his pocket.

"Have you been there?" I asked.

I sensed that Mark was wondering why I was standing outside in the cold having this conversation, but I didn't care. I had moved past believing it was a coincidence that La Sol matchbooks kept showing up in this investigation and onto the decision that I *had* to find that place and check it out myself. Even if it wasn't my investigation.

"Yeah," said Neil.

He was being unusually reticent; almost distracted. I didn't know him well, but the other times I'd interacted with him, he'd been every bit the leading man—gregarious and charming. Even yesterday, his grief and shock over the loss of Thérèse had been tempered by his outgoing personality.

"Is everything all right?" I asked.

"Sure," he said, and flicked the cigarette away. It arced through the air like a miniature comet and landed on a pile of gray-crusted snow. "I gotta get inside. It's almost call."

Mark and I followed him through the door. The general air backstage at the theater was slightly less morose than the day before, but a pall still hung over the place.

"Have you been to La Sol?" I asked Mark as he walked me to the coat room. The backstage area was such a warren of set pieces, clothing carts, props tables, and intersecting hallways that I was grateful for his navigation.

"Sure," he replied with an easy shrug. "It's nothing all that exciting. They've got hookahs, though, which are different. Why are you interested? Do you want to go?"

I was still completely in the dark as to what sort of establishment La Sol actually was—a dance club? A music hall? A restaurant or café?

And what on earth was a hookah?

"Maybe," I hedged.

"Well, let me know. I'll be happy to take you," he replied, smiling.

"Do you know anything about the man who was killed at Thérèse's apartment building?" I asked.

He blinked at my sudden non sequitur and his smile disappeared, but he recovered quickly. "Not really. I just know he was found there on the stairs." Now comprehension washed over his face. "You don't think there's any connection between them, do you? Between their deaths, I mean?"

I shrugged.

Mark stopped and took me by the arm, forcing me to stop as well. "Tabitha, you're not poking around into this whole mess, are you?" His tigerish gaze bored into mine.

"Of course not," I lied. "No, really, but you do wonder, don't you?"

"*I* don't wonder," he said flatly. "And you shouldn't, either. Leave this to the police."

"But don't you realize—it had to be one of . . . one of us," I said, my voice dropping to a whisper. "Someone who was there the other night. Someone . . . *here.*"

His gaze sharpened. "Yes, I know. That's why you shouldn't be poking around in this whole mess. Whoever killed Thérèse won't hesitate to do it again."

"But don't you have any idea *who* or *why*?" I pressed. "You know all these people better than I do."

"Tabitha," he said, and this time he sounded angry. He took me by the shoulders, stopping just short of giving me a shake. "Please don't get involved. Let the cops do their job. I would hate for anything to happen to you. After what happened today, with your bike accident—" He shook his head and heaved a sigh, then gave me a crooked smile. "I'm just getting to know you, and I'd *really* hate for that to get cut short. You know?" He reached out to touch one of my errant curls.

I felt a rush of emotions I hadn't expected: a little shock of warmth that he was genuinely interested in me, a bit of surprise that I was interested, too, and a tiny sizzle of worry.

Did he, like Merveille, think that my bike accident was related to Thérèse's murder? I simply couldn't believe it. It just seemed so illogical and far-fetched.

Suddenly, I remembered what the woman who'd helped me afterward was saying. *The car came right onto the sidewalk. Then he just kept going. If you hadn't stopped suddenly . . .*

I shook my head and Mark's hand fell away. I wasn't in denial; I just couldn't understand why anyone would think that just because I had Thérèse's purse I was poking my nose into things.

Even though I sort of *was.* After all, I had gone to her apartment and looked around. But that was it. Well, I'd scoured the courtyard behind Julia's apartment. *And* I'd been asking Clarice about whether she'd seen anyone walking along the street that night . . .

But no one else knew about that.

Plus . . . how did anyone even know I'd had the purse to begin with?

The only people who knew about that were Julia and Dort. But who knew whom Dort might have mentioned it to, here at the theater . . . where all of the suspects were hanging around.

The bottom dropped out of my stomach and I felt a little sick.

Julia also knew that I'd gone to Thérèse's new apartment. And she'd probably told Dort.

And Julia knew I was going to the 36 to drop off the purse after I went to the Hayeses' house this morning . . . which meant Dort probably knew as well.

"Right," I said. That sizzle of worry had just turned into a blaze of fear.

Mark was still looking at me and I smiled. "I'm not getting involved," I said. *At least, anymore.*

"Good." He gave me one last lingering look, then said, "I'd

best get my medical bag—forgot it in the car—and see if anyone's got a hangnail or hang*over* that needs a little medical
help."

I laughed and now that I knew where I was in the backstage
maze, I started off to find Dort so I could ask whether she'd
been telling people about my so-called investigation.

Just then I saw Thad Whiting. He was carrying something
large and round that looked like a stage light. Despite his slender build, he seemed to handle the heavy, awkward object with
ease.

"Hi, Thad," I said. "How's it going?"

He was the only suspect I hadn't talked to yesterday. I reminded myself firmly that I wasn't investigating anything, but
that little saucy imp inside my head told me I was just being polite in greeting him and that any conversation that might ensue
would be a natural development.

"Hi, Tabitha," he said, giving me a friendly smile.

The idea of Julia describing him as being cracker-like made
me smile: thin, crisp in smile, and sharp in features with snappy
movements. His skin appeared dry, and his hands were cal-
loused and work roughened.

He set the light on a table, and the surface clunked with its
weight. "Dort said you're covering front of house for Thérèse
tonight too. That's really nice. Oh, man . . . I still can't get over
it." His smile faded.

"It's so horrible. Did you know Thérèse well?"

"Well enough, I suppose. I've been here about three weeks—
she was here longer. Hey"—his face brightened and his smile
made him far more attractive than I'd initially thought—"Dort
said you're from Detroit. So am I. Born and raised."

"Actually, I'm from a suburb. I worked at the Willow Run
bomber plant during the war," I told him. I didn't actually feel a
wave of homesickness—who could feel homesick when they
were in *Paris?*—but I did get a rush of affection thinking about
the small town of Belleville where I'd grown up. "Where are you
from near Detroit?"

"In the city itself. Right by the river—we can look over to see Canada anytime we want. My dad worked for Henry Ford, at the stamping plant in Dearborn. Man, you know what I miss over here so much?" Thad said, leaning against the counter with his arms crossed at his waist. "Faygo. Rock & Rye is my favorite, but I dig all their sodas—especially the root beer. Coca-Cola just doesn't do it for me, you know, having been raised on Faygo."

"Oh," I groaned in heartfelt solidarity. "I know. Rock & Rye's my favorite too. Coca-Cola *is* good," I went on, "and I think it's amusing that everyone in France is afraid of it taking over for wine and mineral water . . . but if I had a choice, I'd take a Faygo pop any day."

"Or a Vernors," he said, still grinning. "Man, it's really nice to meet someone from home. I'm looking forward to getting back."

"You're heading home?" I said.

"Yeah. In another week or so. Once I get these lights permanently fixed up for them here, I'm going back. My sister's son's turning seven, and I want to be home to take that kid to Bois Blanc Island for the roller coasters. He's a real daredevil. He's gonna love 'em. I like Paris, don't get me wrong, but I can't speak the language too well, and I miss my family. Your French is really good. How'd that happen?"

"My mother is French," I replied, then I laughed because I'd realized something he'd said. "Bois Blanc Island? You mean Boblo? Maybe the French is rubbing off on you over here if you're calling it that. You know, they officially changed the name to Boblo in April, so you can just forget all that French stuff when you get back."

He shook his head, still grinning. "Don't mind if I say I can't wait for that—and to be able to drink a soda like Coke without being sneered at like they do here."

"Tabitha!"

I turned to see Dort rushing toward me. "Guess I'd better get to the coat check before people start arriving," I said. What

I really wanted to do was find out what Dort had been telling people about my activities.

As I left Thad to pick up the heavy stage light and get back to work, I realized I'd hardly gotten any information from him about Thérèse. In fact, none at all. He'd completely distracted me with talk about our hometown.

Had it been on purpose?

"I heard about your accident," Dort cried when she was still several yards away. Great. Now everyone in the backstage area knew about it. "Are you all right? Thank you for coming tonight—maybe you should be at home resting!"

"I'm okay," I told her in a quieter voice, hoping that she would follow suit and lower her own. "Did you mention to anyone that I was going to the police station this morning?"

"I dunno. I might have. Why? Oh, geez!" The stricken look on her face told me she'd put the pieces together. "You think someone tried to hurt you?"

I shrugged. "Maybe. Who did you tell, and who might have heard about it?"

She looked mortified. "Well, pretty much everyone. I wasn't thinking—everyone was standing around this morning talking about Thérèse and how they'd been interviewed by the cops and everything, and it just slipped out. I'm *so* sorry!"

"Everyone was here? Even Mark?" I had to ask.

"Yes, we were all here this morning. Come to think of it, I was a little surprised to see Mark here because he doesn't usually come until the afternoons. But I guess he was taking out someone's stitches or something. I'm really sorry, Tabs. I won't say anything else."

"Did you, um, mention about me going to Thérèse's apartment? And that it was the wrong one?"

Dort bit her lip. "Probably. I was telling Ivan about it, and anyone could have overheard." Her face was stricken and she took my arm. "I wasn't thinking. I'm really sorry. I'm glad you're okay."

"It's all right," I replied. "No harm done but a crushed hat, a bloodstained pair of pants, and a dead bike. In light of what happened to Thérèse, I'm really quite lucky!" I meant it all sincerely, and I think she read it in my face. But I was also confident that she wouldn't say anything else again.

Not that there would be anything else to say because I wasn't snooping around anymore. I was going to stick to myself and do my job at the coat check tonight, then go home and enjoy leftover *poulet rôti*.

CHAPTER 14

*T*he coat check seemed slightly less of a madhouse than it had been last night. Probably because I was more confident in my work, but I still had to let the customers punch their own tickets so I could get them hung efficiently.

I swore that I saw Mr. Hayes in the crowd, but if he had a coat with him, he didn't check it, and I might have been wrong. I was well into the long, preshow line when a woman rushed up to me.

"There's a lady in the bathroom—I think she needs some medical assistance. Can you please come?"

I hesitated only a moment—health and welfare obviously took precedence over hanging coats. I rose on my toes to make the announcement that the coat check would close temporarily, but just as I was about to shout over the roar of the crowd, I saw Mark.

"Can you run this for a second? And I might need your help anyway, Doctor," I said with a quick smile. "There's a woman in the bathroom who's ill."

He looked confused for a moment, then said, "Ah, sure—but only if I get to keep the tips." He smiled, then got serious. "Let me know if you need help. I'll be right here trying to figure out how to do this."

I didn't take the time to explain my process. Instead, I slammed out of the half door, squeezing past the line of people waiting, and hurried through the throngs still filling the gallery. The woman who'd alerted me sort of pointed in the direction of the bathroom, then went off to find her seat for the show because the lights were blinking the three-minute warning.

When I got to the bathroom, I found a woman sitting at one of the mirrors finishing her lipstick. The rest of the lounge appeared to be empty.

"Is there someone in here who's ill?" I asked, looking under the doors of the three stalls.

"There was, but she left. She seemed okay," the woman told me. "She was making some bad noises in there and was lying on the floor"—she gestured to one of the stalls—"but after a few minutes she came out. She didn't want any help, and she seemed okay."

"All right," I said. "Thanks."

When I got back to the coat check, I found Mark doing his best to keep up with the line.

"She's all right," I told him when he raised his brows in question. He scooted over to let me take my place at the counter. "She was already gone when I got there. How'd it go here?"

"I only knocked the tip jar over once," he told me, grinning. "Thank goodness it didn't break. But I'm glad I don't have to do this regularly. It's a madhouse."

He seemed delighted to get out from behind the counter, and as he went off, I said, "Can you ask Johnny to hold the start of the show for a minute or two?" I gestured to the long line.

He gave me a quick nod and I turned to the next waiting customer, who was complaining loudly about people cutting in line and having to wait forever to hang his coat.

I made soothing noises and explained what had happened while I made short work of his coat and hat.

That turned out to be the most eventful moment of the evening. Everything else ran smoothly after that. I even ducked into the theater and caught some of the production.

It was a pleasure to watch Neil Kingsley and Ivan Cousins

carry the show. They were even better than they had been last night, which was understandable.

Ivan was Sir Lawrence Wargrave, and I could see why Dort was attracted to him—he had great stage presence. Neil, as the young and fascinating Philip Lombard, had the grace and elegance—not to mention the looks—of Cary Grant. I found it interesting to compare his character onstage to the person I knew offstage. I couldn't help but wonder if he had channeled that grace and good looks to lure Thérèse Lognon to her death.

But even if he had, I still hadn't the faintest idea *why* he would. Why *anyone* would.

Thérèse obviously either had some sort of secret that had caused her death—or maybe *she'd* known someone *else's* secret and *that's* why she'd been killed.

I shook my head and thrust away those thoughts. I wasn't getting any more involved than I already had been. It was Inspecteur Merveille's puzzle to solve.

I barely made it back to the coat check before intermission. I didn't expect a lot of people to need their outerwear, but there was always the chance someone had forgotten their cigarettes or a handkerchief or something in their pockets.

By the time the show was over, my knee was throbbing and my body was aching everywhere. It had been a long, active day, and I was ready to head home.

"I'll be finished in another ten minutes," I told Mark when he poked his head around the corner of my counter. "I just want to clean up a little back here, and there are a few stragglers who haven't picked up their wraps."

He gave me a jaunty salute and disappeared into the waning crowd, his ever-present medical bag bumping against his leg. Within another ten minutes, I was ready to go as promised. By then, the front of house area of the theater was empty.

Just as I was closing the coat check door behind me, someone turned off the lights. The gallery went unexpectedly dark except for the footlights that shined on the floor every ten yards or so along the gallery. My heart gave a little lurch, but it wasn't total darkness and I certainly wasn't alone. I could still hear the sounds of people backstage.

Still, I admit that I moved very quickly out of the shadowy gallery and down the hall to the backstage area. Many of the lights were off back there as well. It seemed everyone was in a hurry to leave tonight.

"Oh, sorry," I said when I nearly slammed into Neil as I came around the corner of one of the props tables. He barely paused to apologize as he hurried past me, smelling of cigarette smoke, greasepaint, and sweat. I hadn't even been able to tell him how much I'd enjoyed the show.

It took me several more minutes to locate Mark in the warren of the backstage area, especially with most of the lights off. Everyone else was gone, and it was silent and dark.

"There you are," I said when I finally located him near the stage manager's station.

"I've been looking for Johnny," he said, sounding a little out of breath. "Have you seen him?"

"No," I replied. "I haven't seen anyone for a while."

"I'll check the workshop," Mark said, "and if he's not in there, I'll just catch him tomorrow."

I waited inside by the back door, somehow feeling a little less anxious standing next to the exit instead of in the dark bowels of the looming backstage.

"Couldn't find him," said Mark a few minutes later when he hurried up. "Let's go—hey, did you want to go to La Sol? I could use a drink."

"Sure," I said, forgetting that I wasn't investigating anymore and that my knee was aching. Maybe a cocktail would take away the edge. Besides, I was thinking if things went well at La Sol I might be willing to kiss Mark good night.

He pushed open the door and I went out into the cold night air to discover a flurry of snowflakes swirling in the alley. The temperature had dropped sharply from the sunny, almost warm day, and I shivered. Mark tucked his arm around me and we headed for his car.

When I saw the bundle in the shadows, I thought someone had left a pile of garbage bags in the alley.

But it took me only two more steps to realize the dark shape wasn't trash, it was a person.

And that the dark pool on the layer of snow next to it was blood.

CHAPTER 15

I don't remember if I actually screamed. I probably did, but I'd like to think it was more of a smothered gasp than a full-out shriek. But, to my credit, I didn't turn away or even hide my eyes. I went to help.

Mark and I reached the bundle—the body—at the same time.

He tried to nudge me out of the way, but I had already recognized the still, white face beneath the thick beard.

Johnny.

Mark muttered something short and hard, and his deft doctor's hands were already pulling away the collar of Johnny's shirt to check the pulse in his neck.

But even I knew there was no hope.

"Go inside—there's a phone by Johnny's—the stage manager's—desk," Mark ordered. "I'll see if there's anything . . ."

I slipped a little in the snow as I turned, but despite the protesting twinge of my knee, I dashed for the back door, hoping it hadn't somehow locked behind us.

It hadn't, and I was able to get in, stumbling into the shadowy backstage. "Hello!" I cried into the darkness, trying to remember where the stage manager's desk was. "Is anyone here?"

The only sound was my voice echoing in the hangar-like space and the damp, slapping sound of my shoes as I ran first in one direction, then the other, trying to find the telephone.

I didn't even think about the possibility that a killer might be lurking in the shadows.

At least, not at first.

Finally, I saw a small nightlight that illuminated the desk I was searching for. My hands were trembling and my stomach still pitched a little as I fumbled up the receiver and dialed the operator, asking for the *police judiciaire*. I even remembered to speak in French, and I believe I was mostly comprehensible when I explained what had happened.

It wasn't until the dispatcher repeated what I'd told her and confirmed that a constable would be sent immediately when I remembered to ask for Inspecteur Merveille to be notified as well.

By the time I hung up the phone, my hands were mostly steady and my stomach had settled.

I made my way back to the outside door, which was a little easier this time as I'd neglected to close it tightly behind me and the moonlight and streetlamp filtered in, guiding me through the shadows.

Mark was still outside. He'd removed his coat and placed it over Johnny's face, but he hadn't left the body and was kneeling next to it.

He looked up at me when I approached and rose to his feet. "You all right?" he asked, sliding a supportive arm around me. I could feel the chill in his body even through my coat. The temperature was really dropping.

"Yes," I managed. "You?"

"I've seen my share of dead people," he replied grimly. "Comes with the job."

I huddled next to him, wondering if he'd also been on the frontlines as a medic. Despite his suggestion that I go inside to stay warm, I didn't leave.

"What—happened?" I asked. "To him?"

"Shot. Right in the heart," he said briefly. When I shivered against him, he tightened his arm. "He wouldn't have suffered, Tabitha. He would've died quickly."

I nodded against him, sniffling a little. I hadn't known Johnny well, but he'd seemed like a nice enough person. He'd certainly cared about Thérèse.

I don't know how long we stood there, waiting. It could have been an hour or five minutes, but we were silent as the snow continued to fall and began to blanket the coat Mark had put there.

At last, we heard the sirens and the roar of a car engine. Doors slammed, footsteps pounded down the alley, and two constables came into view, their képi hats throwing long shadows.

"You should go inside," Mark told me. "I'll be right behind you."

He had to be much colder than I was, but I saw no reason to argue. I knew the police would want to talk to me—to both of us. And I was happy to take the weight off my injured knee.

I don't know how long I sat in the dark, waiting. I'd taken a seat in the front row of the theater and was staring unseeingly at the dark, empty stage set of *Ten Little Indians* when a figure came out from behind the curtains. He strode in front of the sofa on-stage, his fedora low on his head, overcoat flapping behind him. He abruptly altered his direction when he noticed me.

"Mademoiselle Knight."

"Inspecteur." I didn't know what else to say. I still felt so shaky.

He made it easy for me, coming down off the stage and sliding smoothly into what I knew was an interrogation of sorts. "Tell me what happened, if you please, mademoiselle." He looked at me closely, and I got the feeling he was assessing my mental and emotional state. He must have been assured by what he saw, for he sat down in one of the chairs, leaving an empty one between us.

I tried to be as succinct and clear as possible, explaining how I'd been waiting for Mark and we'd gone outside together and then found Johnny.

"When was the last time you saw Monsieur . . . Cantrell, is it?" he asked.

"Yes. Before the play began, I caught sight of him walking through the backstage area."

"And you didn't see him after that?"

"No. I was working the coat check, and other than when I sat in the theater to watch a few minutes of the play, I was in that room."

Merveille removed his hat and set it on the empty seat between us. Despite it being nearly midnight, his hair was as perfectly combed as it had been when I saw him several hours ago. He was also fully and neatly dressed. I wondered if the man slept upright in his clothes.

"I didn't realize you were employed by the theater, Mademoiselle Knight." He said it mildly, but I caught an underlying hint of suspicion or annoyance.

"I'm not," I replied coolly. "I was simply helping out by covering the coat check since Thérèse was—is—gone."

He gave a satisfied nod. "Am I to understand you and Docteur Justiss were leaving together? Did you see anyone else?"

"No. Mark said he'd been looking for Johnny backstage . . . I guess we found him," I said sadly.

"Did you hear anything unusual?"

"Like a gunshot? No, but I was in the front part of the theater most of the time and it being a theater, everything is very sound-proofed. Then I was trying to find my way backstage—it's a maze back there—so we could leave."

"Do you have any idea why anyone would want to kill M. Cantrell, mademoiselle?" he asked.

I shook my head. "He seemed like a nice person. I think . . ." I stopped, shaking my head again.

Merveille was silent, waiting. I felt his eyes on me, and I knew he wanted me to continue.

In the end, it wasn't the pressure of his silence that caused me to speak. It was the knowledge that my impressions might help him find the killer.

"As I told you yesterday, I don't know any of these people very well, but I did get the idea that Johnny was hung up on Thérèse. He seemed very upset not only about her death, but he blamed himself because he was supposed to give her a ride home that night. That night she was killed."

Merveille nodded, still watching me in silence.

I hesitated again. Damn. "Well . . . there's something else."

"I thought there might be," he replied.

"Maybe you already know this," I went on hurriedly. "But no one here seemed to realize Thérèse had moved houses. Or at least that she was staying somewhere else, at least temporarily. Even Johnny, who was supposed to drive her home that night. He didn't know."

"What makes you think she was staying somewhere only temporarily, mademoiselle?"

I opened my mouth to make some excuse, but the words dried up. He was looking at me as if he already knew—knew that I had been there, poking around Thérèse's apartment. I felt my cheeks heat under his penetrating stare. Damn.

"Mademoiselle Knight, were you in Thérèse Lognon's apartment?"

"You already suspect I was," I retorted.

"I suspect, yes, mademoiselle. I've suspected since you took more than a day to deliver her purse to me, with, conveniently, the keys to her flat inside. And a book that wouldn't have fit in the purse. And now you've confirmed it for me, *non*?"

I looked at him mutely, but, again, he already knew. He stared me down until I caved. "Fine. Yes, I was there. I was just curious. I didn't touch anything. But . . ."

He waited, seemingly patient and relaxed, but I could see irritation in his eyes.

I spoke quickly, to get it over with. I knew he was going to be angry. "Someone else came in while I was there. Sneaking around. I . . . I hid. They didn't notice me, and . . . they took her gun. I'd seen it, and after they left it was gone."

Yes. He was angry all right. I saw a flash of fury, but it was quickly subdued. "You are very lucky, mademoiselle. Very lucky, indeed. I need not tell you *again* that you will not be so fortunate next time." Those angry-ocean eyes bored into me so strongly I felt the chill in my belly.

I nodded, unable to speak.

I waited for more of a dressing-down, but it didn't come. Instead, he stood and spoke almost gently. "Shall I arrange for a car to take you home, mademoiselle?"

Since I had no idea where Mark was, or if he would be able to leave at the same time, I nodded.

Even though I suspected it would be a long time before I could forget what I'd seen in the alley, I wanted to leave right away—to go home and go to sleep. It had been a long and busy day, ending with almost the most awful thing imaginable. I didn't feel like being around anyone else and having to make conversation.

It was only as my head finally hit the pillow that I remembered what Grand-père and Oncle Rafe had said: *Someone is going to wind up with a bullet in their head.*

Or their heart.

CHAPTER 16

I tried to convince myself that I wasn't doing anything wrong by looking up La Sol in the telephone directory.

So why had I brought the directory all the way up to my bedroom in order to do it . . . secretly?

I was so curious about what sort of place it was. It was an establishment that not only a young French and Polish woman had gone to, but an American doctor, a talented actor, *and* an embassy employee—and who knew who else from this whole sordid mess—had also patronized.

And I didn't know what a hookah was, so I was definitely intrigued. I didn't think it was a slang name for a prostitute.

I found La Sol listed near Place Pigalle in Montmartre, not very far from Thérèse's apartment I'd visited. There was a Métro stop right there if I decided not to spring for a taxi.

I planned to go early this afternoon, just to see what sort of business the place was, and how it looked from the outside. No one knew I was planning to go there—not even Julia—so there wasn't any reason to worry about someone trying to run me down again.

I would just walk down the street where La Sol was located. That was it, I promised myself. If I took a taxi instead of the underground, I could just slip away, take a look, and be back home in an hour.

It was Saturday, so I didn't have any tutoring clients. Julia was usually busy with Paul on the weekends, so she wouldn't be expecting me to go to the market with her. It wasn't even noon—I had slept restlessly and rose early, then went back upstairs to try to sleep some more before my messieurs rose and started asking questions about my night.

I wasn't sure how I was going to tell them that someone else related to the theater had been killed. I was a little afraid Grand-père might ask me to stay home from working the coat check tonight—and if he did, I didn't see how I could disobey his wishes and cause him worry.

So, I thought, it would be best for me not to be seen by either of the older men until after I got back from Place Pigalle. I glanced at the clock by my bed and saw that it was just about noon. I could be back by two o'clock—even earlier if I went by taxi.

I put on my coat, and when I pulled out my gloves—one from each pocket—some papers fluttered to the floor. I stooped to pick them up, wincing only a little due to my tender knee, and frowned. One was a folded piece of paper, and the other was the coat claim check ticket from the theater, which I knew had been in Thérèse's purse. But what about the paper?

It took me only a moment to realize what happened. When I had my bicycle accident yesterday, everything had gone flying, spilling everywhere. People had been handing things to me, and I vaguely remembered stuffing objects blindly into my pocket, including the claim ticket and this paper, which was now crinkled and bent. I realized the paper must have been the bookmark in Thérèse's copy of *And Then There Were None.* Where else would it have come from?

I could have thrown the paper away without looking at it. But of course I didn't, and when I unfolded it to see what was inside, I stared in surprise.

It was a handwritten note . . . in, I was pretty sure, *Russian.*

Thérèse Lognon had been using a note in Russian as her bookmark . . . which implied to me that she read and probably wrote in that language. Still, I didn't know how—or even if—the fact that she knew Russian might relate to her death.

Nonetheless, everything Grand-père and Oncle Rafe had said

about spies came springing into my mind. Though it seemed like a big leap to automatically connect Thérèse Lognon to Cold War—or any other kind of—espionage, I couldn't dismiss the thought. My brain felt as if it were about to explode with all the possibilities.

What if she were a spy? Hanging out with a bunch of Americans might be a good way to get information.

But she'd worked in a coat check at a theater—not really a place where someone might obtain sensitive information. People showed up and sat silently in an auditorium and watched a performance. They didn't sit around and converse, spilling state secrets like they might at a nightclub or café.

But it did occur to me, even at that time, that there was a connection, albeit a very weak one, between a U.S. Embassy employee (Mr. Hayes)—who could conceivably be in the possession of sensitive information—and Thérèse Lognon. Not only had it seemed they'd both been to La Sol, but he'd attended the theater. . . .

Then I realized I'd seen him at the theater *after* Thérèse was murdered. Surely he wouldn't come to see the play twice, so maybe he hadn't been there when she was still alive. So there probably wasn't a connection after all. Still . . . I couldn't completely dismiss the idea. After all, I thought I had also seen him at the play on the second night I worked the coat check. But unless he was a really big fan of Agatha Christie, why would he come and see the play more than once?

Unless it was just a cover so he could meet up with his mistress. . . .

I looked a little more closely at the unfamiliar Cyrillic characters of the note and saw the smallest smudges on some of them— the sort made by a left-handed author whose hand brushed over fresh ink while writing. Feeling very Sherlock Holmes-ish, I nodded with satisfaction. I could reasonably deduce that Thérèse had been the person to write it since I knew she was left-handed.

One thing was certain: My internal sprite wasn't going to stop nagging me until I found out what this note said. For all I knew, it was a grocery list . . . it sort of looked like a list. But it could also be a clue to who'd wanted her dead.

Unfortunately, I didn't know anyone who spoke Russian.

I tucked the note back into my pocket.

I almost threw away the coat check claim ticket, but something held me back. If Thérèse had it in her purse, she must have left a coat at the theater. Though why *she* would need a claim check was a mystery to me—obviously she'd know which coat was hers.

Unless the claim check wasn't for her coat but one that belonged to someone else. I remembered that there had been at least three or four coats left in the room at the end of the night both nights I'd worked. They might even have been the same ones; I hadn't looked that closely at them. A little prickle went down my spine as I looked at the tag: number 35. I'd remember that.

I tucked the claim check ticket into my skirt pocket next to the familiar weight of my Swiss Army knife. I was going to be looking through those leftover coats for number 35 as soon as possible. Maybe I'd go by the theater after I looked at La Sol. Someone might be there to let me in, even though it was Saturday and no one was required to be there until five o'clock.

It hit me, suddenly and forcefully. How stupid I was! Johnny Cantrell—stage manager and set designer—had been murdered last night, there at the theater. Surely the show would be canceled today, even by the "gorgon." That meant I might not be able to look at those coats left behind for a few days.

Hmm. I wondered if Dort had a key to the theater.

It might be worth telephoning to ask.

I'd intended to slip down the stairs past the salon, hoping not to be noticed by Grand-père and Oncle Rafe. Their hearing wasn't the best, which I thought I could use to my advantage. I could go to the telephone in the kitchen to call over to Julia's apartment.

But as I was tiptoeing down the stairs and was just about to continue past the salon and down to the ground floor, Oscar Wilde came alive.

That dog had supersonic ears.

He bounded out of the salon, yipping and yapping and bouncing and dancing in front of me, clearly asking for attention and treats, all the while letting my messieurs know that danger—in the form of *moi*—was lurking. It didn't matter that it was only me, someone who lived there and that he saw every day. M. Wilde was not very discriminating about who he barked at.

I suppose he figured if he made noise for any reason, he'd be shushed with a treat.

He'd been well trained.

"Tabitte? Is that you?" Grand-père called. "If you could come in here, *ma petite.*"

"Good morning," I said cheerily as I came into the salon. "I'm sorry I didn't have breakfast with you this morning. I was tired."

"Are you going somewhere?" asked Oncle Rafe.

"For a little walk," I replied, then tried for a diversion by taking one of M. Wilde's treats from the jar. I made him sit, but his butt touched the floor for only the briefest of instants before he sprang up and began prancing on two feet, eager for his biscuit.

"You're so spoiled," I said as I gave it to him. "I suppose you think you deserve one too," I said to Madame X, who'd slinked nonchalantly into view as soon as I opened the treat canister. She was studiously avoiding looking at me. I think she was still perturbed about being dumped on the floor yesterday.

"We had a telephone call this morning," said Grand-père as I gave his cat a biscuit. "I hope the ringing didn't wake you."

"I don't think I heard it," I said, edging toward the stairway.

"It was Devré," said Rafe.

I stopped. "What did he say? Is there any more information on the case?"

"Apparently there is another dead body," said my grandfather, giving me a pointed look as he lit a cigarette.

I swallowed and nodded.

"Sadly, it was as I predicted," added Grand-père.

"You might have told us," Rafe said to me.

I couldn't tell whether he was worried about me, or just disappointed that I hadn't kept him up to date on all the happenings.

"I . . . didn't have the chance," I replied. Realizing my plan to slip out would have to be aborted for now, I sat down on the sofa, still wearing my coat. At least I could find out what former Inspecteur Devré had to say.

"Are you all right, *ma mie*?" asked Grand-père. He reached over to pat my hand.

"It was a shock. But I'm all right." I crossed my ankles demurely and leaned forward. "What did Devré say?"

"It was the same gun that was used to kill the man at Thérèse Lognon's old apartment building," said Rafe. "The one that was used last night to kill the man at the theater."

I drew in a sharp breath.

"*Alors, chère.*" Grand-père was looking at me with eyes far too sharp for his age. "You understand what that means."

"That whoever was in Thérèse's apartment when I was there must be the person who killed Johnny Cantrell last night," I said.

"And . . . ?" Rafe prompted.

It took me half a second to follow. "And so it might have been Thérèse who shot the man at her old apartment building, since the gun was in her possession."

The two men were nodding at me.

"*Oui.* And that is what Merveille thinks," said Rafe. "They do know that the man who was shot at Mademoiselle Lognon's apartment was not killed on the stairs where he was found. He'd been moved there after and bled to death there."

"Thérèse could have shot him in her own apartment, then dragged him out of it in order to divert suspicion from herself," I said, thinking aloud.

This information put Thérèse in a whole new light. Was she a cold-blooded killer, too, or had she simply been protecting herself?

"What's his name? Did Devré know anything about who the dead man was?" I asked.

"Arthur Coleman, was it?" Grand-père said, looking at Rafe for confirmation. Then he looked back at me. "He worked at the U.S. Embassy, apparently in the area of citizenship services."

"That's . . . interesting," I said. My head was spinning. As I'd mentioned to Merveille, I had been contacted by a Mrs. Coleman a few weeks ago about possibly tutoring her and her daughter in French. But even though I left a message with the maid, no one ever called me back.

If Mrs. Coleman's husband had been shot dead, that would be a very good reason why.

"This is very confusing," I said, then realized I'd spoken aloud.

"What do you mean, *chère?*" asked Oncle Rafe.

Before I knew it, I was telling them about the folded piece of paper. "Now I really want to know what this note says," I concluded, waving the paper in front of them. "I don't suppose you know anyone who speaks Russian?"

Grand-père smirked at Rafe as he drew on his cigarette. "She asks if we know anyone who speaks Russian, *chéri*. What shall we tell the girl?"

My uncle smiled sweetly at me. "That of course we know someone who speaks Russian. We know *everyone*." He held out his hand to me and, only slightly astonished, I handed him the paper.

"You understand I'm not fluent in the language," Rafe said, reaching for the pair of glasses he kept next to his chair. "But I can at least make a start . . . Hmm . . ." He made several thoughtful sounds as he scanned the lettering, nodding as he did so. "Yes, I will have this looked at to be certain, *ma petite*. But for now I can tell you that it appears to be a list of names with some little notes against each one of them."

Now I was even more curious. "Can you tell me anything about the names?" I asked impatiently.

Rafe gave me a quelling look over the top of his glasses. "And where do you suppose this one gets such a great volume of impatience, hmm, *cher?*" he said to Grand-père.

"Certainly not from me," replied my grandfather with a rusty chuckle. "I am the most patient of men. Did I not outwait you and your pigheadedness with all the patience in the world, *mon coeur?*"

Partly amused by their antics and partly writhing internally with curiosity and impatience, I was happy to be diverted when the telephone rang.

I was the closest, so I answered.

"Tabitha? It's me!" Julia's voice rang through the receiver. "You won't believe this. You simply won't believe it."

"What?" I asked, my heart suddenly racing.

"There's been another murder," she said. "At the theater this time."

"There is? Who was it?" My heart dropped. A third person, dead?

"Johnny Cantrell! The one with the beard—"

"Oh," I said, feeling relieved that there wasn't a third body. "I know about that. It was Mark and I who found him last night."

"And you didn't tell me?" Julia's cry had me pulling the receiver away from my ear.

I laughed a little. "I didn't think you wanted a phone call at two in the morning, Jules." Then I sobered. "It was a bad shock. Awful. Poor Johnny. There was nothing Mark could do for him."

"I know. Dort's beside herself. We were supposed to drive to Versailles today, but none of us want to leave the city with all this going on. I'm just going to lock myself in the kitchen and make things to eat. And Dort is saying that the play tonight will definitely be canceled," Julia added. "Even if the owner doesn't want it canceled, the actors are going to rebel. How can you run a show without the stage manager?"

"I'm glad to hear it," I replied. "But, do you know if Dort has a key to the theater? I think I left my gloves there."

"You and your gloves, Tabitha," Julia said with a chuckle. "I'm sure she does. I'll ask her."

"Thank you. Do you want to come over? The messieurs are looking at a note I found in Thérèse's book that's in *Russian.*"

"In *Russian?* I'll be right—" The line disconnected before she finished her sentence.

At that moment, one of the maids appeared in the doorway of the salon. She was carrying a tray with fresh coffee and some cheese and pastries.

"Thank you, Blythe," said Grand-père, gesturing to the round table of inlaid wood in the center of the room. "And we'll need another cup, as Madame Child is joining us."

"Of course, monsieur," replied Blythe with a little curtsy.

I took the opportunity to look at her closely, trying to figure out how I could tell her apart from her sister, now that I knew which one she was. But there seemed to be nothing that stood out about her—no identifying freckles or marks on her face, the same sort of clothing, the same neatly pulled back brown hair, no jewelry . . .

"How can you tell them apart?" I asked in a low voice after she'd gone.

"Hm? Oh, I can't," replied Grand-père as he stabbed out his cigarette. "Impossible to do so. But they answer to either name, and I pay them very well, so, eh?" He shrugged and I laughed.

"All right, then," said Rafe. He looked up at us from over the tops of his dark-framed glasses. "I've deciphered a few of the words, but I need an expert to make certain and to fill in the rest. But there is the word *Detroit*, I believe, on this list," he said, looking at me. He, like Merveille, had pronounced the city name as a Frenchman, not as an American. "And I am certain there is a four-letter name that begins with an *N*—"

"Neil?" I said. "Is that name listed with Detroit?"

Oncle Rafe winced at my barbaric pronunciation. But he nonetheless went on bravely. "No, that is a different line, I believe, *petite.*" He set down the paper. "A different name. Perhaps with a *T*?"

"Thad. He's from Detroit. So she's made a list of people with notes by them—and where they're from?" I said. "Why would she do that? Is *my* name on that list?"

"No, no, I don't see your name on here," he replied. "But you understand, I don't know for certain." Oncle Rafe gave me a steady look. "You must give this note to the good *inspecteur*, Tabitte."

"Oh, yes, of course," I said. I *had* intended to do so, even without his admonishment. "But—"

"But we will make a copy of it first, of course." My uncle smiled.

Just then the door knocker banged enthusiastically, announcing Julia's arrival. I rushed down the stairs to let her in.

"And guess what *else* has happened," she said the moment I opened the door.

"What?" I stepped back to allow the whirlwind that was my friend to enter. It was much colder today than it had been yesterday, and I decided right then that I would be taking a taxi to Montmartre instead of walking to and from the Métro.

"My mayonnaise! It failed again!" Julia whipped off her coat and slung it over one arm while gesticulating with the other. She was still wearing the apron she'd probably had on while making the ill-fated mayonnaise. "I don't understand. Yesterday it was fine, beautiful—creamy perfection!—and then today, again, it was recalcitrant and disobedient!"

"Recalcitrant?" I giggled.

"It's a Paul word. That man is so damned literate, I just want to eat up everything he says. And him too, of course. Anyway, he gave that non-emulsifying, recalcitrant mayonnaise a piece of his mind because I'd promised him some with a bit of that *jambon* we had left over and he was very disgruntled that it didn't turn out." She was laughing about it as she led the way up to the salon.

"Messieurs!" she cried, surging into the room.

Her entrance was heralded by Oscar Wilde's crazy barking and posturing. Knowing the routine, Julia retrieved a treat for the dog. It was a wonder he wasn't fat and round from the amount of food he was fed.

Oncle Rafe was somehow managing to have a telephone conversation despite the yipping and yapping, and he smiled at Julia.

"Madame Child! How good of you to join us," said Grand-père, gesturing expansively for her to sit. "We are having coffee."

"You're both looking very well this morning," she said as she sat. "And how did Tabitha's Madame Poulet *rôti* suit you last night?"

"It was *magnifique*. You will yet make a chef of *ma fille chérie!*" said Grand-père, smiling at me affectionately.

"That is most certainly my intention," Julia replied. "Now tell me about this Russian business."

I filled her in quickly about the note I'd found and what little we knew about Thérèse's Russian notes.

Just as I finished, Oncle Rafe hung up the phone, smiling with satisfaction. "And we will have more information on this Russian business quite soon." When I opened my mouth to ask, he held up a finger. "Tut, tut, *chère*. Patience and circumspection are in order. Now, Madame Child, what can you tell us about Arthur Coleman?"

"Arthur Coleman? Why . . ." Julia's eyes had gone wide with surprise, then narrow with thought. "He worked at the embassy. He died in a street mugging a couple weeks, maybe ten days ago? Paul came home and told me all about it. Everyone was in such shock. I still can't believe it. Paris seems so safe!" She looked at all of us. "Why?"

I had been taken a little off guard by Oncle Rafe's question, but it wasn't surprising Julia knew about Arthur Coleman—especially since he'd been killed. That was the sort of gossip that spread like wildfire, even in a large, complicated entity like the embassy. Besides, obviously Paul knew him, as he had given Mr. Coleman my name as a French tutor.

"Arthur Coleman wasn't killed during a mugging," I explained. "He was the man who was shot at Thérèse Lognon's other apartment. Quite probably by Thérèse herself."

Julia gaped at me. And then she said a very vulgar word.

I nodded in sympathy. "I know. It's hard to believe." I explained what we knew. "But what was his connection to Thérèse Lognon? Do you know what Mr. Coleman did at the embassy? And why would the embassy put out the word that he'd been shot during a mugging?"

"Well, he didn't work closely with Paul, I know that. He was in a completely different department. He was a consular officer, helping American citizens who are here or want to come here with their passports and travel and visas and all of that."

So what would a consular official have to do with Thérèse Lognon? And did it mean anything that Thérèse had listed Thad's name and his city after it? And that she'd had *my* name and address written down, along with the same notation of *Detroit*?

"Maybe Thérèse wanted to come to the U.S.," I said. "And he was helping her. And maybe she was considering moving to Detroit." I felt as if a light bulb had just switched on. "And *maybe* that was why she had my name and address in her pocket—she wanted to talk to me about living in Detroit. Dort probably mentioned to her that's where I'm from, or someone did, and gave her my information. Maybe it was even Arthur Coleman who gave her the note I'd written out."

It made sense. For the first time, *something* made sense.

But there was still something else niggling at me. Why didn't Thérèse just talk to Thad about Detroit, since he was from there as well?

If I'd known Thad was from Detroit, I probably would have talked to him at Dort's party. There was nothing like a shared common interest like Faygo pop—especially a love for Rock & Rye—to spur small talk. I thought it was amusing that he thought of the Boblo Island amusement park as Bois Blanc Island. No one called it by its formal name.

Maybe Thérèse didn't like Thad or had been nervous around him. Hadn't Johnny said something about Thérèse rejecting someone? Maybe it had been Thad.

"That makes a lot of sense . . . except, oh, why would she kill Arthur Coleman if he was helping her?" asked Julia.

That was a question I had no answer for.

"Ah, but you forget *l'affaire de coeur*," said Grand-père, raising a gnarled finger. "There is always ample reason for anger and fury when love—or sex—is involved."

"If Arthur Coleman was having an affair with Thérèse Lognon, and the embassy knew, maybe that's why they put out the story that he was killed during a mugging. To protect Mrs. Coleman from the embarrassment and publicity," I said. I couldn't help but think of Mr. Hayes and the woman I'd seen with him at the theater. "Thérèse was a very attractive woman."

"And something went wrong with the affair and so she killed him? Thérèse, I mean," said Julia. She sounded skeptical. "And then she moved?"

"Maybe *she* wanted to break it off, and he was angry about it and attacked her and she defended herself," I said. For some reason, I didn't want to think of Thérèse as a cold-blooded killer. Which was silly, as I hadn't known her at all. But it was that grim, grimy, bleak apartment that made me sympathize with her—besides the fact that she had been killed.

"Dort said she'd broken up with someone just a few weeks ago, and she'd seemed tense and upset about it. But then again, if she'd simply been defending herself and now the threat was gone, why move?" I said.

"She was frightened," announced Oncle Rafe. "Surely that was it. She was frightened over something and wanted to go into hiding."

I nodded. That did seem the best explanation.

"Well, that is all quite interesting," Julia said. "I'll ask Paul if he knows anything else about Arthur Coleman." She rose. "I've got to get back. Oh, Dort sent this for you, Tabs." She dug into her coat pocket and produced a ring of three keys. "To the theater. You can get your gloves. The show is definitely canceled, so no one will be there."

I didn't hesitate taking the keys at all. "Thank you."

"I want to know if you come across any more dead bodies,

Tabs," she said, giving me a hug, then smacking a kiss on each cheek. "Right away. Even if it's two in the morning."

"Will do," I said, and gathered up my coat. "I'm going to walk Julia out and then I'm going over to the theater to see if I can find my gloves," I told my messieurs.

To my relief, they didn't try to talk me out of it.

Less than five minutes later, I was climbing into a taxi. "Place Pigalle," I told the driver, and settled back into the seat.

The mystery of La Sol would soon be solved.

CHAPTER 17

*T*he mystery of La Sol turned out to mostly be a bust.

I don't know why I thought going to the place, seeking it out and looking at it—even going inside—would help solve the mystery of who'd killed Thérèse and Johnny.

Actually, I do know why I expected that. I'd been spoiled by reading so many mystery novels where that sort of thing would happen to the main character. Follow a clue, follow a trail, solve the crime—or at least come a lot closer to doing so.

But in this situation, La Sol was a big, fat letdown.

The place was nothing more than a shabby-looking night-club. The brightest part about the place had to be the happy yellow matchbook covers that kept popping up in this murder investigation. Even the hanging sign for La Sol was a dingy, weathered yellow. The single front window probably hadn't been washed since the Occupation, and when I peered through it with cupped hands, I could make out only a smattering of tables inside through the dirt and grime.

It was too early in the day for the club to be open for customers, but when my curiosity prodded me, I pushed on the door. It slid ajar.

I went inside, stepping gingerly in case someone accosted me and wanted to know what I was doing there. It was marginally warmer inside than in the breezy wintry chill.

It was dim and shadowy inside with the only illumination

from a few wall sconces with meek bulbs. The place smelled like stale beer and wine, cheap perfume, and smoke. Lots of smoke, as if a cloud of it hung permanently in the room even when no one was there.

And something else . . .

I sniffed. It was the same weird, almost sweet, fermenting smell I'd noticed in Thérèse's apartment after the intruder left.

I still couldn't place what it was, but at least I'd identified the source.

A folding chalkboard sign was just inside the door, probably to be placed on the sidewalk at opening. Someone had written: *TONIGHT: Cherise LaCorte.* Someone else had drawn a vulgar picture in the corner that didn't appear to refer to Cherise—at least, not if she were a woman.

The round tables were tiny and crammed together. I couldn't imagine how servers made their way between them, especially without spilling drinks. There was a counter that ran along one side of the place where the bartender poured drinks and filled small bowls with peanuts or popcorn. From the look of the bottles stacked on shelves behind it, they also poured a lot of cheap wine and vodka.

The stage was the size of a postage stamp, and it was a single step up from the ground. You'd have to be either very close or very tall to see what was happening below the shoulders of anyone on that stage.

"Bonjour, mademoiselle," a voice rang out cheerily.

Ahh, the French proprietor. Always with the polite and sunny greeting, even for the interloper.

I turned to see a tall, very, *very* skinny man standing behind the bar counter. He must have been crouched down behind it when I came in, or maybe he was just so thin I hadn't noticed him at first. It looked like he was stacking glasses on the shelves.

I returned his greeting and threaded my way through the kaleidoscope of tables and chairs to the bar. I had no idea what I thought I could do or say that might produce that great revelation or realization I was hoping for, but I was going to try.

"We're not open, mademoiselle," said the man. "Come back at seven."

"I'm sorry. The door was open and I wanted to see what this place was," I replied. "Some, uh, friends of mine come here."

"Yes, well, we're not open until seven," he said a lot more firmly this time.

I noticed a strange-looking device that resembled a tall vase. It had a little hose-like tube coming out of the top. It reminded me of something I'd seen in an *Alice in Wonderland* illustration where the caterpillar had been smoking on it. That strange smell seemed to be coming from the weird vase-like thing. "What's that?" I asked.

The man behind the counter glared at me. "Hookah."

I wanted to ask more, but he didn't seem likely to answer. "Um . . . is there any chance I could buy a Coke?" I asked, figuring if I were a paying customer he might be more forthcoming.

"We don't sell that poison here," he replied snappishly.

Ooops. "Right. Sorry. Do you, uh, work here every night?" I asked.

"Every damned night," he replied. "For twenty-two years."

"Then you probably know everyone who comes in here," I said, giving him a friendly and, I hoped, encouraging smile.

"No," he said shortly. "They all look the same to me. Don't know anyone. Don't care to know 'em. Just serve their drinks and take their money."

Right.

"I guess a lot of Americans come in here," I said.

"Wouldn't know. We don't open until seven," he said, this time lifting his brows and looking pointedly toward the door.

"All right," I said. "I'm sorry to bother you."

Thus abruptly ended my exploration of La Sol. I had barely stepped back out onto the sidewalk, the door just closing behind me, when I heard the click of the lock.

Well, I thought, if I wanted to find out more about the place— although what I might discover that was important I didn't know— I'd have to come back after seven.

Maybe Mark would want to come.

I was startled to realize that I actually liked the idea of sitting at a little table with him and watching some women do the can-can or whatever sort of dancing they did at La Sol.

Of course, technically he was still a suspect, so that might not be a good idea.

But I couldn't imagine why Mark would want to kill Thérèse—or Johnny for that matter.

The problem was, I couldn't think of any reason any of the suspects would have wanted to do so. To paraphrase Oncle Rafe, I was very thin on motive.

It was a lot harder being an amateur detective than I'd imagined.

I sighed and pulled my coat tighter. It was cold and the wind had picked up, but even so, I suddenly had a taste for a pop.

I walked down the *rue* looking for a taxi and passed a curious building on the corner boasting a large red windmill. MOULIN ROUGE, said the sign, and it was apparently a cabaret of some sort. It, too, was closed in the middle of the day, or I might have gone inside just because of that windmill.

After walking another block, I found a little café that had Coca-Cola for sale (sadly, there was no Faygo), and I bought a bottle to take with me. When I came out, guzzling the drink, I was finally able to flag down a taxi.

I almost gave the cabbie the address to the 36, for I planned to take the Russian note to Inspecteur Merveille. But at the last second, I decided to go to the theater first.

I was already here on the Right Bank, and since I'd struck out at La Sol, I wanted to take the opportunity to look at coat number 35. And if I learned anything, that would be even more information I could give Merveille.

Besides, it was the perfect time to go to the theater. No one would be there, unless Merveille and his people were looking for clues as to who'd killed Johnny.

I knew from my father that the detective often returned to the scene of a crime more than once—not only looking for clues but also in an attempt to absorb the environment, to picture what had happened and how. Maybe something would strike me, too, while I was there.

Whoever killed Johnny had to have done it when no one was around in the back alley, obviously, but it must have been a fairly small window of time between everyone clearing out of the backstage area and Mark and me being the last people coming out to leave.

Mark had actually been looking for Johnny, I remembered. He'd said the stage manager wanted to talk to him.

A shiver of realization took me by surprise. Johnny had wanted to talk to Mark and now he was dead. He must have known something about Thérèse.

Why had he wanted to talk to Mark about it? To compare notes? To ask a question? To *accuse?*

Had someone else overheard Johnny tell Mark he needed to talk to him, and guessed why—and that was what prompted the killer to shoot him?

What a big chance the murderer took—both times. First, to sneak out of the Childs' apartment, stab Thérèse, and then return to the party . . . and then to shoot Johnny right behind the theater when anyone could have come along at any moment. Or heard the gunshot.

I hadn't heard anything that sounded like a shot, but I'd been in the front of the building—nearly as far away from the alley as possible. If Mark had heard anything, he hadn't mentioned it. But a single gunshot could have been mistaken for a car backfiring, which was a common occurrence.

I was finishing the last of my Coke when something else occurred to me. It was such a minor detail I'm not sure even to this day why it lodged in my head . . . except that it turned out to be important.

I suppose it was because I was drinking the Coke—and wishing it was Faygo Red Pop or Rock & Rye—that I thought about my conversation with Thad yesterday.

We'd been commiserating, missing our native Detroit's Faygo

pop here in France. It struck me because Thad had said, *Rock & Rye is my favorite, but I dig all their sodas,* because in Detroit and the Midwest, we called Cokes and Faygo "pop," not "soda."

People in most other areas of the country—like the West Coast, where Julia was from, and the East Coast—called fizzy beverages "soda." While people in the south near Atlanta called them all coke, even if it wasn't an actual Coca-Cola.

I probably wouldn't have thought much more about that except that I remembered Thad calling Boblo Island Bois Blanc Island.

I'd grown up in a suburb of Detroit and I'd never heard anyone refer to the little amusement park isle as anything but Boblo. And Thad had told me he'd been "born and raised" in Detroit—actually in the city. So why would he call it a name that no one ever used? Especially to me, a native?

It was weird.

I was still frowning over it when the taxi stopped in front of Théâtre Monceau. I paid the driver and climbed out.

It wasn't even two o'clock. It was also the first time I'd seen the building in the full light of day. Signs had been posted on the front doors and box office window: TONIGHT'S PERFORMANCE CANCELED.

I had three keys on the ring Dort had given me and could have let myself in through one of the public doors, but I couldn't help myself . . . I walked around to the back, to the alley. I wanted to see it in the daylight.

The alley was empty. I'd half expected to find someone from the *police judiciaire* here, but there was no sign of life. No cars, either. The entire place was, as expected, deserted.

A stain remained on the ground where Johnny had bled to death, but other than that there was no indication someone had been killed here. If I hadn't known what it was, I might have assumed it was an oil or garbage stain. I paused, looking down at the soiled ground, and wished Johnny Godspeed. I couldn't remember if I'd done so last night; I'd been so shocked and horrified.

The second key I tried let me in through the alley door, and I found myself once more in the dark and shadowy backstage area. I fumbled for a light switch, wishing yet again for a small flashlight.

The single, naked bulb that came on illuminated my way only a few steps, but I remembered where the stage manager's station was. I knew there was a flashlight there because I'd knocked it over last night when I called the police.

I managed to navigate myself there and get the flashlight with only one bump to the shoulder and one stub of the toe. Using the flash would be easier than trying to find lights all the way through the maze of backstage to the front of house.

I shined the light around. Everything was so still and shadowy. And silent. Dead silent.

My skin prickling, I made my way out of the backstage area and to the front of house. Even on the street-facing side, I couldn't hear the sounds of car engines or horns through the thick stone walls. The silence was so absolute it was eerie.

The coat room was locked; I hadn't thought about that. I had left my keys to the coatroom in Dort's office as instructed. But one of the keys on the ring she'd given me worked to open it.

I went inside but left the door to the gallery open. There weren't any windows to let sunlight into the theater, even along the gallery, and shutting the door made the coatroom feel too close and uncomfortable. Closed in.

The racks were mostly empty. There were only four coats still hanging way in the back beneath a little sign that said, LOST & FOUND.

One of the coats was number 35. It was tucked in behind the other abandoned items and was the only one with a coat check tag. I almost missed it because a thick scarf had been wrapped around the hanger, hiding the tag.

I got the impression someone had been trying to camouflage it—or the coat itself.

Strangely enough, it was a man's overcoat, not a woman's, as I had anticipated. When I matched the tag on the hanger to the claim check that had been in Thérèse's purse, I noticed that the tag had an extra hole punch in it.

I frowned a little. That was weird. I'd had a few customers who'd also made an extra punch in their tags for any number of reasons: Ineptitude? Nerves? Haste?

It probably meant nothing, but I still noticed it, and it still made me wonder.

The coat on number 35 was nothing exceptional: a regular wool overcoat any man might wear. It wasn't particularly fine or expensive, but it was also fashionable and heavyweight. It wasn't worn or dirty; the buttons were tight, the hem wasn't sagging.

In other words, it was a nice enough coat that the owner should have been missing it.

Why had Thérèse had the claim check ticket for a man's coat in her purse?

I dug through the pockets, hoping to find an identification card or wallet that might give a clue as to whose coat this was.

The first thing I pulled from the breast pocket was a business card. I shined my light on it and gasped when I read the name on it. *Arthur Coleman* and the address was the U.S. Embassy.

That could *not* be a coincidence. *Crap*, I thought. *Crap*.

The question was . . . did the coat belong to Mr. Coleman or someone who simply had his card in the breast pocket of his coat, like Thérèse had had my information in hers?

I dug through the other pockets. There was nothing in the outside ones except a pair of gloves that Arthur Coleman wouldn't be needing anymore.

But when I felt something through the padding, I opened the coat and checked the inside pocket . . .

And pulled out a thick wad of cash.

I gawked at the stack of bills—all American fifties, held in place with a rubber band. I'd never seen that much money in one place before. I counted them with trembling hands and realized I was holding a thousand dollars.

A thousand dollars.

And this pack of money had been sitting here in the coat check room for at least a week or two. The fact that it was American money and not francs was also curious.

Did Thérèse know? Surely she'd known; she had the claim ticket, and who else would have buried the coat way in the back so it wasn't noticed? Obviously, the coat check girl.

It reminded me of "The Purloined Letter": hidden in plain sight.

Was this why she'd been killed? But why had she left the money here for so long? To keep it safe and handy, or to hide it from someone?

It seemed she'd had a lot to hide—she'd even hidden *herself* in a new apartment. Oncle Rafe was right: Thérèse had been very afraid of someone.

My head was spinning. Nothing made any sense. I didn't even know if the money had belonged to Arthur Coleman or someone else.

With this in mind, I turned back to the coat once more. Maybe there was something else that would tell me whom it belonged to. A name inked on the tag would be too schoolboyish for a grown man—not to mention convenient for me—but maybe there was something else . . .

I felt around on the other side of the coat, the opposite side from the inner pocket where I'd found the cash. And I felt something.

Whatever it was was sewn inside the lining, near the hem. And there was more than one of whatever it was. I pulled out my Swiss Army knife and used its tiny scissors to snip the threads and open up the lining.

Then I started pulling out the things that were inside . . . small, booklet-like items that were tucked in all around the hem.

I swore under my breath when I realized what they were: United States passports. A dozen of them. All in different names with different photos. Some men, some women. Even a five-year-old girl. A ten-year-old boy. Rubber-banded to each passport was a corresponding driver's license, social security card, and birth certificate.

I looked through one of the packets to make sure I really saw what I thought I was seeing.

Mr. Darin Cooke of St. Louis, Missouri, had been born in Houston in 1919. He had a driver's license from the state of Missouri and his social security card looked suspiciously new and fresh for him having owned it for more than ten years.

I realized my hands were shaking when the passport slipped out of my grip and everything fell to the floor.

This was something really big.

I wasn't certain what it all meant, but what was clear, however, was that each group of documents were the complete setup for an identity in America. And there were twelve of them. Three had matching addresses and last names, and were for a husband and wife with a five-year-old daughter. There were others that had the same last name—married couples or an older man and a younger man who might be a father and son.

On a hunch, I looked through the passports again more closely, but none of them were for a woman who looked like Thérèse.

Now I was even more mystified, but I also had more theories. Maybe she'd been selling these sets of documents to people who wanted to live in the States. Maybe that was what all the money was from. She'd sold some of her supply, but not all of it. . . .

And maybe she'd been getting the product from Arthur Coleman, who, by working at the U.S. Embassy in citizenship services could have his hands on all sorts of official documentation like passports and birth certificates. No one would think twice if he ordered a replacement passport for an American who'd had theirs stolen.

And maybe his murder had been from a deal gone wrong.

Things were almost starting to make sense.

I tried to remember the photograph in Inspecteur Merveille's office of the deceased Mr. Coleman . . . Had he been wearing an overcoat when he was found on the stairs? If not, then this could be his coat. It made sense—if Thérèse killed him, then she could also take his coat. She must have known what was hidden inside it . . . unless she'd sewn the documents into the lining herself.

I saw no signs of bloodstains. If it was his, Coleman hadn't been wearing the coat when he was shot.

But try as I might, I couldn't remember that detail from the photograph.

I needed to call Merveille and tell him about all of this . . . including the Russian note that had fallen out of Thérèse's book.

I stilled. The Russian note had Neil's name on it, and Thad's . . . and the notation of *Detroit* was next to Thad's name.

And Thérèse had had my contact information in her pocket when she was killed.

I'd thought maybe she wanted to talk to me about moving to Detroit . . . but what if . . .

I felt prickles suddenly erupt all over my body, and I went cold and clammy at the same time as the thoughts began to slip into place like little cogs.

What if she wanted to ask me about Detroit for another reason . . . because someone else she knew was from there—or *said* he was from there . . . and she had reason not to believe him.

Whoa.

I felt as if a ton of bricks had just been dumped on me.

Was Thad lying about being from Detroit? If so, why?

And why would Thérèse care?

And did it have anything to do with fake U.S. identification packets?

By now I was feeling pretty jittery. I needed to talk to Merveille right away.

I started to leave, thinking I'd call him from the stage manager's desk or even Dort's office, but then I hesitated.

I didn't want to leave everything out like this, and I didn't want to take it with me. A thousand dollars in cash was a lot to carry around. I began to stuff everything back into the coat the way I'd found it, telling myself it had been safely hidden there for weeks; it could stay there a little longer.

I put the coat back exactly the way I'd found it—way in the back, tucked behind the others. I started to wind the scarf back around the hanger to hide the ticket, then in the last instant, I pulled off the ticket and—in a moment of brilliance—I put the ticket on a different hanger with a different coat and moved the decoy coat to a different rack, away from the lost and found. If someone was looking for number 35, they wouldn't get near the real coat.

Even though no one knew I had a claim check ticket from Thérèse's purse, I thought one can never be too careful. There was something very funny going on, and though I hadn't completely figured out what it was, I was certain that the key was somehow in this coat check room . . . and possibly involved Thad Whiting.

I wondered if I should go a step further and move the money and documents and hide them somewhere else—like Dort's office—and lock the door.

I was still mulling that option when I heard a noise.

The sound was in the distance, and it wasn't necessarily alarming in and of itself . . . but there'd been an intense, dead silence since I'd arrived at the theater, so any noise was jarring.

Cautiously, I came out of the coat check room and closed the door silently behind me. I turned off the flashlight and listened.

Yes. There it came again—the quiet bump of someone moving about. Someone was definitely here.

It could be anyone.

There could be any number of people here for any number of reasons.

It didn't have to be the murderer.

But it was really difficult to get myself to believe that, considering what I'd just discovered in the coat check room . . . not to mention that the last time I was here, I'd found a dead body in the alley.

And the fact that I devoured crime novels where the protagonist was always being caught alone somewhere by the killer.

I froze and waited, listening to my breathing, and listening for something else.

I was thankful I'd dithered over what to do with the things in the coat, because if I'd been more decisive, I might have already been in the backstage area, announcing my presence by flashlight, footsteps, and telephone call when whoever it was came in. Now, I was on the other side of the building, and there was no reason for anyone to know someone else was even here. . . .

Except that I'd left the back door unlocked and the light on.

My stomach did a slow, ugly roll. If someone was smart, they'd figure out I was here.

I decided my best option was to just wait and see what happened.

I could have stayed in the coat room, in the shadows. But if I was correct that the key to whatever was going on was in the coat room, I didn't think I wanted to be found in there—in a place where I could be trapped.

There was only one door to the room.

Even so, I told myself there was no earthly reason that whoever was here in the theater had anything to do with what was going on with Thérèse, but I didn't believe it.

My skin was prickling everywhere—as if my intuition was telling me I was right—and my heart was thudding.

I should have left right then. I should have let myself out the front door and gone to the closest police station and called Merveille.

But I was curious.

Moving very slowly, very quietly, I gripped the heavy flashlight—a solid weapon, should I need it—and made my way toward the hallway that the cast and crew used to travel between the front and backstage area.

Whoever was here had obviously entered through the alley door, and I could see faint illumination spilling from the opposite end of the hall. It was probably Maribelle, I told myself, checking things out since the theater was closed and the police were gone.

But then I heard voices. They were arguing, and the sound echoed in the vast, high-ceilinged backstage area, bounced around, and filtered down the hall toward me.

That's when I realized they were speaking in Russian.

CHAPTER 18

Maybe it was because it was a different language that kept me from recognizing the voices right away, even though I strained and listened as hard as I could.

They were both male and seemed to feel no need to speak in hushed tones—which I suppose boded well for me, for they must assume they were here alone.

I'm not sure why I crept closer—I wouldn't be able to understand what they were talking about, no matter how close I got. But I wanted to see who it was.

By that time, it seemed obvious to me that Thad Whiting was involved in some way in Thérèse's murder. It was the other person I was also hoping to identify.

I was at one end of the corridor that led from the backstage area to the front of house, where the box office, lounges, bar, and coat room were. There were several offices along one side of the hallway—including Dort's—and on the opposite was a single door that led into the side of the auditorium. It was very dark except for the bit of light spilling from the backstage, and I thought I might be able to get to Dort's office, and the telephone, while the two men were otherwise distracted. At least I could leave word for Inspecteur Merveille.

Listening carefully to make certain they weren't coming toward me, I made myself wait for a few moments. When it seemed the voices weren't moving, I took a deep breath and dashed silently down the hall. I ran on tiptoes with my ears tuned in to the conversation and noticed that it seemed to be getting more intense and argumentative by the moment.

That was good—they were concentrating on each other, not listening for me.

I made it to Dort's office and prayed that the third key on the ring would open the door. With one ear cocked toward the other end of the hall, I fumbled in the shadows to fit the key into the lock. I couldn't see what I was doing and I was so jittery that I couldn't find the keyhole with the metal tip of the key.

Finally, I took a chance and huddled into the recessed doorway as far as I could. Gripping the key ring between my teeth, I held the flashlight by cupping my hand over the front of it to block the light. I was able to turn it on with my free hand, then take up the keys.

I spread my fingers over the front of the flash to allow just enough light so I could see the keyhole.

It took two tries before I found the correct key, and by then sweat was dripping down my spine and my fingers were getting tired. All the while, I listened to make certain no one was coming this way.

When I finally turned the key and I heard the quiet *snick* of the lock opening, I heaved a sigh of relief. But then I lost my grip on the flashlight and it fumbled out of my hands. I barely managed to catch it before it clunked to the floor.

Breathing heavily with relief and clammy everywhere with sweat, I slipped into Dort's office and shut the door behind me. I bumped into a chair on the way to the desk—it was very dark in there—but even to my straining ears, the noise wasn't very loud.

I managed to find the telephone without further incident and dialed the operator. Ducking to the floor, I brought the receiver with me and huddled in the kneehole of the desk, facing away from the door, while I made my call.

I spoke in a quiet but clear voice, stating my name and asking for Inspecteur Merveille. I wasn't surprised to learn he wasn't in the office, so once again I left word for him to come to Théâtre Monceau.

When I hung up the phone, I felt a rush of relief. It might take a while for him to get the message, but eventually he'd arrive.

I told myself I should stay in the office.

Or I could go back to the front of the building and let myself out that way.

Or, my internal sprite reminded me, I could sneak down the hall and try to find out who was speaking in Russian backstage. I would be very, very careful. And very, very quiet.

I replaced the phone and tiptoed back to the door, trying to convince myself it was the best thing to just stay put. But next thing I knew, I was opening the door and peering around the edge.

I could still hear voices, but they sounded calmer. They hadn't seemed to move from the backstage. If anything, they were farther away.

I slipped out of the office and silently closed the door behind me. I still had the flashlight in my hand, but I didn't turn it on as I crept down the shadowy hallway. My heart thudded in my ears, and my palms were slick so I tightened my grip on the flashlight.

As I drew closer, the voices became more distinct. They were no longer speaking in Russian and had moved on to English. And there was a third voice now.

I was pretty sure it was a woman.

That had me stopping in surprise. Now I was *really* curious.

I was about halfway down the hall, but with the light spilling from the direction I was going, I wasn't certain how much closer I could get without being seen. Besides that, I kept getting turned around backstage and I didn't want to get lost, or trapped back there with a murderer . . . or two.

Instead, I darted across the hall to the door that led inside the auditorium. Holding my breath, I pushed down the handle and cracked the door open just a little. The hinges made no sound— not a surprise; creaky doors didn't make for a good theatrical experience—and the space beyond was pitch-black.

Perfect. I slipped through the opening and, keeping close to the wall, I began to make my way down the aisle that ran along the side of the auditorium from the rear seats to the orchestra. It was so dark I could barely make out the shapes of the stage set, but I could see a little glow of light from the wings. I couldn't hear anything more than a rumble of voices until I got to the edge of the stage.

Now I had a decision to make. I could either climb onto the stage and try to creep behind it to spy on the intruders, or I could stay put.

Of course I wasn't going to stay put.

I'd come this far, and the darkness and shadows were on my side—and I was dying to find out who was speaking. Especially the woman, as I'd had no females on my suspects list.

It occurred to me, as I edged toward the stairs on the right side of the stage, that the most likely person was Maribelle—the troupe owner and manager. But for all I knew it could be any of the female actors, or, really, anyone at all.

Keeping low, I crept up the steps on the right, grateful that there were no creaky floors to announce my presence. A pitch-dark, well-maintained theater was a definite boon to a nosy amateur gumshoe like me. As I moved slightly upstage, staying to the right, the voices became more distinct.

Now that they were speaking in English, I knew it would be easier to recognize their voices.

I still didn't have any real proof that Thérèse's and Johnny's killer was here . . . except for the fact that they'd been speaking Russian—which certainly wasn't a crime in and of itself. But I had a feeling my assumptions were right.

I was close enough that I could make out snatches of conversation.

"She *didn't*," said a male voice. I recognized it immediately—it was Thad Whiting. "I talked to her and—"

"You don't know for certain," snapped the woman. The voice did sound familiar to me, but I couldn't place her.

"There's no reason to abort the plan," argued Thad. He sounded desperate. "I've got my tickets—"

"It's too risky," she replied flatly. It was obvious the woman was in charge. "We don't know if she told anyone."

I frowned. I definitely knew that woman's voice. I needed to get closer so I could see who it was.

As most theatrical stages did, this one had the main red velvet curtains that opened and closed in the front, hiding or revealing the entire set. But there were also two rows of black curtains on each side, extending into the wings on a slight angle so that players waiting for their cue could stand just offstage but not be seen by the audience. It was the nearest of these black curtains on the right side that was my destination.

Taking a deep breath, I darted from the front edge of the stage to the closest side curtain, taking care not to touch it and cause ripples that would announce my presence. Fortunately, it was made from heavy material that would resist moving with any shift in the air or slight touch.

My heart thudded as I waited, trying to keep my breathing as quiet and slow as possible.

It took a moment for the nervous roaring in my ears to subside so I could hear the trio speaking again.

"Did you find them yet?" The woman was speaking in a demanding tone and a little prickle went down my spine. *Why couldn't I place her voice?*

I was so close, I could probably peek around the edge of the curtain to see . . .

"Dammit, I've looked everywhere, Rebecca. If Thérèse had them, she hid them well."

My entire body went ice-cold.

I recognized that voice.

It was Mark Justiss.

CHAPTER 19

I barely held back a gasp. My head went dizzy, and that roaring came back, filling my ears.

I couldn't believe it. Mark was involved in this . . . whatever it was . . .

Selling false American identification sets?

And . . . he'd been speaking Russian? He and Thad.

Are they Russian spies?

"We've got to find them," replied the woman, whom Mark had called Rebecca. "Now that Arthur's dead, everything is on hold until we locate the documents."

And that's when her voice clicked into place. It was *Rebecca Hayes* standing there, speaking with Thad and Mark. My student's mother, and the wife of the man I'd seen here at the theater with—I thought—another woman.

To say I was flabbergasted was an understatement.

Mark and Mrs. Hayes not only knew each other, but were working together? Not only that, they'd been working with Arthur Coleman too.

I had to get to a place where I could see them, watch them. I had to get a look to make certain what I thought I was hearing was real.

"Did you search the coat room? She spent a lot of time there— ha, ha." Mrs. Hayes didn't sound amused. "Did you look there?"

"I didn't have the chance to do a thorough check," replied

Mark. "Tabitha didn't want to watch the play, and I could only get rid of her for a few minutes at a time. I had to use that time to place the messages."

"Tabitha Knight. How did she end up involved anyhow?" said Mrs. Hayes. I didn't like the way she said my name. It made the hair on the back of my neck prickle.

"She's only helping out Dort," Mark said. "She's not involved."

"You don't think so?" replied Mrs. Hayes in a tone that told me exactly what she thought about me. "I wouldn't be so certain of that. She asked me about La Sol. She's snooping around."

"La Sol? That's nothing," Mark said, clearly brushing off her concern. "There's no connection to what we're doing. Neil goes there, too, and so do some of the other—"

"The fact remains," Mrs. Hayes went on in a clipped, furious voice, "*you've* jeopardized everything by your rash actions. We've got the *police judiciaire* sniffing around here, and *this* one"—I couldn't see, but I somehow knew she was gesturing to Thad—"has to have his entire mission suspended, or even canceled—"

"No, no," said Thad quickly. "Not *canceled*. I can get a new identity—"

"And how are you going to do *that* with Arthur gone?" snapped Mrs. Hayes. "And that Tabitha Knight chatting you up, asking all sorts of questions? She knows Paul Child, and believe me, *he* knows people. Do either of you *think*?"

"Rebecca, darling," said Mark in a cajoling voice that told me they were more than simply coconspirators. "Please don't worry. It's going to be all right. No one has any idea what's been going on here.

"Even Maribelle and Dort—all of it has been going on right under their very noses for months now, and they know bupkis. Tabitha's a lot smarter than Thérèse, but even she doesn't have the first clue what's been going on in that coat room, and I don't see her being back here when the theater reopens. She was just helping out."

"I think I fooled Tabitha," said Thad. He sounded a little anxious to me. "If I can fool her, then I can fool anyone, don't you think?"

"Thérèse must have had her suspicions about you. *That's* why she wanted to talk to Tabitha," said Rebecca suddenly. "She wasn't sure who was involved, and she suspected you. She was going to blow everything wide open—"

"And that's why I had to take care of her." The tone of Mark's voice chilled me. "Yes. She made a comment that night at Dort's and said, 'People are not always what they seem.' She was looking right at me. I knew she knew, and I sure as hell wasn't going to let her give everything away."

Up until that moment, I hadn't allowed myself to believe that Mark had done anything *really* wrong. He'd even defended me. But hearing the admission in his own words, his own voice . . .

I felt sick to my stomach. To think I'd actually been considering kissing him. A killer.

"But did you have to do it *there?* So that you practically put your name up in neon lights? And—what was his name? The other one," Mrs. Hayes said. She sounded furious.

"Johnny."

"Yes, him. What on earth possessed you to do it *here?* Wasn't it enough that that *inspecteur* was nosing around after you took care of Thérèse?"

"I'm not worried about the *inspecteur*," said Mark in a dismissive voice. "That frog doesn't know his head from his arse as far as I'm concerned."

"I wouldn't be so certain about that. He came around to our house yesterday and started asking questions," Mrs. Hayes said. "Questions about Arthur Coleman. Now how did he connect Coleman to Thérèse if he's so incompetent?"

During this fascinating, enlightening—and, yes, frightening—exchange, I'd been working my way along the black curtain. Taking care not to make it flutter, I got to the end and, thankful for the shadows that still gave me a dark and heavy cover, I peered around the edge of the curtain.

My heart surged when I realized they were closer than I'd realized—though they were still far enough away that I wasn't in great danger of being seen.

The three of them were clustered in a little knot next to the stage manager's desk, where a small, shaded lamp had been turned on. It gave off just enough light to see Mrs. Hayes's face. Mark and Thad were standing with their backs to me, but I recognized their fair heads and the disparity in their builds: Mark's broader shoulders and Thad's skinnier form.

Mrs. Hayes was dressed as smartly and fashionably as she'd been every time I'd seen her—from her cornflower-blue hat to matching gloves to matching purse, perfectly smooth and coiffed hair, and an A-line cut winter coat in a crisp navy. She looked like a very proper society wife, not a killer.

"Arthur's body was found near Thérèse's apartment," replied Mark. "Not a great leap to connect them."

"That's not enough to make a connection. People get mugged on the street all the time and it has nothing to do with anyone living nearby. Besides, Thérèse wasn't even home when he was killed," Mrs. Hayes said.

"Or so everyone believes," replied Mark dryly. "Have to give her credit for fixing up that alibi at least."

Mrs. Hayes scoffed and waved her hand.

"Surely the *inspecteur* is just grasping at straws," said Thad. Now that I knew he spoke Russian, I realized he had a little bit of an accent. It was hardly noticeable unless you knew what to listen for, but now I could hear it and I wondered how I'd missed it before. Or maybe it was just because he was nervous that it had become more apparent. "He can't have put it together that easily."

"She killed Arthur because he couldn't keep his pants zipped and his mouth shut," snapped Mrs. Hayes. "And she tried to make it look like a mugging. Even an idiot could make the connection." She sighed and smoothed a hand over a wing of hair that brushed her chin. "It's time to clean up all the loose ends."

I didn't like the way that sounded.

"Loose ends?" asked Mark.

"Anyone who's been compromised," replied Mrs. Hayes, slipping a hand into her purse. "Or who's drawn any attention. Including my beloved husband. But we'll do it my way this time—not your haphazard, bloody, messy way. Then we're going to have to move our operations to another location."

"Fine, fine," said Mark, holding up his hands. "You're right. We've got to move on."

"Exactly." Mrs. Hayes looked as if she was about to say something, then she froze. "What was that?" She peered into the darkness, her face intent and set.

My heart dropped to my belly. Had she seen me? But she wasn't looking in my direction . . . her attention was over a little ways.

"I didn't hear anything," said Thad. He turned, scanning the shadows. I closed my eyes—as if doing so would keep anyone from seeing me—and remained statue-still.

"Over there. Mark, Thad . . ." Mrs. Hayes sounded urgent and nervous. I opened my eyes, wondering what she was seeing. "In the corner. I thought I heard . . ."

Eager to please, Thad took a few steps toward the shadows. "Where? I—"

It happened so quickly.

Mrs. Hayes wrenched her hand from the depths of her purse. With it came a flash of metal.

I saw the gun. It registered in my brain that it was pointing at Thad's back, and I couldn't stop myself from screaming, "Look out!"

CHAPTER 20

*T*he sound of my shout echoed, mingling with the sharp crack of the gun.

Thad jolted and tumbled to the floor—she'd been far too close to miss—but I didn't see anything else, for after an instant of paralysis, I'd turned to run across the dark stage.

But not before I saw the shocked faces of Mark and Mrs. Hayes gaping in my direction.

"Tabitha!" cried Mark. "Is that you?"

I heard footsteps pounding after me—men's shoes, not the pumps Mrs. Hayes was wearing—and my breath clogged in my lungs as I dashed into the shadows on the left side of the stage.

It was darker here, and I huddled in a corner by the front of the stage, wondering what the *hell* I was going to do now.

Thad was surely lying there, bleeding to death. Or possibly already dead. Mrs. Hayes—I supposed I could start thinking of her as Rebecca—was still holding a gun.

And Mark was coming after me.

I had no illusions about him. He'd killed two people. No matter how nice and boy-next-door he'd seemed, no matter how sweet he'd been driving me to and from the theater, no matter how jokingly self-deprecating he'd been . . . he wasn't going to let me live.

Very ironic, considering he was a doctor. Or so he said.

"Tabitha, it's all right. Come on out," he said in a wheedling voice.

As if that would work on me. I rolled my eyes even as I realized my fingers were shaking. But I still gripped the flashlight, and its weight felt comforting in my hand. My knee was twingeing quite a bit, but I couldn't let that slow me down.

"Turn on some damned lights," Rebecca snapped. I heard her no-nonsense, heeled footsteps clicking around in the dark. "Mark, we need lights. There's too many places for her to hide back here. *How* did this happen? Have you been sleeping with her too?" Her voice was high and tight, almost like a shriek . . . but beneath it, I heard murder.

I shivered and edged farther away from the stage. I wondered if Betty had any idea who her mother really was.

Suddenly, a circle of light burst into the darkness—much too close for comfort.

"He's bleeding all over the damned floor," Mark said from the other side of the stage. Another light exploded, this one upstage from me. "Talk about *rash actions*! What were you thinking, doing that here?"

"Don't worry about it—I've got a plan. But you need to find that bitch *now*!"

My heart was in my throat as I huddled in the darkness, somewhere on the left side of the stage. My thoughts ping-ponged around: do I move, do I stay here, do I run, where do I go, which direction, ohmygod she shot Thad, ohmygod *she's got a gun.*

I could hear Mark coming in my direction. He wasn't waiting for Rebecca to find the lights.

"It's all right, Tabitha," he said in a low, calm voice. "Nobody's going to hurt you. I promise."

I rolled my eyes there in the darkness. Did the man think I was born yesterday? Rebecca had been talking about loose ends. I was certain I qualified.

Another light popped on, but it was far upstage from where I hid. It was a good thing Rebecca was turning on the lights; she had no idea what she was doing.

But I couldn't just stay here, hoping it would remain dark around me. I had to do something decisive. I had to get out of the theater.

I should have left when I had the chance . . . but if I had, I wouldn't know everything I now knew.

I just hoped I lived to tell someone about it. And to find out what was wrong with Julia's mayonnaise.

Good grief. I was becoming punchy, thinking about things like mayonnaise.

There was a soft scuff on the floor and the sound yanked me back to sober reality. I could hear Mark breathing. He was getting closer. If I moved, he'd hear me and know where to go.

I tightened my fingers around the flashlight and considered my options. They were limited, but there were possibilities.

Mark was getting closer, and I was running out of time to act.

I tensed, steadied my thoughts, and braced myself . . . then I purposely bumped into the wall behind me, enough to make a sound.

It worked, and Mark lunged in my direction. It was the hardest thing I'd ever done to stand there and wait for him to get to me. But I did, and when he got close enough, I pushed the flashlight switch, aiming the light right in his face.

The shock of illumination blinded him, and I used the moment to strike out with the flashlight.

It smashed into his face and he staggered back, howling.

I ran.

I left the light on just long enough to see a path ahead of me, then I switched it back off and trusted my memory and luck to get me where I needed to go.

There were shouts and thudding feet in my wake. More lights blinked on backstage as Rebecca shrieked orders that I was pretty certain Mark was ignoring in favor of hunting me down and killing me.

I'd gotten him *right* in the face.

I had a vague idea where I was, and I knew where I wanted to go, and I ran. Mark was behind me, but I had a good head start and he didn't know where I intended to go.

Regardless, it was a miracle I made it to the back door without tripping or slamming into anything. It helped that the light was still on and when I got closer, I could see enough to run at top speed.

I rushed the door and shoved it open, surging into the alley and the waning daylight like a drowning woman surfacing.

Instead of dashing off madly down the alley, I spun back to the door and shoved it closed, dropping the flashlight, then digging into my pocket for my Swiss Army knife.

My fingers were surprisingly steady as I flipped open the corkscrew tool. I heard Mark shouting on the other side of the door and I didn't hesitate. I jammed the corkscrew under the door, the curling, pointy end first, creating a makeshift doorstop with the coil and the body of my tool knife.

When Mark slammed into the door, I felt it heave, but it barely moved in its frame, jammed in place by my knife.

I didn't know how long it would hold, but it would keep him in there for at least a few minutes—and give me a chance to put some serious space between us. Even if he ran around to the front of the theater and came out one of those doors, it would take several minutes to come back around. By then, I'd be long gone.

Just then I heard the sound of a car rumbling down the narrow alley. My heart surged as I turned to face this new potential threat . . . then I sagged against the wall with relief. And because my knees gave out.

The driver got out of the car just as another two more pulled up behind it.

"Inspecteur Merveille," I managed to say in a relatively calm voice. "What took you so long?"

CHAPTER 21

"And so the good *inspecteur*... he did not fully appreciate your assistance, *ma mie?*" Grand-père said with a smoky chuckle.

It was later that afternoon. We were sitting in the salon as usual, surrounded by coffee cups, ashtrays, and a tray of pastries. Of course Oscar Wilde and Madame X were present, ensconced on their respective master's lap.

I was still a little shaky from being chased by a killer, and I was holding a bag of ice against my protesting knee. Oncle Rafe had poured me a very generous serving of brandy, and I was enjoying it very much.

"He looked at me and said, 'Mademoiselle, as you appear to be upright and fully intact, perhaps you could explain to me what is happening there.' And he did that sort of French thing you all do—made a sort of lazy gesture toward the door. Mark Justiss was still trying to get out, so the door was kind of rattling in its frame." I took a large sip of brandy, remembering the way Merveille's steely eyes had swept over me, taking in the scene even before he spoke.

Oncle Rafe smothered a laugh, turning it into a cough as he lifted his own bulb-shaped glass of brandy. Oscar Wilde had settled quietly on his master's lap after I ignored his pleas for a treat, but the dog eyed me with his beady gaze, obviously hoping for some sort of morsel to spontaneously materialize.

"I see," said my uncle. His dark eyes danced with amusement.

"And so I'm certain you explained to him with no delay how you'd escaped certain death *and* trapped the criminals at the same time."

"Of course I did. And then he turned around and sent me home in a taxi! Back *here*—so now I know *nothing* about what's happening at the theater, and whether they caught Mark and Mrs. Hayes, and whether Thad died . . . and I still don't exactly know what was going *on* in that coat check room!"

That probably annoyed me the most.

Here I was the one who'd called Merveille to the theater, who'd given him all of the important clues—the purse, the new address, the information about La Sol (which I still wasn't certain how it connected anyway), the scoop about the *gun*—and he just sent me away.

And on top of that, I'd forgotten my Swiss Army knife!

I was still fuming, even as my messieurs made me tell them again the story about how I'd whipped Mark in the face with a flashlight, ran, then jammed the door so he couldn't come after me. They both found it wildly amusing that I'd managed to hit him in the face and then trap him inside.

"It would be quite fitting if you broke his nose," said Oncle Rafe with great relish.

"But there is little hope we'll see the damage you inflicted, *non, ma petite?*" said Grand-père sadly.

"Unless I visit him in jail," I said sourly.

When someone knocked at the door, I bolted from my chair and bounded down the stairs, ignoring the pain in my knee. But my hope that it was Merveille coming to fill in all of the details was dashed when I opened it to find Julia standing there.

"Are you all right?" She surged into the foyer, balancing a box from which emanated some incredible smells and the quiet clink of a wine bottle. "Dort got a call from Maribelle that something happened at the theater. Were you there? What happened? I brought salmon soufflé as a bribe."

I laughed and gestured her up to the salon as I went in the opposite direction to get plates.

Grand-père and Oncle Rafe were beside themselves with delight, and so was Oscar Wilde. I could hear the enthusiastic greetings—yip-yapping mingled with hearty exclamations and *ooohs* over the delicious smells—from all the way down in the kitchen, where I was loading plates, utensils, trays, and more onto the dumb waiter.

By the time I wheeled a cart into the salon, laden with the serving setups I'd extracted from the dumb waiter, the soufflé had been unveiled and was sitting like a crown jewel on the round table in the center.

I could practically hear the drooling from M. Wilde, Grand-père, Oncle Rafe, and—in a more refined manner—Madame X as they eyed the golden poof rising from its baking dish. Madame X had a particular fondness for salmon.

"Madame Child, please, allow me to open a very special vintage for this beautiful meal," said Oncle Rafe with a smile. He was holding a bottle of very expensive wine from his family's vineyard. The only time I'd ever had a bottle of it was the day I arrived in Paris. "You should sit and sip this lovely Sancerre with our compliments, and allow us to enjoy the fruits of your labor while our Tabitte explains how she bested the criminals."

Julia was delighted to take his suggestion. Having displayed her creation to its best advantage, she now settled herself on the small sofa with a healthy pour of the palest of wines in a slender glass. She poked her nose inside and sniffed, then her eyes went very wide over the top of the rim. "This is magnificent," she said in a hushed voice.

"Ah, and wait until you taste it, madame," said Oncle Rafe with a pleased smile.

As soon as we were all settled with plates of cloud-like salmon soufflé—which was topped with a *pipérade* sauce of red and green peppers and onion—three pairs of eyes focused on me and I set about retelling the tale for Julia's benefit.

"Do you think they could be Russian spies?" I said at the end, asking the question I hadn't been able to ask previously. "Thad and Mark were speaking in Russian, and there were all of those fake identification packets."

"I think that is most likely," said Grand-père. The joviality I was used to seeing in his eyes was gone and had been replaced by a serious, sober expression. "It would not surprise me if the theater—and perhaps La Sol along with it—was being used as a sort of center for communication among these—these Russian spies. They need American identification if they're to be accepted and believed as Americans, *non?*"

That all seemed likely.

"But Mark said something about the coat check room. I don't understand how that was involved—and what Thérèse had to do with it all," I said, sipping my brandy again. "He didn't know she'd hidden Arthur Coleman's coat in there."

"It's quite a mystery," said Oncle Rafe. He made a quiet sound of pleasure as he scooped up the last bite of his soufflé. "Madame Child, will you run off with me and cook for me all the days of my life?" he said, giving her an exaggerated mooning look. "I promise to treat you like the queen you are."

Julia laughed. "But of course I will, if you promise we can stay in Paris forever."

I was considering scooping up the last serving of soufflé for a second helping when I heard the door knocker.

Oscar Wilde accompanied me to the top of the stairs, but stayed up there, barking while I hurried down to see who was calling.

My heart gave a little bump when I looked through the side-light and saw Inspecteur Merveille.

"Bonjour, *monsieur le inspecteur*," I said when I opened the door.

"Bonjour, mademoiselle." He stepped inside and removed his hat, then hesitated even as M. Wilde continued his ecstatic heralding that another potential treat-giver had arrived.

I was just about to speak when Merveille said, "I wanted to make certain you were, in fact, uninjured, mademoiselle." His voice was stilted and formal. "You appeared to be, but . . . ."

"Yes," I replied, more than a little surprised. "My only injuries are from yesterday's bicycle accident."

"I understand that a cat, er, participated in that particular event," he said. We were still standing in the foyer, and M. Wilde was still barking—though not at such a loud volume.

"Apparently, when I stopped abruptly, the car that might have run me completely over merely bumped into me," I replied, feeling a little mystified by this conversation. The Inspecteur Merveille I'd experienced did not indulge in chitchat. "I saw a cat with a broken tail, you see, and I had to stop." I knew I was babbling—the *inspecteur* didn't care about the details.

"Ah, yes, the stray tiger," he replied. "We all know about him on the Île. But he's usually quite reclusive and rarely ventures across the river."

"Well, he was sitting right there on Quai de la Mégisserie when I saw him. Just before Pont au Change," I replied, mystified by the course of this conversation. "Inspecteur, may I invite you up to the salon for some salmon soufflé? Madame Child made it and it's divine. And Oncle Rafe has opened a bottle of Fautrier Sancerre."

"So it will be soufflé, a rare and excellent vintage . . . and, therefore, one must assume, answers, *non*, mademoiselle?"

If I hadn't been paying attention, I would have missed the briefest quirk of a smirk. But it was gone so quickly, I might have imagined it.

"But of course," I replied with a bright smile. "I'm not above using a little bribery to get information. Please, go on upstairs— you know the way—and I'll get a plate for you."

"That is most kind, mademoiselle," he replied with just a hint of irony.

CHAPTER 22

I was polite enough to allow the *inspecteur* to at least taste his portion of soufflé (which would have been my second helping had I not shared) and sample the Sancerre before I began bombarding him with questions.

"Is Thad Whiting dead?" was the first thing I asked.

"I am afraid so, mademoiselle. There was nothing to be done—the shot was at close hand and entered near the heart. I do not believe he suffered long, though," he added.

I nodded, grimacing. "And Rebecca Hayes and Mark Justiss are in custody?"

"Madame Hayes, of course. Docteur Justiss . . . unfortunately, he was required to go to hospital . . . but he was escorted by two of my constables and will shortly be delivered to the Préfecture. His nose had somehow been broken," said Merveille as he lifted another spoonful of soufflé. "I suppose that is only fair, considering he admitted to driving the automobile that ruined your bicycle—and very nearly yourself, mademoiselle."

"Brava!" cried Grand-père, raising his glass in an enthusiastic toast. "Brava, *ma mie!*"

Merveille gave me a look, then returned to his meal. "This is magnificent," he said, looking at Julia.

"Thank you. And I'm honored to share it with such a hardworking public servant as yourself, Inspecteur." She inclined her head regally as she spoke, then gave me an exaggerated, bawdy wink.

I knew what she was thinking and I just rolled my eyes and hid a smile. Julia had a rule for managing husbands: feed them, flatter them, and, er, fornicate with them. (She usually used a different f-word when mentioning the last item of the Rule of the Three Fs.)

Apparently, the first two Fs applied to managing police *inspecteurs* as well.

"And what about—" I began.

"Now, mademoiselle, you must know I didn't come here to be interrogated," said Merveille, setting his empty plate on the table. He'd polished that off quickly. "And you must understand that police business is not meant to be discussed with . . . er . . . civilians."

I gave him a dark look. "You wouldn't have known about the coat with all the money and documents if I hadn't told you about it. I think I'm allowed *some* answers."

"Is that so?" he replied, and sipped his wine. Those ocean-gray eyes were as flat and emotionless as a fork. "The *commissionnaire* might disagree."

I was fit to be tied. Here I'd invited him in, given up what would have been my second helping of soufflé, along with a spectacular bottle of wine—no, *two* bottles, for Oncle Rafe had opened a second one!—and now that the *inspecteur* had finished the magnificent meal, he was going to play this game?

"Now, now, Inspecteur," said Grand-père soothingly. "You must know we have all been discussing the very, very terrible situation for the last three days. Perhaps, at the very least, you might allow our Tabitte to present to you her theories . . . and then you may or may not confirm them. That would be permissible, *non?*"

Merveille didn't actually agree, but he didn't reject the suggestion, either. He merely sat and sipped the Sancerre as if he had all day to sit in our salon.

I thought it was a little strange that he seemed in no great hurry to leave, but then I thought maybe he was off duty if Mrs. Hayes and Mark were in custody. He had to wait for Mark to get back from the hospital anyway, and it was nearly four o'clock on a Saturday. Even police *inspecteurs* could have an evening off—especially if they'd solved a case. And, after all, he was drinking Fautrier wine and eating a Julia Child soufflé. Why would anyone be in a hurry to leave?

"All right, then. Here's what I think," I said in a businesslike manner. "Arthur Coleman was providing fake American documents to—I guess—Rebecca Hayes and Mark Justiss? I'm not completely clear on the purpose, but I assume they were selling the documents to . . . to whoever wanted to buy them and go to live in America." I shrugged.

Merveille didn't even flicker an eyelash. I took that as assent, so I went on.

"Somehow Thérèse found out about it—or maybe she was in-volved—*oh!*" A thought just struck me, and it felt so accurate that my entire body erupted in goose bumps. "They were using the coat check room to disseminate the documents, the fake IDs, right? Somehow they were using that room as the center point of operations . . . but I'm not sure . . . *wait. Wait!*" I said, even though no one was making any move to speak.

Instead, my messieurs were both watching me with affection-ate indulgence; Julia was gaping with wide, excited eyes, having scooted to the edge of her seat . . . and Merveille sat there sip-ping his wine as if we were talking about the weather, not mur-der and conspiracy.

"They were putting the stuff—the fake documents—in their coats! Probably in their pockets; there wouldn't be time for sewing anything into the lining. And when the customer dropped their coat off in the coat check, somehow Thérèse removed whatever was in the pockets—money for the IDs probably. Then she put the documents in the coats in exchange, and *et voilà!*"

I frowned. It made sense . . . almost. But not quite.

"But how would Thérèse know which coats to put the infor-mation in? And what information? She couldn't look through every darned coat," said Julia.

I glanced at Merveille, whose expression remained impassive, damn it. I wondered if that was because I was on the right track, or because he was sitting there, chuckling inside about my wild, harebrained theories.

Or maybe *he* didn't know what was going on and needed *me* to tell *him*.

Much as I liked that last option, I was pretty sure that wasn't it. Which meant there was a good chance I was on the right track with my theory and he knew it . . . so I had to keep going.

And then it struck me. I felt as if a literal ton of bricks had just been dumped on my head.

"The coat check tickets—the ones that I threaded through the hangers . . . some of them had extra hole punches in them," I said, speaking more slowly now as I thought about it. My skin was alive with prickles, which told me I was on the right track. "I assumed it was just people being clumsy or hasty, but what if it was a signal to, I suppose, 'look in this coat' or something?"

Did Merveille give me an imperceptible nod, or was I imagining it?

"So . . . all right, let's walk through this." I was speaking just as much for myself as for everyone else. "Someone shows up at the theater. They make an extra hole punch in the coat check ticket—I guess that was the process that had already been established, so the people who had something in their coat knew to do that under the guise of helping the coat check girl be more efficient."

I remembered the first night a nice man saying to me, *You're new here, aren't you? The regulars know to punch their own tickets when it's busy.* He must have been one of the regulars. And anyone who came in expecting to pass money and accept documents would be told to double-punch the coat ticket.

I took a sip of my own wine, then went further, trying on the theory for size. "So when there was an extra hole in the coat ticket on the hanger, Thérèse knew that there was something in the coat pocket—money probably. And so she took out the money and put the fake documentation in the pocket. And then at the end of the night, the person picked up their coat and went home with their new ID and no one was the wiser."

"Brilliant," murmured Grand-père.

"Indeed," said Rafe. "If only we'd thought to use coat checks for disseminating information during our . . . er . . . displeasure over the German Occupation. Simple and very near impossible to connect people to each other." He gave Merveille a sly, side-wise glance, then lifted his wine to drink.

"But," I said, already seeing a complication in my theory. "How did Thérèse know which ID to put in which coat? The photographs and sex of the documents had to match the person paying, so she'd have to have some way of knowing which coat belonged to which person."

"Perhaps . . ." Merveille spoke, then lifted his glass to sip, surely knowing he kept all of us in suspense as he decided whether or not to continue his sentence. "Perhaps there was some, oh, perhaps a calling card or a note with a name on it in the pocket as well."

"Of course!" In Arthur Coleman's coat—or, at least, the coat I believed belonged to him—there'd been a business card right in the breast pocket. "That would work. Thérèse would pull out the money and the card with the name on it, and then put the correct packet of false documents into the pocket."

"And that was it," said Julia. "You uncovered a ring of fake ID makers and sellers, Tabitha. And you, of course, Inspecteur, were probably already on the trail." She smiled at him, clearly obviously working the second F in her rule. "And we already know that Mark Justiss killed Thérèse—and, I assume, Johnny too?"

I nodded. "Yes, he admitted to it during his conversation with Rebecca Hayes. She was angry with him for doing it in such a way as to draw attention to the theater—which I understand now, since they were using the coat room to pass off the products—so why on earth did *she* shoot Thad right there at the the-ater?"

"And," said Julia, "why did Mark kill Thérèse and Johnny? If Thérèse was in on everything, why did he kill her?"

That was a good question. "I'm not sure why he killed Thérèse." I looked at Merveille.

The *inspecteur* remained silent, and I got the impression he was daring me to continue with my musings.

I huffed a sigh. "All right, let me think. Rebecca Hayes made a comment about Arthur Coleman not being able to keep his zipper closed . . . and we know Thérèse was involved with a man, then moved right after Coleman was found dead at her building. So she killed Coleman because their affair went bad? And she ended up with his money-stuffed coat? And . . ." I shook my head. "I don't know. I'm stumped. Why did Mark kill her?"

I gave Merveille a pleading look. I *knew* he knew what was going on—and he was just sitting there, watching me flounder around because of some misbegotten rule about talking police business with civilians.

The *inspecteur* heaved a sigh and set down his empty wineglass. "That was delicious," he said. "Thank you."

Was he going to *leave?* Leave us hanging without filling in the gaps?

Julia was going to have none of it. "I hope you aren't going to go without telling us," she said, drilling the *inspecteur* with her eyes. "That would be very unfair. Especially since Tabitha gave up her second helping of soufflé so you could have a late lunch."

"Is that so?" Again, I thought I saw his lips twitch. "Then, in that case, I suppose some answers might be in order. Or, at least, some *suggestions*—for as a police investigator, I cannot talk about such things with civilians. Surely you understand."

I relaxed a little. Whatever he had to tell himself to rationalize it was fine with me, if he would just clear up the last few questions.

Unlike me, when Merveille spoke, it was straightforward, clear, and concise. "Thérèse Lognon was *likely* murdered because she knew too much. She most likely did not know precisely what was happening in the coat check room. Did she not spend her time sitting in the auditorium, watching the play in order to improve her English? And so while she was in there, Docteur Justiss would let himself into the coat room to place items in the pockets of those coats with the extra punch in their tickets.

"But," Merveille went on, "and this is only a suggestion, you understand, mademoiselle . . . perhaps there was not only the sale of false documents happening in the coat room but also a network of communications. Messages and funds were exchanged, perhaps, along with the passports and identification cards. Such is the kingpin of a well-developed spy ring."

"Spies! I *knew* it!" cried Grand-père, waving a cigarette. "Those Russkis are everywhere!"

"Indeed," replied Merveille, seemingly nonplussed by his outburst. "Russians that are sent—or, more accurately, embedded in America as Americans must not only have the proper documentation, but also they must be well trained to act like Americans, *non?*"

"That is true," said Oncle Rafe. "Why, there is a small city in Russia—please, do not ask me how I know of this," he said, giving Merveille and me quelling looks—"where the spies live and are trained *how* to be and act like Americans. So when they get to the United States, they have had much practice in acting the part."

"That's *it*," I cried. "That's why Thérèse wanted to talk to me, isn't it? About Detroit. Because Thad Whiting was one of those spies—he was supposed to be from Detroit. That's why he was talking about his mission being aborted.

"Thérèse must have suspected him—or someone—as being not who they said they were. And she thought I might be able to tell for certain, and if I did, that would confirm her suspicions. There *was* something wrong about him, but I didn't realize it until today. It was the Boblo Island thing—that should have told me right from the start."

When I realized everyone was looking at me strangely, I explained about that, as well as the "pop" versus "soda" mistake Thad had made.

"So Thad was going to be sent to Detroit as a spy for Russia?" Julia said.

"No, no, no," said Rafe. "I believe his *cover* was that he was from Detroit, but of course he would be sent to Washington or somewhere else where there would be military or government secrets to be had. But one never knows when one's cover might be blown, *non, cher*?" He glanced at Grand-père. "If M. Whiting had encountered someone else from Detroit while he was under-cover, he could easily have been exposed."

"And so Rebecca Hayes killed him because he was a loose end. Because he'd had his cover blown—or almost blown," I said. "But why do it *at the theater*? She said she had a plan. And that reminds me—how is Mr. Hayes involved? He came to the theater at least once while I was there, and maybe twice—and had an extra hole punched in his coat ticket. Is he a Russian spy too? Or only someone working at the embassy and helping with the fake documents?"

"Roger Hayes is dead," said Merveille quietly. "His body was found in the trunk of Madame Hayes's car. One can only sur-mise that she intended to arrange a scene at the theater—how fitting, *non*?—where it would appear M. Whiting and M. Hayes had an altercation and killed each other . . . thus wrapping up the loose ends of who killed Thérèse Lognon. We would assume M. Whiting was the culprit, and that he and M. Hayes were part-ners in the enterprise and had had a disagreement that ended up in their mutual demise.

"Of course, it is unlikely we would have been fooled, but . . ." He spread his hands in that insouciant manner I found either charming or annoying, depending upon the occasion. I decided to find it charming in this case since he'd actually answered a question.

All of that made sense. Poor Mr. Hayes—he'd been a dupe of his wife's. And their poor daughter . . . I felt a real surge of pity for Betty. How awful for her to lose both of her parents, each for a different reason.

"But how did he know to double-punch the hole in his ticket," I mused. Then answered my own question. "Oh, his wife probably told him some nonsense about double-punching it meant he'd get his coat back more quickly or something. Like being parked in the front row at a theater."

I frowned. I'd just thought of something else. . . . "There was an incident the second night at the theater. I was called to the ladies' lounge to help with someone who was ill, but when I got there to help, she was gone. Coincidentally, Mark Justiss happened to be there when I was called away, so he covered for me at the coat check."

"He probably had been desperate to snoop around in there—or maybe he had to pass on some information in some of those coats—but you never left the coat check during the show like Thérèse usually did," said Julia. "So he needed an excuse to get you out of there for a few minutes."

I nodded. That was exactly the conclusion I'd come to.

By now, I felt mostly satisfied. All of the questions had been answered, and the little events that had niggled at me were explained.

Arthur Coleman had been Thérèse's lover, and she must have suspected something was going on and only put it together after she found what was in his coat.

Mark must have been looking for Arthur Coleman's coat, for he knew Thérèse and Coleman had been lovers . . . and after Coleman died, the coat disappeared. So that's why Mark searched her apartment—and he must have come from La Sol that day, for he'd smelled like the hookah.

"One last question: What about La Sol?" I said. "The cabaret."

Merveille picked up the glass Oncle Rafe had just refilled and sipped. "A meeting place, no doubt. Perhaps initial meetings occurred there, and then instructions were given for attending the theater. And perhaps they even met there outside of business hours for privacy purposes. The owner would be well paid to say nothing, of course."

I nodded. The owner had obviously said nothing to me.

"These are all merely suggestions, you understand," said the *inspecteur* blandly.

"Of course," I replied just as gravely.

"And so why did Mark kill Thérèse again?" Julia asked. "I'm still not clear on that."

"I think . . . I can only make a suggestion of my own," I said, glancing at Merveille, "but it seemed that at Dort's party, Thérèse made a pointed comment about people not being who they appeared to be. She might have meant it about Thad, but Mark couldn't take any chances on her possibly exposing them. Or, she might have figured out what was going on—and that Mark was involved, too—and tried to blackmail him into silence. Either way, it probably sounded like a direct threat, so he had to get rid of her before she spilled the beans—especially to me, an expert on living in the Detroit area." I looked at Merveille for confirmation.

He merely looked interested, which I took to be assent.

"And this Docteur Justiss . . . he is the worst kind of person," said Rafe, his mouth twisting with distaste. "He is an American, and yet he is working with the Russians to spy on his own country. A traitor. I am very glad you didn't find him attractive, Tabitte."

I felt my cheeks heat when everyone looked at me. "I should have known there was something off about him when he made a comment about Maribelle being a regular American capitalist," I said. "The way he said it should have given me a clue that he was a Communist."

"Is he really a doctor?" asked Julia. "And how did he learn Russian? And why did he decide to spy on our own country?"

"I don't know," I replied. "Maybe he became connected with some Russian Communists during the war and came to support their beliefs."

"Indeed," said Rafe. "War can make of men strange bedfellows."

"Then I think that covers everything," said Julia with a gusty sigh. "Just like an Agatha Christie novel—all the questions answered at the end, and the villain is caught, and everyone else is happy—"

"And they have all ended their day with a superb meal and an excellent glass of wine," said Grand-père with a flourish. "What more could one ask?"

"Well, I have one thing," I said, looking at Merveille. "I would very much like the return of my Swiss Army knife when the police are finished with it."

Other than that I couldn't think of anything to add.

CHAPTER 23

"It's just too bad about Mark Justiss being a spy," said Julia.

"And a killer," I reminded her.

"And a killer," she said.

It was early afternoon on Monday, and we were on our way back from visiting the market, where we'd spent more time gossiping about the murders and what we knew than actually shopping.

"But that just means we will have to expand our search for A Man for Tabitha," she said gaily. "Madame Marie is quite invested in it all, you know. She says she has a grandnephew—"

I laughed, shaking my head, "No, Julia, really. I'm not interested in dating anyone right now."

"But you're in *Paris!* It's the city of *love*," Julia said in her bubbly voice. "You need a man to neck with by the Seine . . . to gaze at over a glass of Bordeaux . . . to lick the chocolate gâteau off your fingers and then rain kisses up along your arm . . . and elsewhere!"

I was still laughing. "No, no, really. I'm just fine with my wonderful messieurs. They keep me busy enough."

She scoffed as we turned onto rue de l'Université. "There is always the good *inspecteur*," she said in a wheedling voice.

"Absolutely not," I said. "He's much too uptight and strict for me."

"But those *eyes*," she gushed.

"No thank you," I replied. "Besides, I think he has a woman. There was a photo on his desk."

"All right then, if you insist, but I won't be giving up so easily," she trilled. Then she gusted out a sigh. "I'm so glad all of this is over. Now we can concentrate on your cooking skills!"

"Yes, please," I replied.

We parted ways with a hug and double-cheek kisses, and I hurried inside the house with my market bag.

"Tabitte! You've returned," called my grandfather when he heard me.

"Yes. I'll be up there in a minute. Do you need anything?"

"Not at all. But we wish to speak with you when you can come up here."

I felt a little niggle of worry; he sounded serious. I hurried to put away the fillet of salmon I'd purchased under Julia's eagle eye and assurances that it was difficult to "destroy fish," as she put it. I wasn't so certain, but I could always call her for assistance.

"Yes, Grand-père?" I said when I came into the salon.

Both of the messieurs were there, sitting upright in their chairs, laps covered with blankets, pets curled up appropriately. For some reason, Oscar Wilde hadn't barked when I came into the house, and I wondered if that was a portent of things to come.

Was my grandfather going to gently suggest that I return to the States? After all, I'd just been caught up in a murder investigation and nearly got myself killed. Twice.

My insides clutched hard as a wave of misery washed over me. I didn't want to go back home.

"Please, sit, *chérie*," said Oncle Rafe. There was the faintest twinkle in his eyes, and that eased my nerves a little.

"We have been discussing the fact that your bicycle is no longer with us," said Grand-père gravely. "And that you nearly also met your demise, *petite*, in that awful incident."

I swallowed hard. "Yes. I'm very sorry. I'll pay for a new one—"

"Tut," said Oncle Rafe, holding up a finger. "If you will permit your *grand-père* to finish."

I closed my mouth and nodded.

"Perhaps it is just that we are older than one deserves to be," said Grand-père, "but we did find it quite startling that you should decide it necessary to wear such things as the *trousers* out and about when riding on the bicycle."

Ugh. I nodded but remained silent, mindful of Oncle Rafe's remonstration.

"Riding a bicycle, wearing the trousers, going about investigating murders . . ." Grand-père made his own tut-tutting sound and I sank even deeper into a miserable mood. "Something must be done about all of that."

I was mortified when I felt tears prickling my eyes. I couldn't have spoken even if I wanted to; the back of my throat burned, and there was a lump in my throat. I'd totally messed things up. I'd ruined everything. I should have known—

"And so we have devised a solution," said Oncle Rafe.

"I see," I managed to say.

"If you please, Tabitte—look out there." Grand-père gestured languidly to the window.

Mystified now, I rose and went to do as instructed. The window overlooked the courtyard behind the portico. There was a small stone drive there and a garden that was filled with flowers and herbs during the summer.

Sitting there on the small stone drive was a cheery red Renault.

I stared for a moment, not quite able to believe what I was seeing . . . not quite able to comprehend if what I *thought* I was seeing was what I was meant to see.

"There's a car down there," I said in as offhand a voice as I could manage. "Has someone come to visit?"

Oncle Rafe and Grand-père burst into guffaws.

"Oh, she is a sly one, your *petite fille*, is she not, Maurice," said Rafe, chuckling as he lit a cigarette.

"*Ma chérie,* that is not a visitor's automobile. That is *your* car. We cannot have you riding about the city in the trousers on a bicycle! It's far too dangerous and . . . quite risqué too," said Grand-père with a gravelly chuckle.

"You bought me a car?" I cried, finally believing it. I spun from the window and threw myself at each of them in turn, heedless of the cat and dog on their laps. Tears of relief and delight streamed down my cheeks. "How can I thank you? How? You are simply the most wonderful of men ever, and you have certainly spoiled me for any other man I might ever meet."

"But of course," said Rafe. "That is always our master plan—to woo all of the women away from all of the other men!" His cheeks were pink with pleasure and maybe a little embarrassment. "Ah, and some of the men too, of course."

"But you ask how you might thank us," said Grand-père after a few more moments of my delighted exclamations. His eyes twinkled. "We only ask that you continue to remain very, *very* close friends with Madame Child, and that you spend as much time with her as possible, *d'accord*?"

"That will be my pleasure," I said. "She's already invited me to come to Le Cordon Bleu with her in January for the afternoon demonstrations."

Their eyes widened with delight. "That is an excellent idea," said Grand-père gravely. "A most excellent idea. And now you will be able to drive yourself to and from such events."

Of course I had to go outside and admire the car, and I even convinced Rafe to take a ride with me around the block and over to the Champs de Mar, where we could look at the Tour Eiffel from the seats of my cherry-red Renault.

All in all, it was a wonderful afternoon.

About five o'clock, when I was just gathering up the courage to attack the problem of the salmon, the telephone rang. Glad for a distraction, I answered it.

"Tabitha!" It was Julia on the other end, and she sounded even more breathless and excited than usual. "You've got to come over here! Right now!"

"I do? Why? What's—"

"No, no, please come! You absolutely *must* see this!" She hung up before I could argue further, so I shrugged and slipped M. Salmon back into his wrappings for the time being.

I pulled on my coat and hat and was just adjusting my gloves when I opened the front door.

I stumbled to a halt when I saw Inspecteur Merveille making his way up the walk.

"Oh, mademoiselle," he said, just as surprised to see me as I was to see him.

"Bonjour, Inspecteur," I said. "Did you . . . er . . . need something? I've just been called over to Julia's apartment—she seemed quite upset."

"Perhaps I should go with you," he said, his eyes narrowing in concern. "To make certain everything is all right. And also to return this." He held up a plastic bag with Julia's beloved carbon steel chef's knife.

"I think she would appreciate that, even though I doubt she'd ever actually *use* it again." I paused. "But you were coming here—was there something I can help you with?"

"No, I simply came to . . . er . . . to give you this." He fished in his pocket and when he withdrew his hand, there was a small box in it.

Baffled, I took the box and, giving him a confused look, opened it. There was a brand-new Swiss Army knife inside.

"I regret to inform you that, like your bicycle, your tool knife has gone the way of the dead beneath that door," said Merveille. "I thought perhaps a replacement might be in order, considering . . . well, considering everything."

I stared at the knife, completely shocked by the entire situation. "Thank you," I said after a moment. "That is very kind of you." I smiled, and although he didn't actually smile back, I thought the frost in his eyes might have softened a bit.

As we started walking down the street, he said, "One does wonder, mademoiselle, how you happened to have such a tool at hand. Most women—well, they carry other sorts of tools like the lipsticks and the compacts and the combs . . . not ones like this."

"Well, Inspecteur, let's just say I'm not at all like most women."

"No, indeed, mademoiselle, you certainly are not."

By this time, we'd reached 81 rue de l'Université, Julia's building. I stuck the knife into my pocket and led the way inside and to the lift, which we rode to the third floor, where the kitchen was.

I just assumed Julia was in the kitchen.

"Julia," I called when we came in. "It's me, and I have the *inspecteur* with me."

"Why that is spectacular!" Julia cried when she saw me. She was wearing an apron and brandishing a whisk and something smelled amazing—as it always did in *La Maison Scheeld*. Paul and Dort were there as well, already seated at the small dining table with empty plates and glasses of wine.

I greeted them with cheek-kisses, and Merveille offered polite nods and a hand for Paul to shake. Once these niceties had been complete, the *inspecteur* turned to Julia.

"Madame Child, I believe this is yours." Merveille handed her the plastic bag, and Julia snatched it from him, gathering it up to her bosom like a long-lost child.

"Oh, thank heavens! How I've missed you, dear, dear chef's knife! What an awful experience he has had, hasn't he!" She gave the bag one last hug, then set it on the counter where she gave it a look of distress. "But unfortunately, M. Chef's Knife will need to be retired. I simply couldn't . . . after what happened." She gave a little shudder.

"Yes, I think that's best," I said, eyeing the bagged knife. "Anyway, what was so urgent that you needed me right away?" I asked, looking around the kitchen.

There were bowls and bowls sitting around—all filled with a creamy white sauce.

"Is that . . . is that mayonnaise?" I asked, looking at the bowl closest to me. It was a lush, creamy sauce, and there was the finest sprinkling of green herbs mixed in with it.

"Yes! Tabitha, I've discovered the secret to the mayonnaise problem! Sit, sit, both of you! I'm so glad you're here, too, Inspecteur, for we have more mayonnaise than anyone can eat."

Paul gave a quiet laugh even as he offered his wife an affectionate smile and pat on the butt. "That is quite the understatement, kitten."

Merveille and I did as we were told—who would not obey Julia Child when she told you to sit in her kitchen?—and joined Paul and Dort at the tiny table.

"So what was it? What was the trick?" I asked as Julia set a plate on the table.

The plate displayed sliced boiled eggs topped with arugula and chopped chervil. A second plate followed with cold sliced poultry—I wasn't certain if it was chicken, goose, or some other bird and I wasn't going to ask because it didn't matter. And a third plate followed, this time with egg noodles.

"You must try them all," Julia trilled as she poured mayonnaise over the top of each plate in succession, using different versions of the creamy egg sauce.

"Twist my arm," I murmured with great feeling. "Now tell me: What was the problem, and how did you solve it!"

The others began to help themselves to generous portions of each of the dishes as Julia explained.

"It became clear to me when I realized that on Friday, I was able to make mayonnaise with no problem, but it didn't turn out on any day before or after it. And I asked myself what was different about Friday," she said, bustling around the kitchen.

There was something in the oven that smelled rich and chocolatey and I was hoping it might be a gâteau. I am partial to Julia's Queen of Sheba almond and chocolate cake.

"And . . . ?" I asked, and then I had no reason to speak again for I was immersed in the gorgeousness of fresh, creamy *mayonnaise aux fines herbes* streamed lovingly over boiled eggs, capers, and greens.

"I retraced my steps . . . I was making stock from the ham bone, remember? And I had taken the bowl from where it was sitting next to the stove and I remembered today that *the metal bowl felt a little warm.*" Her eyes were alight and her hands moved and she was simply a *goddess* in the kitchen. "And then I remembered that Friday was an unseasonably warm day . . . and I remembered that *all of my problems* with the mayonnaise had started in December! When it got so damned *cold.*"

I nodded, moving on to serving a portion of the poultry smothered in mayonnaise.

"And that's when I realized that maybe it was all about *temperature*, not the color of the eggs or how hard to whisk them or anything else! And so today, I tried heating the bowl first—I just put hot water in it to take off the edge. And everything else was warm; I set the oil and the eggs on the counter near the oven—I'm making Queen of Sheba cake, you know."

I exchanged delighted glances with Dort, for I knew there would be a piece of that sumptuous dessert in my future. Merveille, if he stayed that long, had no idea what gastronomical pleasure awaited him.

"So the eggs and the oil were not chilled at all. They were room temperature, perhaps even a little warmer than that. And it *worked*," crowed Julia. "It *worked*! I've used a dozen eggs and made six batches of sauce and every time it has worked magnificently!"

"Brava!" I cried, scooping a spoonful of noodles and sauce onto my plate to join the other delicacies. "Brava, Julia!" The others joined me in the congratulations.

"Thank you, thank you," she said, bowing comically to the room at large.

"And so," I said, lifting a glass of wine that had miraculously appeared from the goddess of the kitchen, "we celebrate the solving of two mysteries this week: The Murder With the Chef's Knife and The Problem of the Bad Mayonnaise!"

Even Merveille had to lift his glass in a toast to that.

"Indeed!" cried Julia. "We have succeeded. And now . . . everyone . . . bon appétit!"

HISTORICAL NOTE

*P*ostwar Paris, particularly the 1950s, was a fascinating time. It was as if the beleaguered city was unfurling herself from the cocoon in which she'd been enclosed for the last nearly decade and becoming the beautiful butterfly she'd once been. Many young Americans went over to the city to live, play, and work. In fact, the Parisians deplored the number of cars and people brought by tourists that clogged the city they'd just taken back as their own.

Julia and Paul Child were ecstatic when they learned that he was to be stationed there as part of the embassy's efforts to support the Marshall Plan. Paul had lived in Paris when he was much younger—and poorer—and was looking forward to showing his new wife around and being able to enjoy the finer things in life.

When she first arrived in Paris, Julia was at her wit's end. She didn't have anything to *do*. She tried hat classes, bridge classes, and other social events, and nothing seemed to stick until Paul gave her a huge tome of French cookery (in French, of course). Her determination to cook from that book led to a decision to take classes at Le Cordon Bleu . . . and eventually, as we know, she cowrote a cookbook about French cooking for American women and became a television celebrity.

Tabitha Knight, a completely fictional character, was in a similar position as many young women after the war. She'd been doing all sorts of "masculine" work, but now that the troops were returning, women weren't needed in those jobs. She, like many of her peers, felt lost and unnecessary and uncertain about her future. The war left nearly everyone utterly changed, and it's no surprise someone like Tabitha would take the opportunity to visit her *grand-père* in one of the most beautiful cities in the world.

Tabitha's work at the Willow Run bomber plant as a "Rosie the Riveter" hits very close to home, as I grew up within two miles of the plant and airport. My great-aunt Rosie was a literal Rosie the Riveter, and the history of that airport has always been a source of fascination for me. I look forward to sharing more about Tabitha's work building bombers in future An American in Paris mysteries.

—Colleen Cambridge, May 2023